Passion's Rival

"You think with a ring on your finger you'll be able to let Buchanan touch you without drying up inside?" he demanded harshly. "You think you're ever going to be happy with him?"

"I won't talk of this with you," she said, closing her eyes tightly and shaking her head. She balled her hands into tight fists, fighting the feelings stirring in her at Logan's closeness.

"I wonder how you're going to feel when he gets into bed with you and starts putting his hands where mine have been."

She gave him a stricken look and tried to pull free.

He held tight to her. "It won't be tender kisses in an open field, then, will it, Beth?" She pushed at him, and he forced her back against the wall. "It'll be in earnest then. No high-necked dresses, corsets, tiers of petticoats, pantaloons. Just you. Naked. Under him!"

"Stop it!" she choked.

"Are you going to be as warm and willing with him as you were with me?" he demanded, relentless. "Or are you going to die a little inside every time he takes you?"

FRANCINE RIVERS
OUTLAW'S EMBRACE

CHARTER BOOKS, NEW YORK

OUTLAW'S EMBRACE

A Charter Book/published by arrangement with
the author

PRINTING HISTORY
Charter edition/September 1986

ISBN: 0-441-64449-X

Charter Books are published by The Berkley Publishing Group,
200 Madison Avenue, New York, New York 10016.
PRINTED IN THE UNITED STATES OF AMERICA

Chapter One

SOFT PUFFS OF dust rose from the road as a rider rounded the last wooded bend before reaching Kilkare Woods. The first house that came into view was neat, small and white with blue trim and geranium-laden window boxes and potted flowers along the front porch railing.

The simplicity of the dwelling was lost amidst the glorious garden. Red, yellow, and pink-kissed white roses stretched perfect blooms above the low, whitewashed picket fence. Down the sides of the tightly bordered yard lay a profusion of sweet peas, daisies, snapdragons, roses, wild but nurtured poppies and lupins, pungent marigolds, and sweet alyssum.

The front door opened and a young woman emerged, carrying a heavy, cloth-covered tray. She was like the house, small and simply dressed. Yet, on second glance, she displayed a certain understated elegance.

Black passementerie decorated the hem of her plain

brown skirt. Delicate pin tucks, shadow embroidery, and
crocheted lace adorned the prim white high-necked,
mutton-sleeve blouse. Her wheat blond hair was brushed
into a modest chignon, while her oval face was dominated
by a pair of wide-set, shining hazel eyes. The soft smile
curving her generous mouth seemed to reflect some deep
inner acceptance of both life and self.

Balancing the tray on her hip, she closed the door behind her. She came down the front steps with a grace that
seemed to come naturally rather than through balancing
books for hours. She paused once as she walked along the
narrow raked pathway to the front gate. As she came
through the gate, the hem of her skirt caught.

It had happened before, and she dipped her right hip and
turned her body slightly to tug the skirt free. It remained
caught. She dipped again and still it held. Dismayed, she
balanced the tray on her hip once more and carefully bent
at the knees to try to free the brown material from beneath
the rough wood gate stakes where it had snagged. The tray
swayed precariously; dishes rattled beneath the cover. She
grasped it quickly and straightened while uttering a soft,
exasperated sigh.

Trying once more, she dipped, turned, and gave a small
hop as she lightly kicked at the skirt hem. The gate swung
shut, trapping a thick fold this time.

"Oh!"

Hearing an approaching horse, the young woman
glanced back and up. The stranger was approaching
slowly, but even at this distance she could see that he sat
big in the saddle. He was dressed in dark clothing, even to
the hat pulled low over his eyes. Wearing a gun was not
unusual, but this man wore his strapped low and tied down
against his muscled thigh. A rifle was secured to his saddle. She saw that it was a repeater, a gun that could be
drawn from its scabbard with one hand and cocked with a

snap of the wrist before firing.

He either expected trouble or was looking for it.

When the man edged his horse toward her front gate, the young woman's heart stopped.

"Trouble, ma'am?" His voice was deep, resonant, and amused.

"Pardon me?" She tipped her head, trying to see his eyes beneath the shadow of his hat. She noticed instead his finely shaped mouth curving into a faint smile. His body shifted, leather creaked, and she realized with heart-knocking alarm that he was dismounting.

Mexican spurs jangled as he walked slowly toward her, his catlike tread revealing inherent male power. When he stopped in front of her, he pushed the rim of his hat up an inch.

Bold, blue eyes looked straight into her startled ones as his hands rested lightly on his lean hips. "Seems you're in something of a predicament."

Her lips parted, but no sound came.

The man's smile deepened, lines crinkling about his eyes and deepening in his bronzed cheeks. He didn't move for a second, but surveyed her from head to foot. She didn't know what else to do but stare back into those compelling, half-laughing, very watchful eyes.

He leaned toward her, one arm extending. She drew back with a soft gasp.

"Relax, I'm only going to open your gate," he said, grinning. "If you'll just stand a little to this side," he told her, putting his other hand beneath her elbow and drawing her stiff body in the direction he wanted her to move. She felt the strength of those lean fingers even in gentleness, and her heart pounded faster.

When he bent down, she drew back again, the dishes beneath the cloth rattling noisily.

"Don't drop it on me," he said, and she looked down at

the top of his dark, dusty hat and at the strong back muscles that moved beneath the taut cotton shirt he wore. He
straightened again, and her hands whitened on the tray.

"Thank you," she managed shakily, and tried to smile.

"You're welcome, ma'am," he said very formally, his
mouth twitching as he touched his hat brim. He nodded
toward the quiet main street of town. "Kilkare Woods?"

"Yes, it is."

"So . . ." He studied the small town spread out before
him, a muscle working slowly in his hard, square jaw.
When he looked at her again, his blue eyes were darkly
enigmatic. She sensed that deep emotion lay beneath that
secret look, but of what sort, God Himself only knew. It
frightened her somehow. He smiled again, and it hit Beth
Tyrell right in the pit of her stomach just how handsome he
was.

"Is there a place to stay?"

"The hotel." She nodded toward the street. "It's toward
the other end of town, just past the tack shop and across
from the sheriff's office." She thought that information
would send him on his way, but he seemed in no great
hurry to leave her.

"No boardinghouses?"

Missus O'Henry ran one down on Maple Street, but
Beth knew she wouldn't even open the door to a man like
this one, let alone allow him in her house to rent one of her
small, comfortable rooms. What could she say?

His mouth curved again. "The hotel it is, I guess.
Clean, I hope."

"I'm sorry. I can't tell you. I've never been inside, but
I'm sure it's very nice. My father goes there each evening
for a whiskey and a visit with the men from the ranches
around town." She glanced at the man's lathered, dusty
horse standing in the street. "If you're staying the night,

there's a good livery down Oak Street. It's right near the train station. Dan Trader is very good with horses, and he'd see yours was grained and curried."

He gave her a curious look and nodded slowly. "Much obliged, ma'am."

She watched him walk back to his horse, take the reins, and mount. He looked down at her again. She'd never had a man look at her in quite this way before, and she felt the warm tide rush into her cheeks, try as she might to prevent it.

She turned hastily away and walked quickly along the edge of the street until she reached the boardwalk. All the while, she heard the slow hoofbeats of his horse and felt him watching her intently.

Four-year-old Terence dove out of his father's general store, his mother's voice following. "Not another piece of candy! Do you hear?" Beth paused as he darted past her and hunched behind the rain barrel. His mother came to the doorway, an exasperated look on her plain face as she looked for him. Seeing Beth instead, Faith Halverson smiled. "I swear, that boy is going to send us to the poorhouse with the amount of candy he steals out of that jar." She came out, brushing her hands on her apron, her brows lifting in interest.

"Somethin' smells mighty good, Beth," she remarked, and lifted the edge of the white cloth covering the tray. She chuckled. "McAllister, hmmm?"

Beth laughed.

The stranger came even with them, and Beth glanced at him. When she looked back, Faith's face was wide with curiosity. "Haven't seen one of them around here in a long time," she murmured softly. "Oh, dear, he's stopping off at the hotel. Well, your father'll see he goes on his way quick enough."

Unease trembled through Beth at the suggestion. "I'd best take this along," she said, and headed down the boardwalk again.

The stranger had dismounted and looped his reins around the hitching post. Standing by his horse, he untied the saddlebags and swung them over his broad shoulder. He took the rifle in its scabbard as well. Pushing his hat back, he looked directly across the street at her and smiled slowly before turning toward the front steps of the hotel.

Beth averted her gaze quickly, embarrassed to be caught studying him, and kept walking until she reached the sheriff's office. Balancing the tray on her hip, she opened the door.

"Beth! There you are," her father greeted her with a wide smile. He swung his feet off his desk, and the front chair legs slammed to the floor. "Smells good." He took the tray from her and set it on the table.

"Stew and dumplings?" came a loud, raspy voice from the jail cells in back.

"Yes, Mr. McAllister," Beth called, smiling.

"By damn! I timed it perfectly again," he called out jubilantly.

Beth's father laughed and shook his head. "You get yours after I get mine!" he taunted.

"Watch how he divvies up, Miss Beth," McAllister shouted.

"I will," she called.

"What kept you, honey?" her father asked quietly. "You're late."

"Just a few minutes, Papa. I was finishing the dress for Sally Daniels's little girl. I wanted to have everything done so I can concentrate on Avery's wife when she comes in for her fitting this afternoon."

"Edwina Carlile again?" Her father scowled. "Seems that girl must have dresses for a lifetime by now."

"Don't complain. Where would I be if people stopped wanting new things?"

"You always have a headache when she leaves. Nothing is good enough for that girl. Why don't you send her on to Missus Abernathy? Let her put up with her tantrums."

"Edwina's just unhappy," Beth said in defense of the girl. "It's hard to live out here after you've spent all your life in an eastern city."

"Well, she's trying to make everyone else unhappy too, from what I've been hearing," he snorted. "She doesn't help Hannah Carlile, and she makes Avery's life a plain misery."

"You know how Avery's mother can be, Papa. It can't be easy on a young girl."

"True enough, I suppose, but that don't give her reason to take things out on you every time she comes into town. She gives you any trouble today, tell her to make her own damn dresses. That'd give her somethin' to do."

Beth took the bowl he was holding and filled it with stew. She spooned dumplings on the top and handed it back to him with a faint teasing smile. "Why don't you just eat and leave my worries to me?"

McAllister began running his tin cup back and forth against the bars. "Where's my stew? Hey! Is Frank out thar eatin' it all, Miss Beth?"

Beth laughed softly as she filled a second bowl with chunks of succulently seasoned beef, carrots, potatoes, celery, sauce, and dumplings.

"Shuddup back there or you'll be on bread and water. I oughta charge you room and board!" her father shouted back, winking at her.

"Ha! You old goat! You know you like my company! What else you gotta do round here, Frank? You don't earn your pay no more. Only time you do anythin' attal is when I give ya a little excitement at the saloon!"

Beth ladled out stew into a bowl for the other prisoner, Mac Slate. He was in the back cell, silent, dark-eyed, back against the wall, legs stretched out as he waited for his noonday meal.

Beth's father took the loaded bowls and went into the back room. McAllister continued his needling, and Frank Tyrell answered in kind and then some. Their voices dropped as the insults coarsened. Both laughed.

When her father came back into the office again, Beth wondered whether to mention the stranger. If the man was staying, her father would know soon enough. Nothing passed his attention, and a man like that one would be hard to miss.

"Now the animals are fed, we can eat in peace!" he said loudly. McAllister guffawed from the back.

"What did he do this time, Papa?"

"Got drunk and raised hell as usual. Broke a chair and threatened a drummer for insulting General Lee. War's been over fifteen years, and that damn reprobate is still waving the Stars and Bars." Frank shook his head.

Beth ladled herself a modest portion of stew and dumplings. She said grace for them both.

"You're a damn fine cook, honey." Her father nodded, chewing contentedly on a chunk of rich beef. He forked another and added innocently, "Saw Doc this morning."

Beth gave him a careful look. "How was he?"

"Missy Connor seems to like him right well," he went on, not meeting her eyes. "His southern drawl is charming, she was telling him at the general store."

"It is."

He looked at her. "He's a gentleman, Beth. Got an education, good family blood in his veins."

"Eat your stew, Papa."

He set his fork down. "He asked after you. Seems mighty interested."

Beth sighed heavily but said nothing.

"Took you to that ice cream social, didn't he?" her father continued. "He sat right next to us in church two Sundays ago. Now, that's interest!"

"He's very nice."

"Nice!" he muttered. "Sounds like a curse the way you say it." He lifted his head. "Half the women in town have their eyes on him, and he's got his eyes on you. Do you give him any encouragement? God, I never thought my own daughter would end up on a shelf."

"Are you worried about your pride or my happiness?" she countered without rancor.

His mouth tightened. "You damn well know the answer to that. You should have a home of your own, a man to take care of, children. You're twenty-one. Half the girls in this town were married by sixteen and the rest by eighteen. You ought to be, too. If it weren't for—"

"Who'd take care of you?" she cut him off, trying for levity.

Frank was having none of it. "Doc Buchanan is a fine young man. Good-looking, solid. He's going to do well for himself and any family he gets. The man wants you, if you can't see it for a sunrise, Beth. Open your eyes, girl, before life walks right on by you."

Seeing he was in another of his worried moods, she set her fork down and reached across to cover his big, hard hand with her own pale, softer one. "Papa, my eyes are wide open. You told me what it was like between you and Mama before she died. That's what I'm waiting for. A deep, abiding love. I won't settle for less. Adam is good-looking and nice and solid and charming, yes. He's wonderful, but I'm not in love with him." She took her hand away from his.

He said nothing, nor did he hold her gaze. They finished their meal in silence, hers easy, his grim. Beth glanced out the window several times. From where she was sitting inside, she could see the dusty roan stallion still standing at the hitching rail before the hotel.

Her father looked at her over the rim of his coffee mug. He flatly refused to drink from a cup and saucer. He said he preferred to have something he could hold on to, and only one finger would fit through Beth's china cups. "I wish you didn't have to work at all. It isn't right," he grumbled.

"I enjoy it," she said truthfully. She took great pleasure in the creativity of her work, and there were few occasions when her labors went unappreciated. It was true she dreaded the confrontations with Edwina Carlile, but there were other women who made up for the unkind, often unfair, criticisms Edwina made. The extra money she brought in was a great help. It took some of the strain off her father, and they were able to have a few extras that they never would have had otherwise.

"Maybe if I'd done something else for a living," Frank said almost to himself, "something that paid better, things would have been easier on you."

"I've never suffered," Beth said.

"Maybe not, but I'd like it a whole lot better if you didn't bow and scrape to someone like Edwina Carlile."

"She pays better than all the others."

"She doesn't pay a thing! It's Avery that pays. I wonder when he's going to put his foot down on her squandering money the way she does. Two dresses last month, and three the month before that, and not a practical one in the bunch. Frilly, silly things. And where the hell is she going to wear them? But then, from what I hear, the young missus doesn't do much at the Double C except sit around on her well-shaped little rump."

Beth dimpled. "I didn't know you noticed things like that, Papa."

Frank Tyrell eyed her balefully, knowing she was trying to draw him off the subject. She didn't like him speaking ill of anyone no matter who they were. Seeing the look in her eyes, he relented. He gave her a rueful half smile. "I'm not dead yet."

Far from it. Frank Tyrell was a big man, big in size and big in the respect he commanded in the small community. His coloring was very different from his daughter's. His white-gray hair had once been very dark. His eyes were brown and could turn black when he was angry. He had a jutting, stubborn jaw, and a beaklike nose that had been broken several times in his youth.

Lines were deeply cut about his eyes and mouth, and his skin was permanently brown. He wasn't handsome by anyone's standards, but he had a compelling quality about him that still drew women's interest. A man's man, he was honest, dependable, and hard. Kilkare Woods had become a quiet little town after Frank Tyrell took on the job of sheriff following a grim episode in the hotel across the street eighteen years before.

"My plate's empty!" McAllister hollered, and ran his tin cup along the bars again.

"So what!" Frank shouted back, and grinned at Beth. She laughed softly, knowing what was coming.

"You old tin-badged crowbait!"

"Watch what you call me, you dumb cowpoke! If you had the brains of your donkey, you wouldn't be in my jail again!"

"You couldn't shoot your way out of an outhouse if your life depended on it!"

Beth suppressed a laugh as she stood. "I think I'll be leaving, Papa, before you two get too warmed up with your insults."

"Faraday is coming by later," he told her. "I'll send him on down with the dishes."

She glanced back. "Why is his father in jail this time?" she asked softly.

"You don't want to know," he told her firmly, thinking of the condition in which he had found Faraday's mother. He suspected Slate had broken another of her ribs, but she refused to see the doctor. "That man is just plain miserable mean. If someone saw fit to shoot him through the head and put his family out of misery, I might just look the other way."

Beth frowned. "I've never heard you talk like that before."

Her father's expression remained uncompromising and unrepentent. "Some people aren't worth buzzard droppings." He opened the door for her and kissed her cheek. McAllister shouted at him, and he turned back into the sheriff's office again.

Beth hadn't taken more than a few steps when she saw the stranger on his horse again, in front of the hotel, and coming in her direction. Stepping down from the boardwalk to cross Santa Rita Street, Beth was overly aware of the horse and rider just a few feet behind her.

"Miss Tyrell," the stranger said, and her heart leaped. Before thinking better of it, she stopped and looked up at him as he came even with her. He moved his roan so that her way was blocked.

He looked down at her, the previous warmth in his blue eyes gone.

"How did you know my name?" she asked.

"I asked. At the hotel."

Beth blushed.

He leaned forward, resting his forearms on the pommel. A slow smile curved his sensual mouth. "I wanted to know who the pretty little lady was who lived on the edge of town. They told me she was the sheriff's daughter."

His manner and tone sent a shiver through her. His eyes

changed slightly, not cold anymore, but disturbed, half-angry. He straightened slightly. "Where was that livery stable you mentioned?"

She put her hand to her throat unconsciously and then pointed. "Turn up the next street to your right. You can't miss it."

He gave her a brief nod and backed his horse a few steps. He tipped his hat again.

It was a moment before Beth realized she was staring after him. She lowered her eyes quickly, mortified, and began walking again, measuring her pace carefully to keep her distance well behind him as he walked his horse.

He turned up Oak Street, and she saw him glance back at her. She paused before the milliner's window and pretended interest in the plumed hats.

As soon as he was past the building on the corner, Beth began walking again. She paused and looked down the street at his dark, broad back, then crossed quickly. Several townspeople called out greetings to her as she headed for her small house. She smiled and waved back, pausing several times to speak with people.

Reaching the gate, she drew her skirt well out of its way before opening it. She went inside and shut the front door, leaning back against it. Her heart was still racing.

Standing there, she tried to sort out her jumbled feelings. Nothing so very momentous had happened. A stranger had come into town and freed her skirt hem from the gate. He had spoken a few words to her. That was all!

She put a trembling hand to her chest.

Had he really thought she was pretty? She raised cool hands to her warm cheeks. She wasn't. She was quite ordinary.

She straightened and walked to her worktable, opened the armoire next to it, and removed Edwina's green dress. She forced her thoughts away from the stranger and tried to concentrate. She hoped the dress was right this time. Hanging it on the wall hook, she caressed the soft green percale of the flowing skirt and made sure the lace lay properly. It was her very best work and more beautiful than anything she had ever made before.

Beth walked to the front windows and drew back the lace curtains to look for Edwina. She was always punctual and it was just a few minutes before one.

Beth leaned forward and looked down Main Street again. She wondered who the stranger was, why he had come, and how long he would be staying.

Even more than that, she wondered if he would speak to her again.

Chapter Two

"I DON'T LIKE it at all, Elizabeth." The shapely brunette's dark, heavy-lashed eyes flickered over her reflection in the full-length mirror. The green dress fitted perfectly, the cream lace and velvet piping accentuating Edwina's perfect figure and complexion.

"It's worse than before. I thought you understood what I wanted! I made it clear. You didn't ask any questions. You just nodded your head and said, 'Of course.' If you didn't understand the King's English, you should have asked. Now I've wasted another trip into this . . . town. Just look at this!" She plucked at the offending lace around the scooped neckline.

Beth knew Edwina was working herself up into a rage, and she sighed inwardly, wondering why the girl was so consistently disagreeable to her when she treated others with at least courtesy. It would do no good whatsoever to defend herself and remind the spoiled girl that her instructions had been followed explicitly. In fact, defense would incite further abuse. Beth knew from past experience. Silence was her best and only course. Then, at least, the harangue ended more quickly. Why did the girl dislike her so? It made no sense, especially since she kept coming back. Beth had tried hard to be friends with her in the beginning, but her every invitation had met with hostility and refusal.

If it weren't for Avery. . .

"It looks cheap and gawdy. I can't wear a thing like this," Edwina snapped. She flashed a resentful look over her shoulder. "You should sell your needles and pins and work behind a store counter." She turned around fully, her head tilted in open challenge, waiting for Beth to answer the insult. When Beth didn't, the girl frowned faintly at her silence. She looked into Beth's eyes and then away, her own overbright.

Standing in front of the full-length mirror, she looked at the dress again, from neckline to hem. "In Philadelphia, there were seamstresses from whom one could choose. And in Paris, there were the finest in the world." She looked up in the mirror again, meeting Beth's quiet gaze. "Have you ever been to Europe, Elizabeth?" she asked arrogantly.

"No, I haven't. It must be a marvelous place, but I've never been further than ten miles from home," she admitted without envy.

"So you don't know anything about fashion really, do you?"

"Only what I've seen in magazines I've sent away for and what you've told me."

"Well, this effort of yours shows you haven't learned much," Edwina attacked again.

Beth had heard it all before and tried to understand what provoked it. The East was Edwina's Mecca. The West was the end of the earth.

Or was there more that brought such discontent?

Avery had married Edwina in the East. It seemed he had planned to stay there forever but then his father died and his mother had sent word to him that he was needed. Avery came home with his pretty, finishing-school wife and put his law books away for good, donning his old leather chaps instead. He took over the Double C, glorying in being home again. He said more than once that he had missed California and had never gotten her out of his blood.

"I suppose I could travel to San Francisco," Edwina said, casting a cool look at Beth's pale face. "At least there I would have some choice."

San Francisco was a good two-day trip from Kilkare Woods. Beth laced her fingers together in front of her and remained silent. She had known Avery from childhood. And she knew his mother. Avery might agree to letting Edwina go, but Hannah Carlile would raise Cain.

"But it'd be a miserable trip on that stagecoach," Edwina said glumly. She lifted a graceful hand to the French lace she had insisted upon Tuesday, and which today she found so loathsome. She caressed it and then, seeming to catch herself, she stiffened. "I want this off." She plucked angrily at the expensive lace, and, fearing she would damage it, Beth stepped forward quickly. Edwina drew in a sharp breath and brushed past her.

"Please, Edwina . . .," Beth said, and gasped in dismay when she heard the sound of ripping cloth as Edwina yanked the dress back off her shoulders and shoved it down over her slender hips, letting it drop in a heap on the floor. Beth looked from the dress to Edwina.

Edwina quickly moved away to the screen, where her brown and gold day dress hung.

Beth knelt and picked up the green dress. She bit down on her lip to hold back tears. She tried not to think of all the hours she had spent on it and now how many more hours it would take to redo the bodice. Some of the precious lace was ruined. Avery wouldn't object to the cost, but the waste was appalling.

Edwina came back from behind the screen and stood in her own dress, her hands at her waist. "I need help with this," she said, avoiding Beth's eyes. "Avery will be wondering what's taking me so long."

Beth showed as little of her feelings as she could as she walked across the room to assist Edwina in buttoning her dress. Edwina fidgeted impatiently, then stepped quickly away as soon as the task was done. She paused before the mirror to put on her wide-brimmed ostrich-plumed hat at just the right tilt. She was the only woman in town who could wear one and make it look elegant rather than ridiculous. She was remarkably beautiful and poised, but she had such a horrid temperament. She wasn't at all the kind of girl Beth had expected Avery to marry.

"I suppose now I'll have to make another trip back here just because you couldn't get things right this time." She turned. "Do you know how far it is into town from the ranch? Seven miles!" She made a small, disgusted sound. "Seven miles in that awful carriage Avery's mother thinks is so grand." She sniffed. "You should come to the ranch for my fittings just the way the seamstress did back home."

"I don't have a buggy," Beth responded simply, making no point of the time involved or that she had a business to run and other customers to see to.

"You could rent one!"

"It would make your dresses very expensive, Edwina, since I would have to raise the price to cover my additional expenses," she said.

Edwina's eyes grew cool and disdainful. "You're too expensive as it is, in my opinion, though Avery doesn't quibble about the money I spend." She picked up her beautifully beaded drawstring bag and lacy parasol. "At least when he brings me to town, I'm away from . . ." She stopped, and a small, painful frown crossed her face before she looked away.

It was no secret that Avery's young bride and mother did not get on well together. Hannah Avery Carlile was a strong-willed woman who had helped Web Carlile carve out a ranch forty years before. No other woman would reign as a first lady on that ranch until Hannah was dead and buried.

"I'll return next Tuesday at the same time, Elizabeth," Edwina said. She opened the door. "Have a pleasant day," she said, and banged the door shut behind her.

Beth listened until the front gate closed. Relieved that Edwina was finally gone, she held up the green dress again to reassess the damage. Closing her eyes at the depressing sight, she sat down on the settee and crumpled the soft material on her lap. When Edwina saw the large bill for the dress, due to the damage she herself had caused, more abuses would come.

From the first, Beth had realized Edwina didn't like her. She suspected it was because of the longtime friendship she had shared with Avery when they were children.

"This is Beth, darling. She's the girl I've told you so much about. The one that used to fish with me down by the river," he had said with a laugh.

Beth had become immediately aware of the cold scrutiny of Edwina's brown eyes.

Edwina had been very polite, but after their first meeting, each invitation Beth extended to the young woman had been met with refusal.

Beth had always been very fond of Avery, and those feelings had not changed. He teased her unmercifully as he had when she was twelve and he was fifteen. Edwina was always courteous when he was present, and even pretended a certain friendliness. It was only when the two women were alone that her true sentiments were revealed.

"She's plain jealous of you, Beth," her father had told her.

"Why should she be?"

"Because of Avery."

"Oh, Papa. He dotes on her. How could she possibly be jealous of me?"

"Because he loved you long before he ever laid eyes on her."

That had startled her. "It wasn't that way at all, Papa."

"Yes, it was. Why do you think Hannah Carlile sent him east?"

"To go to Harvard."

"Avery never wanted to be a lawyer and you know it. He wanted to be a rancher just like Web. Hannah sent him east to get him away from you."

"We were friends, nothing more. And you're wrong."

"I'm dead right," he insisted angrily. "She figured her son was too good for the likes of a sheriff's daughter. So she sent him where he'd meet highfalutin ladies instead. And don't you sit there and tell me you didn't care. You moped around for months after he went away, and he wrote to you steady for the first three years he was gone."

"I was fourteen," she said. "We were fond of each other."

"Given a chance, it would've grown into something a lot more, and Missus Carlile knew that," he said doggedly.

There was no use arguing with her father, and realizing that Edwina might believe the same nonsense, Beth had begun to treat Avery differently. Fond as she might be of him, he was married and she didn't want to be the cause of dissension between him and his wife.

Laying the green dress aside, Beth went into the kitchen to put on her long apron and get her gardening gloves. She needed time in the sun with her flowers to dissolve the depression over Edwina's visit. No one else was expected today, and she had an hour before she needed to begin dinner.

Working among her roses, she glanced down the street toward the hotel and wondered again about the stranger. Perhaps he had gone after all. Kilkare Woods wouldn't have much to offer a man like him. A nice, quiet little town was all it was.

She saw Faraday coming with the tray of dirty dishes and went to open the gate for him. Most people in town avoided him. "Takes after his father," was the usual defense, but her own instinct was to mother him.

"Frank sent me along with these," the boy said flatly. He was thirteen and already taller than Beth. He had a lanky frame, fair hair, and a perpetually sullen expression.

"Thank you, Faraday. Would you please take them into the house and put them in the kitchen?" She didn't follow him. He came out a moment later with a big apple and tossed it up and down while looking at her squarely. Someone else would have accused him of stealing it.

"How's your mother, Faraday?" Beth asked, ignoring his challenge.

His eyes narrowed and his mouth tightened as he looked away. "Fine." He stopped tossing the apple up and down.

Beth removed her gloves and tucked them into one of her apron pockets. "If you'll wait a minute, I have something for her."

"What?"

"A shawl. It's pink. It would look very pretty on her, I think. You wouldn't mind taking it to her, would you?"

"Pa wouldn't let her keep it. He don't want charity from no one."

She frowned. "It's not charity, Faraday. It's a gift."

"You keep it. If you give it to her, Pa'd just—" He stopped, his eyes darkening. "He don't want her having nothin' he don't buy her hisself, that's all."

Beth knew Mac Slate worked only when abject poverty demanded coin to put bread on the table.

The tall, lean boy stood in her garden, a heavy scowl on his young face as he looked away from her clear eyes. He was proud and defiant, and carrying a deep anger within him. She knew he idolized her own father, who treated him fairly even when he caused trouble at the school or with shopkeepers. Once Frank had shoved the boy's head underwater at a horse trough when he'd begun swearing. Yanking him up sputtering, his arms flailing, Frank had told him quietly that he wouldn't put up with foulness on a public street.

"Say your piece square and I'll listen, but keep your mouth clean, boy."

Oddly enough, after that Faraday had said his piece in the sheriff's office frequently, and sometimes he walked with Frank Tyrell as he made his rounds of town after sundown.

Beth knew her father thought she didn't know anything about the Slates, but she had learned of Mac's brutal temper and of a meanness that went deeper than the resentment that shone in his eyes. That, and the shadows beneath Annie Slate's eyes, told a great deal about her personal misery.

Faraday looked into Beth's clear eyes again. His expression lost its arrogance and he held out the apple.

She didn't smile, knowing he'd take insult. "You earned it, Faraday. Thank you for bringing the dishes."

Frank Tyrell sent his deputy, John Bruster, for the dinner tray. John was a quiet, soft-spoken man in his late twenties, and Tyrell didn't worry about his bothering Beth. He was a good man, and not too aggressive. On the draw, Bruster was too slow with a gun, but once clear of leather he could shoot the whiskers off a retreating raccoon. His conversation with Beth was usually limited to, "Good evenin', ma'am. Thank you. Your pa should be along soon," before he left.

Just as well. Hannah Carlile wasn't the only parent around who wanted the best for her offspring. Frank Tyrell wanted a doctor for his daughter, not a deputy.

When Bruster returned, Frank took his hat and left the jail to walk the boardwalk, pausing to talk to townspeople. He bought another pouch of tobacco from Thomas Halverson before the store doors were locked for the night.

Looking up the street, Frank saw Beth clipping flowers in the front yard, and he headed slowly toward home. She always arranged a fresh bouquet for the mantel and another for the small dining table she had bought with her hard-earned sewing money. With her earnings from the delicate work she did creating pretty things for the better-off ladies in town, she managed to make the little house shine.

Not for the first time, Frank wondered how he, a rough-looking, rough-talking man without education, had ever sired such a gentle creature as his little Beth. She seemed satisfied with her life, even happy, and he could understand that least of all. She needed a man, children, her own place. All she had was her work, the little white house at the end of the street that went along with his being sheriff, and him. Not much, to his way of thinking.

Love was what she was waiting for. He knew why she believed it existed, and wondered if he had made a mistake after all. She couldn't wait around forever for some imaginary Prince Charming. All the men around Kilkare Woods were married, attached, or not worth a turn of her head. Save the young doc.

And the young doc was interested, Frank knew. He had watched them at the ice cream social. Everyone had wanted to talk to him, and Beth had stood by, watching all the fuss with an amused smile. She would make a fine doctor's wife for she had patience aplenty.

But she didn't know anything about encouraging a man who was interested. When the young doc sat next to her in church, she had been clearly embarrassed by his overt attention rather than pleased by it. Since then, she had insisted upon sitting at the end of the pew away from the aisle so that he couldn't do it again. It was no wonder Buchanan had backed off some. He just needed to understand that it was shyness that prompted her actions rather than rejection.

And Beth needed a good nudge.

Beth opened the gate for her father. "Everything fine?" she asked in an odd tone.

He frowned. "Same as always," he remarked, searching her face. "Anything wrong?"

Either the stranger had left or her father had already had words with him and made his position clear. "No, nothing," she said, relieved.

He went up the steps ahead of her and opened the door. While she went into the kitchen at the back of the house, Frank relaxed in his wing chair in the living room. Beth came out a few minutes later and put a shiny tin pitcher full of flowers on the table. He wished she had a porcelain vase. She ought to have a cabinet full of them. And nice dresses, too, like the ones she made for other ladies.

"Is something the matter, Papa?" she asked quietly, frowning slightly in concern.

"No, no," he grunted, shaking his head.

They shared a quiet evening meal, and Frank settled himself again into his chair to read the Bible.

Beth noticed he had to hold the book almost at arm's distance now and wondered why he was so stubbornly set against getting spectacles. She finished washing and putting away the blue willow dishes and came back into the parlor to work on her sewing. When she sat on the settee opposite him, he lowered the book slightly.

"She didn't like it?" he asked gruffly, nodding at the green dress on which she was working.

"She decided against the lace." She shrugged, not meeting his eyes.

His mouth tightened. "Why don't you tell her to go—"

"Papa," Beth said, smiling slightly as she gave him a reproving glance.

The mantel clock struck the half hour. Listening to it, Frank heard the front gate open and close and footsteps come up the front steps. He glanced surreptitiously at Beth as she gathered a few things from her cabinet at the back of the parlor that doubled as her shop. "I think someone's here," he said innocently, raising his Bible as a tap was heard against the door. "Would you get it, honey?"

She passed by his chair, set down a spool of thread on the arm on the settee, and opened the front door.

"Doctor Buchanan," she said in surprise.

"Good evening, Beth." The man standing on the porch was of medium height, well built, and well dressed. His light brown hair was brushed boyishly against his forehead, and his brown eyes crinkled at the corners when he smiled. It was the same smile that had the women in town in such a twitter.

She noted he was carrying his doctor's black case with him in one hand and his hat in the other.

"I came by to check on your father," he said in his honeyed southern drawl.

Beth glanced back at Frank, who avoided her gaze. She opened the front door wider and admitted Adam Buchanan to the small, cozy room warmed by the fireplace. She looked at her father again in growing suspicion. "Are you feeling ill, Papa? The doctor is here to see you."

He shifted uneasily in his chair. "Nothing serious,

honey." He had complained of a few aches and pains lately, and now Beth realized he had used them as an excuse to get Adam Buchanan here this evening. She suspected the young man knew of the subterfuge but had welcomed some assistance in getting the courtship moving in the right direction.

Frank closed his Bible and set it quickly aside as he stood. Extending his hand to Adam, he smiled. "Glad you could come on by, Doc. How about some coffee? Beth makes the best in town."

Suspicions confirmed, Beth turned and avoided the doctor's smiling look. How could her father do this to her? She wanted to kick him.

"Where you going, Beth?" her father asked, surprised by her coolness.

"To get coffee," she muttered, beating a hasty retreat to the tiny kitchen at the back.

"Sit down, sit down," she heard her father saying. "Make yourself comfortable, Doc."

Beth yanked open the cabinet door. She set cups and saucers briskly onto a tray. She didn't care if she broke the lot of them. After splashing coffee into the blue willow cups, she slammed the tin pot back on the stove.

Coming back into the parlor, Beth felt Adam's amused brown eyes watching her. She didn't meet them as she offered him coffee. When she bent over her father with the tray, she debated spilling the contents into his lap. He had the good grace to look sheepish. "Now, honey," he whispered.

"Just wait, Papa," she breathed. "If there isn't something wrong with you now, there will be!"

Adam Buchanan coughed, and Beth was mortified to realize he had heard her.

Sitting in embarrassed silence, Beth listened to her father and the young man discuss town affairs. In his four months in Kilkare Woods, Adam had learned a lot of the town's doings. It was obvious he enjoyed his vocation and the people who came under his care.

"Your father's right," Adam told her. "You do make the best coffee in town."

Her father's smug expression made her want to throw something at him. Did he seriously imagine a man married a woman for her coffee? Had *he?*

Beth smiled back at Adam. "Thank you. Would you care for more?"

"Please," Adam said, leaning toward her as he slid his cup closer to the tray on the narrow table.

Frank stood up. "I have to make my rounds," he explained too quickly. Adam stood as well. "Sit down, Doc. Sit down. Finish your coffee. Don't think you have to leave. I won't be gone long enough to cause any lifted eyebrows. Sit a spell and visit with Beth."

Before anything more could be said on the matter, Frank was out the door. Beth put a hand to her blushing cheek, wondering what on earth she could possibly say now. If her father had wanted to be subtle, he had failed dismally.

All the women in town with unmarried daughters plotted unmercifully for Adam Buchanan's attention. But none as openly as her own father, she thought grimly.

Turning, she gave Adam an embarrassed smile. "I'm sorry, Adam," she murmured, seeing his amused, sympathetic smile and knowing there was no point in pretending she didn't know what her father was up to. It was more than clear that Adam knew of her father's ruse.

"You needn't be embarrassed, Beth," he said. "Your father just wants us to—"

"Yes, I know what he wants," she interrupted quickly.

"He worries about you. An affliction of most fathers, I suspect," he teased.

"He needn't worry in quite this way. I'm doing very

well as things are without his well-meaning assistance."

"Yes. You maintain a thriving business and handle the household for him, as well as cooking and cleaning for any prisoners he might have in his jail. I was told that Darrel McAllister always times his arrests for Monday because he knows Tuesday is stew and dumplings."

She laughed. "You do hear a lot, don't you?"

His eyes studied her face in leisurely interest. "A doctor sometimes acts as a patient's confessor."

"Then it won't shock you greatly if I tell you I could strangle my father for embarrassing you like this."

"I'm not the least embarrassed. I'm flattered by his approval." One side of his mouth tipped at her look. "Since he didn't allow me the opportunity to check him over as he asked this morning, I may have to wait until he returns."

Her color rose sharply and she looked down at the coffeepot, shying away from his flirtation. "Are there many like my father who pretend an illness in order to have you come to call?" she teased back lightly.

"Mostly females," he admitted. "Mothers pose the greatest threat."

She laughed again. "Yes, I can imagine."

They fell silent for a moment. He nodded at the green dress. "You do beautiful work. You would do quite well in a large city, Beth."

"How does a doctor come to know so much about ladies' clothing?"

He grinned. "I had three spoiled sisters and a father who enjoyed pandering to their every desire. And Mother had impeccable taste," he added in a smooth, humorous drawl.

"You were very outnumbered."

"I had two younger brothers to help me when necessary. Things worked out fairly evenly. Father always had the last word."

She laughed softly. "You miss them, don't you?"

"We correspond. I'm needed here, and that's what is important. To be needed."

"Yes," she agreed, wondering if her father understood that.

"Have you ever thought about leaving Kilkare Woods?"

"Oh, no." She shook her head. "I can't see myself anywhere else. And Papa's here. I wouldn't want to leave him. Kilkare Woods is all I'll ever want."

"It does have a decided appeal, I agree, but I thought most young women longed for . . . well, more." He watched her face intently.

She smiled. "Young ladies in these parts learn homecrafts from their mothers and grandmothers, go to school to learn to read and write some, and then marry and have babies."

"And you don't want that?"

"More coffee?" she asked softly.

"No, thank you."

"Perhaps I should clear this away, then," she said.

He stood as she did and followed her into the kitchen. She glanced back at him as he leaned against the doorframe and watched her work at the counter. He wanted an answer. "Yes, I want all those things, too," she admitted. "But a woman shouldn't feel pressed to marry just because she's eighteen or twenty . . . " She dimpled. "Or older."

"Twenty-one," he said, eyes dancing. "I asked."

His words brought the stranger to mind, and a quickening of her heartbeat. She looked away. "If you hadn't, I'm sure Papa would have volunteered the information," she said in faint amusement.

"I read all of Doc Wingate's files. You had measles when you were six and had to have a fishing hook removed from your left shoulder when you were eleven."

She blushed. "Oh!" She wondered if he had read as far as her menses starting when she was thirteen. Doc Wingate had had to explain all that to her because her father had been embarrassed even to try. When she had told him something was wrong and what it was, he had taken her straightaway to Doc Wingate and said, "She needs you to talk to her about . . . the woman thing." And he had left.

"You've had me intrigued since the church had the potluck dinner to welcome me to town," Adam said, his mouth curving. He moved aside to let her step by him and followed her back into the parlor. "You were the only woman there who didn't invite me home to dinner."

She glanced back and laughed. "Father did say you were doing quite well for yourself, and you've been here for Sunday dinner." She sat down on the settee again and folded her hands sedately. He sat down closer than he had before.

"On your father's invitation. Not yours."

"It was from both of us, Adam."

"Then it's my turn to reciprocate."

"You did," she murmured, embarrassed once more. "You escorted me to the ice cream social."

His eyes widened slightly in comprehension. "That was not out of any sense of duty," he said clearly. "And you spent almost the entire afternoon by yourself because everyone kept wanting to tell me their medical history." His expression was ruefully apologetic. "I'm afraid I made a very bad impression."

"I enjoyed the day very much," she said sincerely.

"As did I, but I would have preferred a little more time with you." He put his hand over hers. "It would give me the greatest pleasure if you would accompany me on a carriage ride Saturday. I have a few calls to make and would like your company. We would have plenty of time between visits to talk without interruption."

"Are you asking because my father—"

"No," he said, not even letting her finish. "I seem to

have your father's blessing to come calling on you. All I need is yours."

Several weeks ago, on the Sunday following the social, he had sat down next to her in church. She had seen the speculative looks from half a dozen women in the congregation and had heard the twittering. Her father sat on her right, arms crossed over his broad chest, almost grinning. Creating gossip had never been in Beth's nature, and after that, she had been careful to sit at the far end of the pew. She wondered now if Adam had misunderstood entirely. She liked him very much and had meant no rebuff.

"I . . . I would like for you to call on me," she said, and lowered her eyes. "But I . . ."

"People will talk anyway, Beth," he told her, and she was surprised at his sensitivity.

She sighed. "I suppose they will."

"They do so in a kind way."

The front door opened and her father came in again. He saw Adam's hand over Beth's and smiled at them. "Did you offer him one of your tea cakes, Beth?"

"No. You ate them all before dinner."

Adam laughed and stood.

"You aren't leaving, are you?" Frank asked, obviously dismayed.

Adam glanced at Beth's exasperated expression and winked at her. "No. First I want you to strip down in your bedroom so I can check you over."

Frank reddened to the roots of his hair. He cleared his throat. Adam laughed and slapped him on the back. "Never mind, Frank. I'll be back on Saturday if I have your permission to take Beth for a carriage ride."

Frank's face cleared immediately and he grinned broadly. "I think you're a man I can trust with my daughter. Permission granted."

Adam bade them good evening and left. Her father

closed the door and turned to her, hands on his hips. "Well, that all turned out for the best, now, didn't it?"

"It could have been an absolutely impossible situation," Beth said in annoyance.

"He wasn't being polite. He likes you. I told you that before. He asks after you every time we meet."

"Is that why you found it necessary to create some imaginary illness just to have him come to call?" she added dryly. "Oh, Papa, I've never been so embarrassed. If he wants to come by, he will. I don't need you prodding him on with a poker."

Her father snorted. "You keep yourself cooped up in this little front-room shop of yours from dawn to dusk. The only time you ever come out for air is to bring meals to the jail, run your errands in town, attend church, and work in your flower garden out front or vegetable garden out back. You need someone of your own!"

"I have you."

"God in heaven, Beth!" he boomed, shocking her. "I'm sorry," he said gruffly, "but I'm not going to be on this earth forever. I'd like to know when I die that my only child has a husband and children and a full, rich life. All you have now is me and this little house that doesn't even belong to us. It belongs to the township and goes to whoever is sheriff. You know that. What if something happens to me? What would happen to you?"

"We live in a quiet town, Papa. What could happen?" Her eyes widened and darkened. "You aren't really ill, are you? It *was* just a ruse when you asked Adam to come by?"

"I'm fifty. That's what's wrong with me. I'm getting old. You're the one that keeps after me about needing spectacles." He turned away. "Damnit, I never did get my drink," he muttered, grabbing up his hat again. He hesitated, playing the rim through his fingers.

He let out a deep sigh. "Beth, you've got to stop living for me. You've got to start living for yourself. That's all I'm asking. That, and for you to give that young doc a chance. He's a right fine fellow. You couldn't do better."

He looked old and tired and Beth wanted badly to say something that would ease his worries on her behalf. She was happy. Granted, she wasn't married, nor did she have babies of her own, but perhaps that would come in time. For now, her life was full if he could but see it. She had her work. She helped at the schoolhouse on occasion, and she was active in the church. Why was it so hard to explain to him that she didn't feel deprived? Her father viewed any unmarried woman as incomplete.

Or perhaps a failure?

He bent and kissed her lightly on the forehead before going out. She went to the curtained window and watched him go down the path and open the gate. He always stopped there and rolled a cigarette. He drew heavily on it for a moment and then headed down Main Street for the saloon. He would not have more than a whiskey or two, but he would linger over them for an hour, taking in all the news of Kilkare and the surrounding ranches.

She thought about the stranger again and pressed a hand to her quivering stomach. Was he still there? What would her father do about him?

She turned away and tidied the parlor, washed the cups and saucers in the kitchen, and put them away on their shelves. She ironed several of her father's shirts. Her evening chores finished, she sat again and worked on Edwina Carlile's green dress.

The clock chimed eleven.

Beth frowned. It was not usual for her father to be this late. Perhaps he had joined in a game of cards, as he sometimes did. She went into her small, spartan room off the kitchen, took off her blouse and brown skirt, and folded them onto a chair for washing in the morning. She removed her petticoats, pantaloons, camisole, corset cover, and corset, and left the thin chemise on as she found the lightweight flannel nightgown in her dresser. After removing the last layer of clothing, she slipped the gown quickly over her head.

Sleep wouldn't come. She kept listening for the front door to open. The clock chimed once for half past, then again later for twelve.

Where was he?

She thought of the bold-eyed stranger again, the manly way he had looked at her. She sat up in bed, hands over her face. Swinging her legs from beneath the heavy quilt, she pulled on the robe she kept at the foot of her bed. Her bare feet felt the chill of the wood floor as she crossed to open the door into the kitchen.

She wasn't sure what to do. She couldn't go out looking for her father at midnight, and if something had happened, someone would have come.

Worry coursed through her, a nameless, reasonless unease.

The front door clicked open. A sense of relief that was almost physical swept over her, and she quickly wrapped the robe more tightly around her as she pushed the door open into the parlor. Her father's bedroom was off the parlor at the front of the house.

He hadn't gone there, but was standing before the low-burning fire, his hand on the mantel. His head was down and he looked to be in pain.

"Papa, are you alright?" She crossed the room quickly and put her hand on his arm. He straightened, looking down at her with a tightly veiled expression that was entirely alien to her.

"I'm fine. What're you doing up this late?"

"I was worried about you. Was there some trouble?"

"No trouble. I just felt like having a long walk." He looked away. Stooping, he picked up a log.

"It's past twelve," she said.

"I know what time it is."

"Aren't you going to bed?" The log he was putting on would burn for hours. Usually they let the fire burn down at night and relighted it in the morning.

"No."

"Something did happen," she said, frightened.

"Stop nagging and go to bed!"

Her eyes went wide and filled with tears. He had never spoken to her so harshly. "Good night, Papa," she said, and turned away.

He caught hold of her shoulders. "I'm sorry," he rasped. "It's nothing to do with you, honey. I've just got to figure things out." His hands fell away from her.

She turned and looked up at his craggy, grim lined face. "Does this have anything to do with the man who came into town today?"

His eyes darkened to onyx. She'd never seen that look on his face. "What do you know about him? Did he stop you? Talk to you?"

"My skirt snagged on the gate and he helped me."

"He *touched* you?"

"No," she said, staring up at him. "He freed my hem, asked if this was Kilkare Woods and if there was a place to stay. I mentioned the hotel."

"That's all? He didn't say anything else? Ask you anything?"

"No." It was not what the stranger had said but how he had looked at her that had been so disturbing. "What would he want to say to me?"

He shook his head. His fingers kneaded the back of his neck and he looked exhausted. "That sort of man might say something offensive to a lady."

"Is he a gunfighter, Papa?" He had looked it, every lean, powerful inch of him.

"Yes. He's got some notches on his handle," he said derisively.

Her stomach plunged. Hadn't she known already? Why this feeling of grievous disappointment? "What's he doing in Kilkare Woods?"

Her father made a sound in his throat. "Looking for trouble."

"You asked him to leave?"

"I asked. He said no. Long as he stays peaceable, I can't run him out or lock him up." He obviously wished things were different.

"Maybe he's just passing through town," she murmured, thinking of the man again and of the look in his eyes that had made her heart race and her stomach flutter so strangely.

Her father didn't answer. He just stared down into the flames with a look of bitter sadness etched deeply in his tanned face.

"Who is he, Papa?" Beth asked, unable to entirely extinguish her interest in spite of knowing what he was.

"Logan Tanner," he said flatly, and straightened. He glanced at her, worried. Reaching out, he cupped his hand at her nape beneath the heavy braid that hung to her waist. "You stay clear of him. Understood? If he's walking one side of the street, you cross to the other. If he tries to talk to you, you just keep walking and don't even look at him."

Her lips parted and she searched his eyes.

His hand tightened, knowing what he asked was entirely against her nature. He drew her against him in a brief, hard hug. He looked haggard when he let her go. "You'd best get to bed, honey."

"Papa?"

"Just go to bed. I've got some thinking to do. Nothing for you to worry on, honey. I swear. Nothing that has anything at all to do with you. Now, go on."

Whatever it was, he was telling her he would handle it in his own way. He wanted no interference from her or anyone. He never had.

Obedient, she nodded and went back to her room.

But she couldn't sleep for thinking about Logan Tanner.

Chapter Three

BETH WAS UP with the sun, but her father's bedroom door stood open. "Papa?" She peered in. He was gone. He never left this early.

Trying to still her worries, Beth went about her usual morning chores. She made bread dough and left it to rise on the kitchen table while she took the rugs out back to air. She polished the wood furniture with beeswax.

By the time she had finished her polishing, it was time to get a breakfast of scrambled eggs and fried potatoes ready to take down to the jail.

Her father wasn't there. John Bruster was still sitting at the big desk looking over a pile of wanted posters that had come in on the morning stage.

"The Widow O'Keefe sent for your pa early this morning," John said. "She said someone was making off with her cattle again." He caught her curious look and shrugged. "Your pa asked me to look through all these and see if there was anything on that new fellow in town. Tanner." Beth waited till John had gone through the entire file before leaving.

On her way home, she stopped off at Halverson's. Little Tammy Whiler, whose father cleaned out the livery stable, was standing before the counter, staring longingly at the mason jars filled with an array of brightly colored candies. Faith ignored her as she worked on a high ladder stacking canned goods away. "What can I do for you, Beth?" she called down.

Beth bent and whispered next to Tammy's ear. "What'll it be, sweetheart?"

Big, limpid blue eyes gazed up at her. "Peppermint, please, Miss Beth."

Beth straightened. "One peppermint stick, please."

Faith climbed down and brushed off her hands on her white apron. She held out her hand for a penny and Beth placed one in her palm. Faith opened the jar and took a peppermint stick out and handed it across. Tammy's thin face glowed as she took it. She gripped Beth around the hips and squeezed her before darting out of the store, the treat clutched in one tight little fist.

Faith shook her head. "She comes in here every morning and just stands there looking at all that candy."

"She's a dear," Beth said.

"She's a little thief's what she is. In another second, she'd have lifted the lid and snatched one of those peppermint sticks. I was watching her out of the corner of my eye."

"It might be a sensible idea then to place the candy jars back there on the shelf, where they can be easily seen but not reached," Beth suggested, knowing Faith's own son was the worst offender.

Faith laughed. "I think you're right. Lead us not into temptation, is what the Good Book says, and here I am putting temptation on the front counter." She put her hands on her ample hips. "Now, what can I get for you this morning? More tobacco for your pa? You know, he smokes too much. He was standing outside his office early this morning smoking and looking at that hotel. Three cigarettes right in a row, he smoked."

Beth handed over her short list.

"Must have something to do with that new man in town," Faith went on, glancing back over her shoulder at Beth. "Thomas said he saw your pa talking with him last night in the saloon. Thought there was going to be trouble. Then your father stood up and left." She set a sack of dried beans on the counter.

Beth listened intently while trying to show no particular concern. Faith would ask more questions if she did.

"Looks like a gunfighter, my Thomas said," Faith told her, putting dried peppers in a paper sack and twisting it closed before laying it by the beans. "Can't imagine what a man like that would want to come here for, but Thomas said word's out he's staying awhile. Paid for a week's lodgings." She measured out coffee beans. As she set the sack on the counter, she looked at Beth closely. "Did your father tell you what they talked about?"

"No."

"Didn't say anything? Thomas said they talked for some time. Said your father looked white as a ghost for a while and then red as an Indian before he left. Mad as hell, most likely. Thomas said after your father said his piece, that stranger just sat there smiling at him cool as you please." She brushed her hands off on her apron again. "What else can I get for you, Beth?"

"That's all for today, thank you." Money was short at the moment, but several customers had promised to pay by next week, and Beth knew she could always count on Avery.

While Faith tallied the total, she went on talking. She

was the main well of town gossip. Patsy Longford was pregnant again, though Faith couldn't for the life of her understand how the woman could be so foolish. With eight mouths to feed already, how could they possibly afford another? Sam Hamilton was paining again. It was his stomach, but Faith was sure it was all in his head. Every time his sister came to visit, Sam got sick. "Just trying to keep her here to wait on him, probably." Maybe the new doctor could give him something. Speaking of the new doctor, wasn't he handsome? That southern drawl of his made a woman weak at the knees even when she'd been married well on ten years now. But then, Beth should know all about that since the doc seemed to have his eye on her.

Beth was embarrassed by the last remark. She made noncommittal replies as Faith went on, and tried not to listen. She thought of her father and how late he had come home last night and how weary he had looked. How early had he left this morning? Had he slept at all? What had been said between him and Logan Tanner?

She opened her small drawstring purse to extract money for Faith, then carried the small box of goods out of the store and back up the boardwalk toward the cottage. She stopped off at the Polks' butcher shop for two chickens. She made another stop at Maddie Jeffrey's for a couple of eggs. Loaded down, she returned home and stored everything away.

She spent the morning working on Edwina's green dress. She had a fitting with another lady at ten. Everything went well, with no further alterations needed. She wrapped up the dress carefully and was paid.

Beth delivered two loaves of fresh bread, sliced beef, cheese, and fruit to the jail at noon. Her father was still gone. Another customer came at one and asked her to make a dress like one she had seen in a magazine. The lady requested blue Henrietta, which Beth had on hand. They were discussing trims when a messenger arrived to inform Beth that a large crate had come in on the noon train. The lady departed.

Taking her handcart from the woodshed, Beth started for the station. She was sure the crate contained the bolts of myrtle green and cardinal Henrietta she had ordered from San Francisco some weeks before. She was eager also to see the wine brilliantine, black lisle voile, and shadow-stripe batiste. Cambrick, muslin, sateen, and percale were standard fare, and she had ordered them as well.

She stopped by the sheriff's office to enlist her father's help, but he still had not returned. Dismayed and worried, she went along to the station by herself.

When Beth reached it, at the end of Oak Street, she saw that the manager, Matthew Galloway, had placed her large crate just outside his office door. It would be far too heavy for her to handle, and he always helped her when her father was unavailable.

Opening his office door, she peered in. "Mr. Galloway?" He wasn't there, and she guessed he was still at home having his lunch with Mary. She would have to wait until he returned.

"Can I be of help, Miss Tyrell?" drawled a deep, familiar voice.

Beth swung around, startled, and stared up at Logan Tanner standing a few feet behind her. "Wherever did you come from?" she gasped, closing the door.

His mouth curved sardonically. "I was at the livery stable when you passed by. Thought I'd say hello."

She put a hand to her throat and gave a self-conscious laugh. "You walk very quietly for such a big man, Mr. Tanner. I didn't even know you were there until you spoke."

"Took off my spurs. Walking quiet can keep a man alive," he said cryptically. "I apologize for frightening you."

He looked even more handsome today with the dust and sweat of hard travel washed away. He wore dark brown pants, a clean plaid shirt, and a leather vest and jacket that made him look much like other citizens of Kilkare Woods. Yet, his gun remained buckled low on his hips and tied down on his thigh. There was an alertness in his expression that was unnerving.

His smile deepened. "I asked if I might be of help to you, ma'am."

"Oh!" The potent virility of his look made her catch her breath and look away. She glanced back at Matthew Galloway's closed door, wondering what she should say. Her father's firm warning of the night before was still in her mind.

Tanner made the decision for her. He stepped forward. "You just stand aside, ma'am, and I'll put your crate in your cart for you," he said, putting his hands to her slender waist and moving her out of his way. She stood back shakily and watched him tip the heavy, large crate effortlessly onto her cart.

"Thank you, Mr. Tanner."

"You're welcome, Miss Tyrell," he mocked, a sparkle in his blue eyes that made Beth wonder if he was laughing at her. His eyes softened slightly at her bemused, questioning look. "I'd better see you home with that thing. It's far too heavy for you to manage."

"There's no need for you to put yourself out. I can leave it here and have Mr. Galloway bring it around. Or my father . . ."

An uncomfortable silence fell between them. She sensed he was insulted.

"Aren't you curious what's inside this? You'll be the

first woman I've ever known not to want to open a closed box," he remarked.

She wondered how many women he had known. "I already know what's inside. Bolts of cloth," she answered simply.

"Ah, that explains your lack of interest." He leaned one hand against the wall and hooked a thumb into his holster. All she could stare at was his gun, ominous and dark and part of his lean, hard body. She raised her gaze to his.

"I should be going," she told him softly.

His eyes narrowed. "Afraid of me, or just don't want to be seen in my company?" The cynical bite of his words and a darkness in his eyes moved Beth oddly.

Shun him, her father had told her, but something about him made that utterly impossible. "I'm not exactly afraid of you, Mr. Tanner," she said.

"Who told you my name?" he asked in amusement.

"My father told me he'd spoken with you last evening."

His smiled chilled and his dark eyes glinted. "Did he also tell you what we talked about?"

She said nothing for a moment, then answered. "He said he asked you to leave town and you refused. Beyond that, he said very little."

A knowing look in Tanner's face made her color rise.

"Beth!"

Logan's body stiffened, and Beth saw the almost imperceptible movement of the hand above his gun before he glanced back, saw no threat, and relaxed into his indolent pose again. It had all happened in a second's time, but Beth's heart raced in alarm.

A big, barrel-chested man with a curly mane of sandy hair, thick muttonchop sideburns, and a sagging mustache stepped up onto the train platform and strode toward them.

"Hello, Mr. Galloway," Beth said.

"I'm sorry I wasn't here when you arrived," he apologized, stopping close to her and looking at Tanner speculatively. He ran a hand down his black suspenders and frowned heavily. "You're new in town, aren't you? Haven't seen you around before." It was half accusation.

Logan's veiled, cold eyes were faintly amused. "Yes." He waited, his expression mocking.

Galloway stiffened, eyes narrowing in hostility.

"Mr. Galloway, this is Logan Tanner. He helped me with the crate," Beth interceded, feeling the tension mounting.

Galloway made a noncommittal grunt, then said, "Planning to stay long?"

"Depends."

For a man who only moments before had been encouraging Beth to ask questions, he now seemed very reticent. "Mr. Tanner is just passing through, Mr. Galloway," Beth volunteered to prevent further interrogation. This time Logan surprised her with a broad, suggestive grin.

"I didn't say that at all, Miss Tyrell. Are you trying to put words in my mouth or parroting your father?"

She blushed painfully.

Galloway's mouth flattened out. "Then you're planning on staying for a while."

Logan looked Beth over from head to foot. "Maybe."

"Kilkare Woods doesn't have what you're looking for, Mr. Tanner."

Logan laughed softly. "I wouldn't say that. I think it has just what I'm looking for." He winked at Beth.

Matthew Galloway's mouth opened slightly as he glanced at Beth. His face was a thunderous mask, and Beth knew that Logan's remarks had only incited his temper. Seeing trouble coming from her father's longtime friend who had a reputation for acting on emotions rather than thought, and more than sure Tanner was capable of swift retaliation, Beth reached out and put her hand lightly on Logan's arm.

Logan glanced down at her in surprise.

"Would you please help me take this home now?"

"Beth!" Galloway protested sharply.

"You're busy. I saw what's in your office. And Mr. Tanner did offer."

"Can't turn a lady down when she asks, now can I, Galloway?" Logan said, bending to the handles of the cart. Angry color came into Galloway's ruddy face as he stared after them.

Logan glanced at Beth as they went up Oak Street. One side of his firm mouth lifted. "Who were you trying to protect, Miss Tyrell?"

"Both and neither."

"He's a stuffed shirt."

"He's a friend of mine and my father's and I will thank you not to speak ill of him. Why were you baiting him if you're so quick to take offense?"

His brows arched and she felt a shiver of apprehension at her own temerity. He gave a low laugh. "I guess I'm just disagreeable by nature. Comes from the company I've kept."

"Mr. Galloway is usually more polite."

Logan grinned. "He didn't want me near you."

"People are friendly here, Mr. Tanner. They don't take exception to anyone unless they have a reason to."

"What have I done wrong, ma'am?" he asked, eyes glinting dangerously. "I rode into town easy, asked a pretty lady directions after helping her free her skirt from a gate, then put up at the local hotel. First thing I know, the sheriff's telling me to get out of town. I don't like being ordered to do anything. Now, look at that woman on the porch over there staring at us. This town is anything but friendly." He stared at the woman across the street with hard intensity and raised his hat slightly, giving her a cold, insolent grin. Missus Becket retreated quickly into the quiet coolness of her house. Beth closed her eyes for an instant.

"It's understandable that people will be curious about you," she told him as they walked. "Not many men ride into Kilkare Woods looking armed for trouble."

He laughed again. "Never know when you might be in the middle of a war, Miss Tyrell. Your father came close to starting one with me last night in the saloon."

She paled. "He was only trying to do his job."

"Does he order every stranger out of town?"

"It's only that you look . . ." She flushed.

One dark brow rose. "Look?" He waited, his expression filled with grim amusement.

"Perhaps if you left your gun at the sheriff's office, he might . . ."

Logan's eyes went cold. "Guns are my business."

Her step faltered. She stopped and looked up at him, her eyes wide and apprehensive.

He let the cart thump down as he straightened and faced her, his manner arrogant. "Still want me to manage this load for you, ma'am?" His eyes were dark and enigmatic. "I could give one shot and half the town would be running down here in seconds. Fine, upstanding gentlemen like Mister Galloway back there or that Doctor Buchanan."

Her lips parted slightly as she searched his face. He put his hand on his gun, angry defiance darkening his eyes. Did he really mean it?

"I can't manage it without you," she told him softly, "unless you'd rather not help me, of course."

He hadn't expected that. A faint frown flickered and his blue eyes narrowed in curiosity. A muscle locked in his jaw as he bent and took up the handles of her cart again. He walked wordlessly to the small cottage at the edge of town and thunked the cart down at her gate. He turned to leave with a gruff, "Good day, ma'am," and tip of his hat.

"Mr. Tanner?" He glanced back at her. "Why are you here?"

"That's a personal question," he said without expression, "and not one I'll answer." He gave her a cynical smile. "But rest assured, pretty little Beth Tyrell, that even a man like me has a code he lives by."

She took a step toward him, her head tilted as she searched his hard, withdrawn face. "What is your code, Mr. Tanner?"

"I've never killed a man who didn't deserve to die." He turned and strode away.

Chapter Four

"I TOLD YOU to stay clear of that man!" Frank boomed at his daughter.

Beth stared up at him with wide, frightened eyes, her needlework lying in her lap. He slammed into the little house and began shouting at her immediately.

"But Papa—"

"I wasn't back in town five minutes before I heard about you walking right down Main Street with that damn gunfighter!"

"I—"

"Then Matt comes running from the station to tell me you *asked* Tanner to help you!" he accused, his face red with anger, the vein in his neck pounding visibly.

"But—"

"Did you listen to what I said to you last night?" he railed, his anger feeding on itself, and her wide-eyed look making him want to shake her. "I told you to stay away from that scum. What do you think everyone in town will say about this? My God, you won't let that nice young doc sit next to you in church, but you ask a gunfighter to see you home in broad daylight, the whole town watching you!"

"That's not fair," she managed. "I didn't encourage—"

"What do you call it when a woman asks a man to do something for her?"

She blushed crimson, wondering what Logan thought of her. Surely he had understood her motives. "Mr. Galloway wasn't there when I arrived. I couldn't load that crate myself. He offered—"

"You could have left it and waited."

"Yes, but Mr. Tanner appeared and put it on my cart. Then Mr. Galloway arrived and acted like a surly bear looking for a fight. He as much as told Mr. Tanner he wasn't welcome."

"He's not! I want to see the back of him."

"Yes. You already made that clear to him at the saloon," she said after a pause. "Did John find anything in those wanted posters you gave him this morning?"

"No. But that doesn't mean anything," he said grimly, raking a hand back through his thick gray hair and then standing arms akimbo, glaring down at Beth. "Matt said Tanner was standing in front of you, blocking your way, when he arrived."

She saw the ominous darkness in her father's eyes. "He was talking to me."

"I told you not to talk to him!"

"He had just loaded my crate, Papa. How could I be rude to him?"

"Rude, hell," he snarled, forgetting himself entirely and swearing at her. "Sensible, damnit!"

She blinked, shocked. "Why are you so set against him? He's done nothing."

"He will."

"You don't know that," she protested.

"I can't believe you're defending that rattlesnake!" He bent slightly, his chin jutting. "Just what did go on?"

Her face went very pale at his tone. "He was kind and I was polite. Nothing more," she defended herself.

"Well, I'm telling you right now that you won't speak to him again. Do you understand me?"

She stiffened. "I am not a child, Papa!"

"You're not a woman with a lick of sense, either!" He knew the moment the words were uttered that he had made a tactical mistake.

Two spots of color appeared in Beth's cheeks and her eyes changed. She lowered her head and began sewing again.

Frank stared down at the top of her head grimly. He watched in growing fustration as each careful stitch of blue silk thread was sewn into the blue bodice of some woman's new dress. He thought of Tanner walking her down Main Street and a muscle locked in his hard, uncompromising jaw. Her silence didn't fool him. She might appear placid, but he could almost feel the resistance she radiated.

She had never bucked him in the past. She had obeyed as a loving, dutiful, sensible daughter. She had to listen this time. It was too important.

"Beth, I want you to promise not to speak to Tanner again," he said quietly. She had never broken a promise to him.

She didn't raise her head.

"Beth!"

"No."

He gaped. "No?" He couldn't believe she was defying him.

She raised her chin, the color still high in her cheeks. "I will leave it to you and Mr. Galloway and the rest of Kilkare Woods to snub Mr. Tanner if you so wish. But you will not order me to do so. He is due the same respect as anyone else, and I will not treat him with deliberate disrespect and unkindness."

Frank stood silent for a long moment. "You don't understand, Beth."

"I do understand that unkindness begets unkindness, Papa."

He had gone about it all wrong. He frowned as she lowered her head again and went on with her needlework as though he were not even there. A woman's silence could be a damn wearing thing, worse than any man's outburst of temper, he thought with annoyance.

"Beth," he pleaded, and sat down in his easy chair. He leaned forward, hands clasped between his knees. "That man is here to cause grief."

"You don't know that."

"I know." A muscle worked in his jaw. "You only have to look at him to know."

She laid her sewing aside and stood up. "Whatever his reasons for being here, Papa, I'll treat him as I would anyone else." She turned away. "I'd better start supper."

Frank watched her walk toward the swinging door to the kitchen. "Beth," he said in exasperation, and stood. "He lives by that gun he wears."

She looked back at him. "So do you, Papa." Turning away, she left the room.

He swore vehemently. Tanner hadn't been in town twenty-four hours and already there was trouble, right here in his own home between himself and his own flesh and blood.

Later, at the sheriff's office, Frank sent John back to the cottage for the lunch tray instead of having Beth carry it to the jail. A friend stopped in to talk and reported that Tanner was at the hotel playing poker. He was winning a sizable amount of money and he wasn't cheating.

"That man's got the luck of Lucifer."

At suppertime, walking up the boardwalk toward the cottage, Frank saw Beth watering and fussing over the window boxes filled with flowers. The foul taste of their earlier argument haunted him. He'd never spoken to her the way he had today, and he remembered the hurt he'd seen in her eyes.

Beth turned as he reached the gate. He looked tired, his shoulders hunched, his expression grim as he met her eyes.

"Hello, Papa," she said softly.

He came up the steps slowly. She opened the door for him. He unbuckled his holster and hung his gun on the brass hook just inside the door. "I'm hungry."

"Everything's ready. Sit down and I'll serve."

He was quiet through the meal.

"Papa, I'm sorry," Beth said quietly, gazing at him sadly. "I just can't—"

"We won't talk about it anymore," he said gruffly. "You know how I feel and why. You just think about it some."

"I didn't encourage him," she said again, hurting at the distance between them.

He said nothing for a moment, then reached out and patted her hand.

Since Avery had returned from the East with Edwina, her father had had bouts of ill temper with her, but nothing so violent as today. She could only guess his reasons. She knew that he had harbored hopes of her and Avery's marrying eventually. She had dreamed of it herself during their idyllic summer. But she hadn't really been in love with him. If she had, she wouldn't have gotten over loving him so quickly, or felt so little when she saw him again.

She acknowledged Logan's danger, though not in the same way as her father. The danger that threatened her was from his devasting attractiveness. Each time she glimpsed him, strange new sensations moved swiftly through her body. He looked at her and her heart raced.

When her father had ordered her to avoid him, some deep, thus far unknown feeling in her had reared up in hot defiance.

As father and daughter sat there in tense silence at the table, Adam arrived. This time her father's surprise matched her own.

"I didn't have the opportunity to check you over last night," Adam said in way of explanation.

Frank looked from the doc to his daughter. "Never mind. I feel just fine today."

"It'll take but a few minutes, Frank. Come on in here and take off your shirt." He stood at the bedroom door off the parlor, waiting, his black leather bag in his hand.

"Alright," Frank said impatiently.

Beth smiled slightly and cleared the table. She heard the two men talking for some time in her father's bedroom. She was working on Edwina's green dress again when they emerged. Her father shrugged back into his leather vest.

"Would you like some coffee, Adam?" she asked.

He smiled and set his bag down on the long table before her. "I would like that very much."

Frank cleared his throat.

"You're invited, too, Papa," Beth said, her dimples flashing.

"I'm going round town now," he said, and looked pointedly at Adam.

She glanced questioningly at Adam. "He isn't ill, is he?"

"Called my bluff, that's all," Frank said grudgingly, and then gave a sheepish, lopsided grin.

Beth laughed. "I hope you gave him a good scare, Adam."

"Just what he deserved," Adam remarked.

Frank reached for his holster and buckled it on. He looked at them. "Maybe you two ought to sit out on the porch."

"So the whole town can see us?" she teased.

"That's right," he said, and went out.

Her lips parted and, looking embarrassed, she glanced at Adam. "I'll go make the coffee," she said, and went out to the kitchen. He didn't follow this time, but waited on the porch outside.

She brought the tray out and set it on the wide rail. Looking down Main Street, her mouth tightened slightly. She glanced back, forcing a smile for Adam as he rested his hip against the rail a few feet away from her. His smile was gentle. "I don't mind, Beth."

She lowered her eyes. "Would you care for a macaroon?"

"Sit with me," he said softly, straightening and moving toward her.

"If I sit with you on the porch swing, the town will have us married by summer," she told him.

He looked squarely at her. "Sit with me."

Warmth rose up into her face.

He reached out and took her hand. "Remember our agreement?" He lifted it lightly and kissed it, his eyes twinkling.

She moved the tray to the small table at the end of the porch, then sat down with Adam on the big swing. She served him coffee and macaroons and they listened in silence to the crickets. She asked him finally about his day, and he told her anecdotes about several patients.

Gradually, she relaxed in his easy company.

"You were upset earlier," he said, startling her. "Were you and your father arguing?"

"We seldom argue," she countered.

He made a soft sound and smiled disbelievingly.

"Well, almost never," she amended, smiling back. She frowned slightly. "Actually, he's become quite short-tempered lately." When Adam volunteered no remark, she looked at him carefully. His expression invited confidence. "He treats me like a child."

"He's your father. You are a child in his eyes, and will be even when you're married and have children."

She shook her head and looked away.

"Did something happen today?"

"There's a new man in town," she said slowly.

"The gunfighter. Yes, I've heard. An arrogant man by the looks of him."

Somehow, Adam's tone grated. She glanced up at him. "He was at the train station when I was there and loaded my crate onto my handcart. He offered to see me home with it, and I accepted his offer."

Adam looked at her assessingly but said nothing.

"Papa heard about it and was furious."

"And no wonder. It doesn't do for a lady like you to be seen with a man like that, Beth. It could hurt your reputation. If you ever have anything to pick up at the train station, send word to me and I'll help you if your father can't, or I'll see that you have the help you need."

Beth fell silent.

Adam changed the subject.

It was several moments before Beth felt the earlier rapport with Adam return.

He stayed for two hours. "I look forward to our carriage ride tomorrow, Beth," he said, smiling down at her as she walked him to the gate. "Missus Michaels is packing a lunch for us so we can picnic on our way back to town," he told her, mentioning his housekeeper.

"That will be nice," Beth said sincerely. He closed the gate as he went out. "Good night, Adam." She watched him walk away, his leather satchel as much a part of him as the gun was a part of Logan Tanner.

She went back up the front steps and gathered the cups together and put them on the tray. Pausing at the rail, she looked down the street for sight of her father. He was probably at his office with John, or having a whiskey at the saloon. He always strolled along the boardwalk on the way back, checking each shop door to make sure it was locked securely.

A man was leaning against a store pillar just down the street. She saw the glow of a cigarette and lifted her hand, thinking it was her father. Slowly, the man straightened from his indolent pose and turned away; he walked back along the boardwalk away from her.

With a shock, Beth realized it was Logan who'd been watching her. She stared after him, her heart racing. He went up the steps of the hotel, paused, and flickered his cigarette back into the street. He glanced back in her direction once more and then went inside.

It was a perfect morning for a carriage ride. The sun made the dew glisten on new grass and new leaf while the flowers opened their faces to its caressing warmth. Everything was alive, and Beth felt the same energy stirring in herself. Looking into Adam's brown eyes, she saw it there as well. She felt it in his hands as he lifted her to the seat of the buggy rather than let her stop up from the box.

"We'll take our time," he told her, flicking the reins expertly and starting off at a smart pace that drew laughter from her.

They passed the hotel where Logan Tanner was staying, and she found herself looking up at the second-story windows wondering which room was his and if he was friendly with the women who lived there.

Adam was full of talk, eager to share everything with her. Twice he told her she looked pretty and she felt the color come warmly into her cheeks. He laughed and teased her. "Does it bother you to have a man tell you you're pretty?"

"A little."

"Nonsense."

They stopped at the Garcias' small farm and he checked young Miguel, who had been ill with a stomachache. "Don't give him an emetic, Maria. You're taking his strength from him," he told the young, concerned mother. She nodded deferentially and gave him a chicken as payment for the visit. It squawked raucously until stuffed into a sack and placed with due honors on the seat beside Beth.

Next, they checked in at the Hardestys' to see how the grandmother's arthritis was doing. Adam suggested tea made with alfalfa, four to five strong cups each day. "I'm not sure it will work," he admitted to Beth as they left, "but an uncle of mine swears by the remedy."

"Fine doctor you are," she teased.

He drew the horse well to the side of the road and up near a huge valley oak. A meadow stretched back toward the rolling hills. Poppies, lupins, mustard flowers, and buttercups splashed their color on the landscape.

Adam jumped down, then lifted Beth to the ground. He reached under the set for a gingham-covered basket and a thick blanket. He spread the blanket beneath the shade of the tree and set the basket at Beth's feet.

She sat and uncovered it. She found a bottle of fine wine, some cheese, bread, freshly picked strawberries, and sliced beef with Missus Michaels's special seasonings. Two beautiful crystal glasses were carefully wrapped and were so exquisite that Beth was almost afraid to hold them. She had never seen anything like them in Kilkare Woods.

"My mother packed them up for me before I left home. I've a set of eight, and china as well. I said to her, 'What does a bachelor need with all this?' She said a doctor wasn't meant to remain a bachelor."

She avoided his eyes. "I've never had wine before, Adam," she admitted. "I don't know if you should waste it on me."

"It's excellent for the digestive system." He smiled, pouring some and handing her the glass. She cradled the glass carefully between her hands.

"Like this, Beth." He held his high and then sipped, eyes bright as he met hers over the rim.

She did as he instructed.

"I hope you like it. It's a fine vintage. My father ships me a case when he receives his order from France."

She knew he came from a wealthy family. Adam Buchanan was used to the best. It was apparent in the cut of his clothing, his horses, his buggy, the way he carried himself. This was no simple country doctor, and Beth wondered, not for the first time, what had brought Adam so far from home and the life he was used to. In her usual guileless way, she asked.

"I wanted the freedom California has to offer. I love my family, but they were smothering at times." He shrugged. "I like it out here."

He talked of his brothers and sisters and made Beth laugh. She listened to his worries about his practice and the hesitance some patients left toward him after years of taking their health and personal problems to old Doc Wingate, who had died two months after Adam arrived. He had been ailing for a long time.

"A cancer," Adam told her grimly, and refilled her glass. "He was a fine man. We corresponded for some time before I decided to come to Kilkare Woods." He smiled slightly. "Family pulls until the end."

"Are you ever sorry?"

He looked into her eyes. "Not anymore."

She looked away, shy at his open courtship. "No matter

how hard I work in my garden, how many varieties of flowers I plant, I can't match the glory of one meadow," she remarked, changing the subject and admiring the countryside.

"There's a much larger hand at work," Adam said, and took hers. Startled, she looked at him. He turned her hand palm up. "You could play the piano. You have the hands for it." He caressed the small calluses she had gained from hours of sewing.

Beth drew her hand away carefully, embarrassed.

"More wine?" he offered, raising the bottle.

"No, thank you, Adam." Her head felt light already from what she had drunk.

Adam poured the rest of the bottle into the grass and put the empty bottle back into the basket. What the bottle of wine had cost probably would have put food on Annie Slate's table for several days, possibly a week, Beth thought.

"We'd better get back," he said, and he held his hand out for her when she finished putting the things away in the basket. He shook out the blanket and folded it, then set it beneath the buggy seat again.

She felt easy with him on the ride back to town, thankful for his sensitivity. She wasn't used to a man's overt attention. Odd that Adam's touch hadn't stirred her senses as much as one look from Logan Tanner, but she didn't want to think about that.

"May I see you to church tomorrow morning?" Adam asked, seeing her to the front door rather than leaving her at the gate.

"I'm afraid not," she said, surprised that he would want to make such a public connection between them as that, and so soon. Perhaps he didn't understand what people would think under those circumstances. "I have to be there early to arrange flowers for the altar and to get the trays ready for refreshments. And Sunday school is earlier than the service."

"Then I'll see you after the service at the social hour," he said, half in question.

Beth dimpled. "I'll be with the macaroons."

Adam laughed softly. "Once they're gone, where will you be?" he asked suggestively.

"Most likely home, doing the work I put off today." She grinned.

"Miss Tyrell, we will have to discuss your schedule," he drawled.

Frank opened the door, surprising them both. "How were things on your ride?" he asked, looking at them, pleased they seemed to be enjoying one another.

"Wonderful," Beth said, and mentioned the wild flowers.

"Wonderful," the doc said, and looked at her.

Once he was gone, Beth set about fixing the evening meal. Her father followed her into the small kitchen. "You enjoyed yourself," he said, looking at her speculatively as she peeled potatoes.

"Very much." She laughed. "Don't look at me like that. You have all your hopes hanging out like Monday-morning wash."

"You do like him."

"Very much," she repeated.

"You aren't telling me much."

"Papa, there's nothing to tell. We had a very nice ride and talk. I like Adam's company, but we don't plan to make arrangements to talk with Pastor Tadish." Her eyes sparkled with laughter at his annoyed look.

After a moment, he grimaced sheepishly. "Can't blame a father for wanting the best for his daughter, can you? He's a fine man. You couldn't do any better."

"Seems to me you're in a terrible hurry to be rid of your

only child," Beth teased, thankful he was back to his usual self again and not wearing that tired, grim mask.

"I don't want to be rid of you," he protested. "I want to see you in a man's safe keeping." His mouth twitched.

"Like a prized cow locked away in a barn, I suppose," she responded.

"A little more care than that, but much the same idea." He grinned unabashedly.

Beth shook her head. "Poor Mother. What she must have had to contend with, with a man like you." She chuckled, cutting potatoes into the pot. At his silence, she glanced up and saw the stone-stillness of his face and the bleakness in his eyes.

"Papa?"

His expression cleared. "Do you plan on seeing Doc again?"

She searched his face before answering. "That's up to him, but I think so. Papa—"

"Good," he said briskly, and turned away before she questioned him. "I'll set the table for you." He left the kitchen.

They ate in silence. "Are you alright, Papa?"

"Fine," he muttered. "I told you Doc was just paying me back for embarrassing you."

She frowned. "I meant the way you looked in the kitchen. Was it what I said about Mama that upset you? I was only teasing."

"No," he said, and looked pointedly at the sideboard. "Apple pie?"

"Berry." She knew he was putting her off, but she was afraid to pursue the subject after the two strained days they had had. She sensed any further questioning might bring back his anger again. She didn't know what was going on with him, but she didn't want to put undue pressure on him to find out. Surely it couldn't all have to do with Tanner and her own spinsterhood. He kept saying he was getting old.

She looked at his gray hair and lined face, his callused, tanned hands, and the slight bulge at his waist where he had once been hard as granite. She knew he was in better health than most men his age.

He is fine, she told herself. He will live to be an old, old man, God willing.

Whatever it was that was bothering him, he would tell her in his own time. He had always confided in her before. Why should now be any different? They were all the family each had.

Beth sat with her father during the church service. A rush of twittering ran through the congregation just before Pastor Tadish took his place at the pulpit. Her father glanced back and she felt him stiffen. She looked up at his rigid face and stole a glance back over her shoulder.

Logan Tanner sat by himself in the last pew.

She turned around quickly again, heart racing, breath high in her throat.

When services ended, and Beth had left the church, she couldn't see Tanner in the crowd filing out the doors into the yard. Then she saw him as she came out. He was standing by himself, indifferent to the uneasy and blatantly curious glances he received from the parishioners. She could hear the whispers like the crackling of an approaching storm. He looked at her. She avoided his eyes, busying herself with setting out refreshments on the long, linen-covered table.

Adam came and received his coffee and cookies and lingered to tease her, enjoying the giggles of ladies who overheard his flirtation. He was drawn aside by a young rancher's wife well into her last month of pregnancy.

Frank talked to Howard Polk and George Mason, two

town leaders, both merchants. Neither wanted to ask Tanner to leave. The women were all looking at him with interest. The Carliles had come for Sunday services, but remained slightly off to themselves. Edwina studied Logan Tanner openly. Hannah stood with her and Avery, her face lined with years of hard work and the hauteur of earned success. Avery smiled at Beth.

Beth's nerves stretched taut as she saw Logan walking toward her at the long table. People moved back from him to let him pass. She couldn't look away from those compelling, glowingly cynical blue eyes.

He stopped in front of her, looking relaxed in his fine, dark western suit. "Hello, Miss Tyrell," he said in a deep, low voice.

Her heart thumped and a quivery feeling fluttered in her stomach. She smiled. "Mr. Tanner," she said, and nodded her head in greeting. "Would you care for some coffee and cookies?"

"Just coffee. Black." He made a slow, provocative appraisal of her in her blue percale dress. It was her best, enhancing her pale creamy skin and the wheat color of her coiled hair.

Her nervousness subsided. "I didn't expect to see you in church," she teased when he made no move to leave.

His smile grew exceedingly wry. "Why not?"

"I didn't mean to imply you weren't welcome," she said, answering his tone rather than his words.

Logan looked around him, and she saw the hardness in his face, the contempt darkening his eyes. His face held challenge and cold arrogance. Some deeper emotion twisted painfully inside her breast at that look.

"Am I?" he drawled coolly, and faced her again. He frowned. "Why are you looking at me like that?"

"Yes, you are welcome."

His eyes flickered, and then he gave a curt laugh and

jerked his head. "I don't think everyone here shares your sentiments, Miss Tyrell."

Beth saw her father coming their way, his face rigid with barely concealed rage. She glanced quickly at Logan Tanner and her heart thundered at the look in his eyes. He was looking at her father with a cold, insolent smile that both chilled and frightened her.

He looked at her again and casually lifted the cup and saucer. He sipped coffee, his eyes mocking her sudden discomfiture.

Beth looked from him to her father and felt everyone watching as well. She tried to catch his attention as he stopped at the table, but his gaze was focused on Logan Tanner.

"What're you doing here?" he growled. Beth had never heard that rough, hard tone from her father before.

Logan smiled and winked at her. Turning slowly, he calmly put the cup and saucer down and assumed that deceptively relaxed stance. "I took your pretty daughter's advice and left my gun at the hotel." Beth felt, rather than saw, the hostility emanating from the younger man as he went on in a mild voice. "Unless you prefer I wear them to church, Sheriff."

"We both know you're not here for the sermon."

"Do we? Why should I get less out of one than you?"

"I want you to leave. Now," Frank snarled.

"And if I refuse again, what will you do, Tyrell?" Tanner said very quietly, still keeping that cold smile on his handsome face, though his blue eyes blazed.

"Papa, please," Beth murmured.

Frank glanced at her mortified face with impotent anger. He could go no further with Logan Tanner without publicly humiliating her and making her seem the cause.

Avery appeared and slapped him on the back. "Hello, Frank. How're things?"

"Fine," he muttered curtly, glaring at Logan.

"Beth, any more coffee?" Avery asked.

"Of course," she said, striving for normalcy. She gave him a grateful look. Her father stepped back slightly. Logan looked back and forth between her and Avery. His eyes lingered assessingly on Avery before finally returning to Frank. He moved back from the table and said something in a low voice to her father, then laughed mockingly.

People stared.

Logan turned slightly. "Good day, ma'am," he said, touching his hand to his brow in a gallant salute to her for all to see. "And thank you for the Christian welcome." His gaze swung around to the rest of the members of the congregation in one slow sweeping look that stopped on her own father. He grinned incitingly, and Beth's heart stopped at the look of rage on her father's taut face. He clenched his fists. Logan looked at them, raised a brow, waited, then shrugged indifferently. He turned and sauntered away.

Beth looked at her father's white, lined face and thought suddenly how old he looked. Feeling her gaze, he glanced at her briefly and shook his head, his eyes bleak. He turned and walked off in the opposite direction Logan had gone.

She let out a slow breath of relief.

"Was that man bothering you, Beth?" Avery asked, nodding toward Logan, now walking down the hill toward the hotel. Beth looked after him. He had a distinctive walk, a loose-limbed grace that held virile power. She remembered his quick reflexes when Matt Galloway had startled him at the train station.

"No. He just wanted some coffee," she answered, and belatedly poured a cupful for Avery.

Avery was tall and leanly built, with thick dark brown hair that fell boyishly across his square brow. His brown eyes were thoughtful as he contemplated her. "Your father seemed to think there was more to it than that." He accepted the cup she offered, his fingers lightly brushing hers.

"He was wrong if he did." She glanced in the direction her father had gone, vaguely distressed. He had come down on Logan Tanner like an angry bull, and Logan had not been the least bit cowed.

"He's a good-looking brute, isn't he?" Avery said, and Beth realized she had turned to look at Logan again just as he turned around the last building and disappeared from her sight. Her face warmed, and she glanced up at Avery's questioning expression.

"I suppose he is," she answered, and lifted a plate. "A macaroon, Avery?"

He took one. She wondered where Edwina was and looked for her. She spotted her. Hannah was talking to her, and Edwina was staring solemnly at the ground.

"Edwina thought he was very handsome," Avery remarked. He waited, but Beth made no comment. He let out his breath. "Why can't we talk the way we used to, Beth?"

"We're still friends, Avery, but I'm not fourteen anymore, and you're married."

"I'd like you and Wina to become friends."

What could she possibly say to that?

He sighed. "You know, sometimes I long for those old days, Beth. They were so uncomplicated." Lines deepened around his dark eyes in self-mockery. "I wonder what would have happened with us if I hadn't gone east."

She frowned. "Nothing would've happened. You know that better than I do."

He looked into her eyes. "Do I? Sometimes I think I made a mistake ever leaving at all."

"Why?"

"People treat me differently now. You especially."

She poured coffee for several others and Avery stood by, waiting. She frowned, glancing at him in concern. He came close again. "Wina said you refused to come to call at the ranch. Why?"

Beth thought of Edwina's imperious suggestion that she rent a buggy and drive back and forth the seven miles each way for her fittings. She would hardly call that an invitation to come to call.

"She did invite you and your father to come for dinner, didn't she?"

She searched frantically for something to say that wouldn't cause trouble between him and his wife. "She did invite me to the ranch, yes," she said carefully, "but you see, Avery, I'm very busy right now. It's hard to even keep up."

"You manage time for Doc Buchanan, I hear."

She wondered at the harshness of his tone.

He looked sheepish. "I'm sorry. Dog in the manger. He's a good man." He glanced at Adam, surrounded by townspeople. As he looked back again, Adam's familiar face took on the old expression he'd sometimes worn as a boy when talking of his dreams to run a ranch like the Double C. "Do you remember how we used to talk down by the river, Beth? You told me once you never wanted me to leave."

She smiled. "That was a very long time ago," she said, lowering her head. Why was he bringing up the words of a passionate, heartbroken child? She had been a girl on the brink of womanhood, and he her knight in shining armor. He had been seventeen, full of pride and ambition. She had been hurt when, in that patronizing tone he could take on, he had said that she would get over him.

He had been right.

"Beth, I have to talk to you."

She saw his drawn expression, the intentness in his eyes. "What's wrong, Avery?"

He laughed softly, sounding somehow bitter. "Everything is wrong, but I don't want to discuss it here. Meet me at the river tomorrow. At one."

"I can't do that." She was amazed he would suggest it.

"You remember where we used to go. We've been there together a hundred times before, Beth. It'll be just as innocent this time as it was then."

"We were children, Avery. Things are considerably different now," she reminded him.

"Beth, it's important or I wouldn't ask. I need to talk to you. I need to talk to someone, and I can't talk to mother. You know how she is," he said grimly.

He looked so unhappy that she faltered. She thought of how many years they had shared their special friendship.

Avery pretended light conversation as several people came close for more macaroons and coffee. As they moved back, he leaned closer. "Please, Beth." He seemed so desperate, she gave in.

"Alright."

His face relaxed immediately. He smiled, this time with feeling. "At one," he said again.

"Two is better."

He nodded.

Edwina was watching them, and though Avery seemed unaware of his young wife's animosity, Beth felt it shrouding her.

He moved away from the table and talked to others. Edwina wove through the crowd of parishioners and looped her arm with his, saying something to him. His mouth tightened and he nodded. When he started to move away, Beth knew they were leaving.

Beth wondered how big a mistake she had made in agreeing to meet Avery down at the river.

Chapter Five

BETH PINNED UP Grace Patterson's russet dress while listening sympathetically to her family problems. After a small glass of apple cider and cinnamon cookies, the lady left in better spirits. Beth rushed about the house putting things in order before she left to meet Avery.

It was almost two miles to the secret place she and Avery had discovered and shared as children. She remembered running freely then, but now the tight corset and layers of women's clothing made her walk more sedately. She longed to raise her skirts and run again. She had climbed that valley oak over there and sat on a high branch to taunt Avery when he wouldn't follow.

Reaching the thicket of brush, with grape ivy and vines growing in overhanging trees, Beth pushed her way in carefully. It was not as easy now as it had been to negotiate the thicket. As a young girl, she had been able to duck and dart in and out of the tangle of greenery.

Her hair cascaded about her shoulders in disarray when

she made it through to the sandy riverbank and clear pool that lay below a small falls.

Avery was already there, sitting on the large rock from which they had dived as children. He turned from his serious contemplation of the swirling pool, and a smile of relief lit up his face as he stood. "Beth!" He jumped down from the boulder and strode toward her, hands outstretched. "I was afraid you'd changed your mind." He clasped her hands and grinned down at her. "God, you're a mess."

She took her hands away and quickly began tidying her hair. "I know. Everything has grown over through the years."

He watched her comb through her tangled hair, picking out leaves and twisting the tresses back up into a neat coil. She searched blindly in her hair for the pins to hold it securely in place. "I liked you better in pigtails," he said ruefully, an odd look in his brown eyes.

"And you in knickers," she retorted, her dimples deepening in her cheeks.

He sat down on the bank and patted the sand next to him. She sat down beside him. "It's been years since I came to this place. Not since I told you I was leaving," he told her, his forearms resting on his raised knees.

"I came back for days after that, hoping you had changed your mind," she admitted.

"I know."

She glanced at him. "You knew?"

He pointed up the hill. "I watched from up there. I thought I was letting you down easier by not coming down again," he said wryly. "You said a lot to me that day, Beth."

She blushed hotly and gave a soft, self-conscious laugh. She could laugh now, the pain long since forgotten. "Yes, I did, didn't I? And you were so very adult to tell me it was all childish infatuation."

"I was right, wasn't I?"

She smiled softly. "Don't sound so disappointed." She linked her hands about her knees and looked at him. "Would you have had me carry on an unrequited love?" she teased.

His expression was grimly serious. "It wasn't entirely unrequited. I missed you like hell when I went east."

"But quickly forgot."

"As you did me."

She frowned and searched his face. "I never forgot you, Avery. It's just that people do change, just as you said. People grow in different ways, have different needs and dreams. You know that."

"How have I changed?"

She felt something eating at him and felt sad. "In appearance. In your eyes especially. You're not the wild, carefree boy you were then. You're a man now with the responsibility of a large ranch, the men who work for you, your cattle, your mother." She paused and looked into his eyes. "Your beautiful young wife."

He looked away. "What about you, Beth?"

"What about me?" she asked, confused. What was worrying him?

"Remember how we used to laugh together? Do you laugh with anyone that way now?" He searched her eyes again.

She thought of Adam Buchanan, the warm afternoon and talk they shared. Yes, she could laugh with others and did. Smiling, she touched Avery in a gentle way. "My life only revolved around you for a short while."

He frowned heavily. "Then why haven't you ever married?"

Her eyes lit in comprehension. "Oh, dear," she sighed mockingly, "not you, too."

"I'm serious."

"Yes, I see you are. For heaven's sake, Avery, I'm only twenty-one. That isn't so very old."

"All the girls you knew are married. Most of them have babies."

"Have you been talking to Papa?"

He gave her a half-angry look. "Why haven't you married, Beth?"

He really wanted to know. "Because I've never met a man I loved enough, and no one has ever asked."

He turned and looked directly into her eyes with an intentness that surprised her. "Beth, if I hadn't gone east, would you have loved me enough?"

"What a thing to ask now."

"I have to know."

It was not a question to ask or answer lightly. She sighed and looked at their river pool and remembered those idyllic days piercingly. "I used to think about it," she admitted softly. "At fourteen, yes, I'd have married you. At fifteen and sixteen, I don't know."

"Then the answer is no?"

"The answer is no," she agreed gently.

He gave her the lopsided smile she remembered. "It's one of the things I always liked so much about you, Beth. Your honesty. You say what you feel. I never had to wonder what was going on inside your head."

She laughed. "No, I guess you didn't."

"You didn't say one thing while meaning another." He wasn't smiling anymore. "I didn't appreciate that then, not as much as I should have. I do now."

What did he mean by that? Who was dissembling with him now? Edwina? His mother? There was a tension in him that still hadn't relaxed. She watched as he stood and walked to the river's edge. He tossed a couple of pebbles.

She rose and walked down to stand by him. "What did you want to talk about, Avery? Were you entertaining worries that I might be pining away for love of you?" she teased in her old way.

He laughed softly and gave her a rueful look. "Wretch. Maybe I was hoping you were."

"No, you weren't. Now, what's the matter?"

"I was worried about you," he said frankly. He gave a slight, humorless laugh and shook his head. "But you know exactly what you're about, Beth. You always have, I think. There's joy in you. It's there, in your eyes. And it doesn't seem to come out of being in love with anyone. It's just there. God, how I wish I had that."

"Why aren't you happy, Avery?" She frowned.

He tossed pebbles again. "I suppose I am."

"Suppose? Aren't you sure? You have everything."

"Do I?" He sounded as sullen as he had as a boy when his mother would make demands of him.

"Your ranch that you always dreamed of running; control of your own life; a very beautiful young wife."

"Who won't adapt to life out here!" he said, and flung the rest of the pebbles.

Beth's eyes widened. And no wonder, she thought, but she could hardly say anything without bringing up Avery's tyrannical mother. "Maybe she needs more time."

"She's had time! She's had almost a year."

"How long did it take you to adjust to the East after Kilkare Woods? Or did you take to it like a duck to water? I seem to remember a despairing soul in some letters I once received."

Avery looked at her. His expression changed. "I don't think I ever did adjust completely."

"Then don't expect things to happen so quickly for Edwina. Give her time and love, Avery." She dropped her seriousness and dimpled. "How can she help but adjust? All of us will wear her down with our country charm."

He laughed.

She put her hand on his arm. "She loves you. That's obvious. That will make all the difference if you just have patience with her." And a firmer hand, she wanted to add.

He reached out and touched her cheek, the old teasing Avery shining from his dark eyes. "I hear you've been gallivanting with the young doc."

She blushed. "One ice cream social, two visits to the house, and a carriage ride don't necessarily constitute a courtship."

He grinned. "In Kilkare Woods that makes you practically married." His expression softened. "Do you think you could love him enough, Beth?"

"It's a little early to even think about it," she said, but sensed she knew the answer already.

"But you do like him?" His mouth tipped slightly. "You ought to be married, with a dozen children running around."

"I suggest you work on building your own family," she countered, eyes sparkling merrily. "Who *did* put you up to this interrogation? Papa?"

"We hardly speak," he said simply.

"Oh, dear," she murmured.

"His manner around me is what made me wonder... well, if I was to blame."

"For me being a lonely old spinster?" She laughed and hit him lightly. "Well, now that you've found it's just my nature, you can go back home with a clear conscience."

He took her hand. "If you ever need anything, you come to me, Beth. Promise?"

She smiled. "I don't want for anything, Avery."

His hand tightened and a hesitant look came into his

eyes. "One bit of advice from an old friend?"

She tipped her head, curious at his concern. "What?"

He put his other hand over the one he held. "Avoid that Tanner fellow like he was the plague," he told her seriously. "Beth, a man like that would make mincemeat of your heart."

She withdrew her hand. "I only gave him a cup of coffee."

Conversation between them became stilted. Gradually, the tension eased again as both turned their talk to the past.

Beth watched him step carefully from rock to rock to cross the wide stream below the river pool. He disappeared into the shrubbery on the opposite side. A few minutes later, he appeared again on the hill where he had tethered his palomino. He mounted, turned the horse back, and raised his hand to her before riding away.

Bending, Beth picked up some flat stones and tossed them. Satisfied she could still make them skip, she laughed and turned toward the thicket and home.

It was difficult getting back through the thicket and when she had almost reached the end of it, she heard a horse whinny close by. Pushing her hair back from her face, she peered through the veiling of grape ivy and branches and drew in her breath softly.

Leaning against the trunk of a great cottonwood barely a few yards beyond the thicket stood Logan Tanner. He was watching her, a mocking smile on his handsome face. She felt a rush of hot color in her cheeks.

She stood frozen among the tangle of vines, not sure what to do or say, if anything.

"A tryst with a lover, Miss Tyrell?"

At that, she pushed through the last bit of greenery and stood in the clearing. "No," she said stiffly, and pushed her hair back. Dismayed, she began repinning it again. Her gaze brushed his with embarrassment, seeing he watched with interest and open sardonic amusement.

He nodded toward the hill. "Who was the man on the horse?"

"Avery Carlile."

"Married, isn't he?"

"Yes. Very happily."

He laughed. "Not all that happily if he's meeting you in a secluded place by a stream well away from town and prying eyes."

"He wanted to talk," she said, stung by his implication.

"Talk?" He straightened and walked slowly toward her with that measured, arrogant male stroll. He was wearing his gun again.

Beth backed a step, heart racing. "Talk! We've been friends for years."

"Never more that that?" He kept on coming.

She kept backing. "No." She gasped as she felt the vines at her back. "Avery wouldn't be interested in anyone else but his wife."

"That dark-haired sulky little tart, you mean? She'd be hell to live with."

"You don't even know her."

"Pretty is as pretty does, Miss Tyrell, or haven't you heard that before?" He stopped right in front of her, hands resting lightly on his hips. His gaze swept down over her body. "She's a peacock, and I'm guessing your Avery has his eyes on a nice tasty little quail."

She caught her breath. "That's a vile suggestion, Mr. Tanner," she said shakily.

"Such innocent eyes," he drawled. "No one would ever guess what depths lie hidden in them, now, would they?" He grinned.

"You're being insulting."

"Insulting? I find this makes you all the more intriguing. Tell me, what would Papa say about your meeting a man out here?"

His tone made her heart pound in alarm. The look in his blue eyes was sensual and caressive, openly speculative.

"Nothing," she managed truthfully. "I intend telling him." She half suspected her own father had put Avery up to it anyway, after the warning he had given her concerning the man standing in front of her now. "He would understand just how innocent the meeting was."

Logan's brows lifted. "What about the rest of town?"

Beth's eyes went wide as she searched his. "Avery and I met here so there wouldn't be talk. It would hurt his wife for gossip to start."

"And you," he said pointedly. "It'd tarnish that angelic reputation of yours, wouldn't it?"

"Yes. But why would you want to hurt me?"

Something inside him was moved at the look in her eyes. He forced it down. "One kiss will buy my complete silence."

She stared up at him in alarm and backed another step. "No!"

Logan looked down at her and wondered how anyone could seem so innocent and look so guileless when just caught in a blatant indiscretion. He could well imagine what they had been doing in the bushes. He came closer.

She drew back sharply, the tangle of vines embracing her from behind.

He laughed softly and raised his hand to her cheek. "Oh, come now—"

She slapped it away and tried to duck around him.

Logan caught her arm and swung her around to face him again. "Miss Tyrell, so much—" She slapped his face this time. Stunned, he narrowed his eyes fiercely. "Bitch!" He caught hold of her with iron fingers.

"Don't!"

Her soft cry of fear and revulsion sent his temper soaring. He yanked her against him and took her mouth savagely. When she tried to fight him, he hurt her deliberately, to teach her he was a man and not that besotted fool doctor she played with coyly while meeting a married man in seclusion. His own desire mounted sharply at the feel of her body against his, at the clean fresh taste of her. He caught her hair, slanting her face against his, and forced her mouth open.

Beth Tyrell's body was still against his. He could feel the shock running through her veins as her heart pounding wildly against his own.

It had not been pretense.

He loosened his arm around her, giving her support rather than imprisoning her. His hand in her soft hair gentled, cupping her head rather than gripping it. He drew back slowly, just enough to look down at her. Her face was deathly white. Her breath came in soft gasps—partly the fault of one of those damnable corsets that cinched so tightly any exertion or excitement could send a woman into a swoon. But he knew well enough now that the greatest fault lay with himself.

She made weak, uncoordinated little pushes against him to gain her freedom. He let his hands fall away from her. She stumbled back from him, and he thought she was going to faint. He reached out, wanting to steady her. She froze, eyes closing tightly, expecting another assault. He didn't touch her again.

"Perhaps you should sit down," he suggested hoarsely, his chest rising and falling with the effect she had had on him before he'd come to his senses.

She raised trembling fingers to her swollen mouth as her

eyes filled and glistened with barely restrained tears.

His face tightened. "My apologies. I made a mistake about you."

She drew herself up with difficulty, getting her breath back. Her chin trembled, but she looked straight into his eyes with those clear, hazel ones of hers now glimmering with deep hurt. "Why did you want to believe the worst of me?"

It wasn't what he had expected. Another woman would have been screaming hysterically, or railing shrill accusations at him, or sprawled under him, legs wide, taking him in and giving everything she had. But Beth Tyrell was everything she seemed and more, and something inside Logan squeezed tight and hard with pain and self-recrimination.

She was right. He had wanted to believe the worst of her. She was the daughter of that sanctimonious, son-of-a-bitch sheriff. He thought of his first night in town, facing that badge across the table and a bottle of whiskey.

"Get out of town. Just mount up and ride out easy-like. What you want you won't find here," Tyrell had said.

But this was exactly where he would find what he wanted. He would fulfill something that had been tearing at his guts for years, eating him up inside, spurring him on from town to town, hunting, forever hunting.

"Why?" Beth murmured again.

Logan looked at the slender young woman with wide hazel eyes staring into his with confused hurt. What was this desire in him to pull her close again and soothe her this time rather than attack her? He couldn't afford to feel this way about anyone.

His mouth curved in a cold smile. "Your father would call me out for what I just did to you, wouldn't he?" It wasn't a question. He knew.

Her lips parted.

He turned and strode toward his horse.

"I won't tell him, Mr. Tanner," she said from where she stood near the thicket.

Logan mounted and turned back toward her. "No," he said softly, "I don't guess you would." He swung his roan stallion round again and spurred it into a gallop.

Chapter Six

"WHAT'S BOTHERING YOU, Beth?" Adam asked, his voice no louder than the soft squeak of the porch swing on which they sat. She felt him watching her and forced a smile.

"Nothing," she said, and leaned her head back to gaze up at the clear, star-studded night. Somewhere close by a bullfrog was making throaty garrumphs, seeking a mate.

It had been three days since Logan Tanner had insulted and kissed her down by the river. She hadn't been able to forget about it, nor the look on his face before he'd turned away. She lay awake at night remembering that dark, hot glow in his eyes when he had grasped her, the bitterness that had shone before he'd turned away and ridden off in such a wild, fierce manner.

Why? What had she ever done to deserve such treatment from him?

"Your father seems in better spirits," Adam remarked.

"Yes." Logan Tanner was gone, and with each one of

Adam's visits, her father's worries lessened. He was cheerful, almost smug.

Would Logan Tanner come back? Why did she feel certain that he would?

"Something's on your mind, Beth. Do you want to discuss it?"

"No. It's nothing important." She was making entirely too much of the incident. Logan had misunderstood what had gone on between her and Avery and had tried to take advantage of her because of it. When he realized his mistake, he had apologized. She was mistaken; he wouldn't be back. What was there here for him? Surely a man like Logan Tanner would look for a more exciting place than Kilkare Woods.

Why wasn't she glad that she would never see him again?

"That gunfighter left town, apparently," Adam said, startling Beth. She glanced at him and caught his curious look. Resting her head against the back of the swing again, she hoped she hadn't given away her secret thoughts. Why did the mention of Logan set her heart thumping so fast?

"Yes. Papa is quite pleased at his departure. He never did find out why Mr. Tanner came here in the first place."

Adam put his arm along the back of the porch swing. "For no good purpose, I'm sure." His fingers brushed Beth's shoulder. "You must be relieved, too," he said, watching her closely.

She was grateful for the darkness that concealed the rush of warmth in her cheeks. "Me? Why?"

"He seemed very interested in you."

"That's ridiculous, Adam."

"Why?"

"Whatever would a man like that find of interest in a woman like me?"

Adam laughed softly, his eyes crinkling. He caressed

her cheek briefly. "Beth, you amaze me. You've no awareness of your attraction, have you?"

Embarrassed, Beth turned the conversation to Susan
Whitsett, a school friend of hers who was expecting a
baby. She didn't want to discuss Logan nor become involved in too intimate a flirtation with Adam.

"Susan is doing very well," Adam said. "Better off than
her husband. She has a couple of months to go before the
baby is due, and Charles is already talking about moving
her into town so she'll be close to me."

"Is there some problem?" Beth asked in concern.

"Absolutely none. Susan is healthy and strong. It's her
doting husband who's falling to pieces." He shook his head
in amusement. "They aren't far enough out to worry, but
Charles is sweating blood just the same. He must think a
baby falls out with the first contraction."

Adam went on to talk enthusiastically about his first
delivery in the East. Beth's face went from hot red to pale
coldness until he realized some of the details of childbirth
were too personal a topic for her. He shifted to country
medicine and talked about herbal remedies passed down
through generations and learned from Indians.

It was after ten when he left. Beth entered the cottage,
taking the crocheted shawl from her shoulders and folding
it across the back of the sofa. Her father looked up from his
Bible and smiled.

"You and Doc seem to have plenty to talk about."

"Stop being so obvious, Papa."

"Couldn't find a better man, honey. He'll make a good
husband for a sensible woman."

Beth shook her head in exasperation. "You're impossible." She bent and kissed him lightly on the forehead.

He glanced up and grinned. "Pleasant dreams."

Beth's dreams were anything but pleasant. Her father
was shouting at her, and Adam was somewhere in the

background calling her name over and over again. Logan
Tanner was standing in front of her, blocking her way, his
blue eyes glinting darkly. He reached for her, his head
coming down, his lips parting.

She sat up, breathing hard and fast, her body damp with
sweat. She blinked, disoriented, and slowly sank back
against her pillow. She stared up at the ceiling, her heart
still racing. She closed her eyes and raised her fingers to
her lips, remembering that it had been more than fear that
had sung through her body when Logan Tanner held her
and kissed her. It was hours before she could sleep again.

Edwina arrived early on Tuesday. Avery brought her in
the road wagon, apparently intending to pick up supplies
for the ranch. Beth saw them arrive. The tension between
them was noticeable. Avery wore a tightly withdrawn look
as Edwina spoke to him. She hadn't even finished when he
stepped down, lifted her to the ground, stepped up, and
snapped the reins.

"Avery!" Edwina cried, and stared after him. When he
didn't look back, she swung around and snatched open the
gate, then entered and slammed it shut with a force that
made Beth wince. Their meeting was going to be fraught
with displays of temper.

Beth opened the door and Edwina stormed in without
even looking at her. "Good morning, Edwina," Beth said
carefully to her back.

Edwina swung around. "Were you watching us from the
front window? I suppose you're gloating because we ar-
gued."

"Of course not," Beth said, surprised at her vehemence
and dismayed by the girl's animosity.

"Is the green dress ready or not?" Edwina demanded,
taking off her kid gloves.

"Yes. It's behind the screen, ready for you to try on."

Beth tried to swallow her rising impatience with the girl. She was Avery's wife, after all, and she wanted to like her. "Do you need help?"

"No!" Edwina disappeared behind the screen. There was an ominous silence. Beth waited to hear the rending of cloth and popping of buttons. She heard instead a soft sniff and a shaky indrawn breath. A moment later Edwina emerged, holding the dress about her slender waist. She gave Beth a mutinous look. "You will have to button it. I can't reach after all."

Beth complied, thankful Edwina hadn't taken out her spleen on the garment again. The task finished, Beth stepped away. She positioned the full-length mirror for Edwina and crossed her fingers behind her back, praying that Edwina would be happy with everything and she wouldn't have to deal with the girl again for a few weeks.

This time it fitted perfectly. The rich color enhanced the girl's creamy skin and dark hair. The brown eyes searched up and down, seemingly desperate for some flaw. Beth held her breath. Edwina's expression fell. "It's fine," she said with a sigh. "Though it probably would've been better if you hadn't chosen to rip away all the trim. I only said I wanted a little removed from around the sleeves."

That was a bald-faced lie, but Beth said nothing. The dress had to be paid for, and she suspected Edwina was looking for some excuse to leave her in the lurch. Beth would never go to Avery for money, knowing it would cause further dissension between the married couple. And she had no intention of being in the middle of their problems—or a part of them!

Beth turned away and breathed deeply, counting slowly to ten. She picked up the sampler and her tape measure.

"What are you doing?" Edwina exclaimed.

Beth gave her a bland look that didn't reveal the taut nerves beneath the surface of her apparent calm. "I'm going to measure where you want the trims and show you what I have available. Then you write out your instructions so there won't be another mistake." She handed Edwina the sampler. "Which is your preference? And where exactly would you like it?" Beth knew exactly where she would like to sew it!

Edwina thrust the sampler away. "I said it was fine."

Beth gritted her teeth. "No, you said it would look better with lace. So I'll do as you wish and put lace on it again."

"I said it wasn't necessary," Edwina said, her eyes overbright. "Now, forget about it, will you?"

"No. Not this time," Beth said firmly. "I want you completely satisfied with this dress. When you leave here today with it wrapped or on you, I want to believe you're pleased with it. I don't work long hours for mediocre results, whatever you seem to think, Edwina, and you wouldn't want to pay for something you didn't really like." She had never said so much to Edwina before and was dismayed by the look of moist-eyed misery on Edwina's face.

The girl's shoulders slumped. "The dress is just perfect as it is. A New York designer couldn't have done any better." The compliment was uttered so bitterly it was almost an insult.

Beth put the sampler aside. "I'm sorry, Edwina," she said softly. "Would you like a glass of lemonade?"

Edwina's chin tipped sharply and her dark eyes brimmed with angry tears. "No."

Beth said nothing for a moment, then sighed heavily. "Would you like me to wrap it for you?"

"I'll wear it. After all, Avery will want to see your latest creation."

If this was the girl's usual attitude about everything, Beth could well imagine Avery's difficulties. Hannah could be hard enough to handle without another termagant in the household.

"Alright," Beth agreed quietly. "I'll wrap your other dress."

Edwina stood by watching as Beth carefully folded the pretty apricot dress and wrapped it. "What happened to your beau, Elizabeth?"

Beth glanced up. "What beau?"

"Oh, don't look so innocent. You know who I mean. Avery made straight for you the moment that gunfighter started talking to you at church."

"If you're referring to Mr. Tanner, he's gone, and he was certainly never my beau."

"He had his eye on you. Too bad he didn't stay."

After tying the last string, Beth picked up the package and handed it to Edwina. She named the price for the dress after the final alterations, and Edwina's brow rose haughtily.

"You'll just have to wait. Perhaps sometime next week. I didn't bring any money with me today."

"I'm sorry, but that leaves me with no choice but to ask Avery to settle your bill today," Beth bluffed, suspecting Edwina was lying.

Edwina's face flushed. "You would do that, wouldn't you? You'd like nothing better than to make trouble between us."

"He brought you here today. He knows I'm making a dress for you. What possible trouble could I make by asking to be paid for my materials and labor?"

Edwina snatched up her drawstring purse, opened it, and dug around in it angrily. She thrust some money at Beth. "Here. Take it. There's a dollar extra for work well done," she said, her face pale and twisting up like that of a child ready to cry.

Beth accepted the money but handed back a dollar. "Thank you, but what's due is all I ask."

Edwina hesitated and then took the dollar back with shaking fingers. She didn't look at Beth, but her tension was still noticeable.

"Edwina," Beth said as the girl turned away to walk to the door. Edwina bristled immediately and glanced back coldly. "The next time you want a dress made, please go to someone else."

Edwina's mouth fell open and her face drained of color. "But Avery won't like it."

"Avery has nothing at all to do with this," Beth said impatiently. "This is between you and me."

Edwina swung around. "And what am I supposed to tell him when he asks why I can't come to you?" she demanded, sudden tears glistening in her dark, beautiful eyes.

"I don't really care what you tell Avery," Beth said wearily. "Put the blame on me, if you wish. Tell him that I was insufferably rude to you every time you came here."

Edwina's face flamed scarlet. "You know he would never believe that. He thinks you're absolutely angelic! Your patience is legend!" She wiped an escaping tear from her cheek with an angry swipe.

"Hardly. My patience ended five minutes ago where you're concerned. I suggest you treat Missus Abernathy with more courtesy than you've shown me, because if you don't, she'll show you the door on your first visit."

"I'm sure you'll change your mind, things being as they are," Edwina said cryptically, and went out the door without another word.

Beth released her breath and rubbed her throbbing temples. It was the last time she would work for Edwina and put up with the endless criticisms. She and Papa didn't need money that badly. They could do without covering the settee, and the repairs to the roof could wait one more year. Papa had told her long ago to refuse to do business with Edwina, but she hadn't wanted to hurt Avery. Now it had come to that anyway. She wondered what story Edwina would concoct for him. What did it matter?

Beth went for her gardening gloves and bucket. She donned the long white apron that protected her gingham dress. Working outside in the sunshine always warmed away any coldness inside her. She went down the front steps thinking that if anyone came to discuss work, she'd be right there and not miss them.

She bent and pulled up overcrowded flowering plants. Pinching off dead leaves and flowers, she tossed them into the tin bucket to save for the compost pile behind the small woodshed out back.

The sun was warm on her shoulders. She scorned the bonnet most women wore, liking the sun on her face. The garden hummed with bees, and Beth brushed one lightly away from the damp curl against her temple. The scent of roses and sweet peas was heady delight to her.

Some of her bulbs had died, and she knelt, working down deep to remove the dead ones. She decided to move several that were still alive, and she worked them out of the ground with her fingers rather than go back for the trowel. After carefully brushing the roots free of dirt, she tucked two bulbs in her apron pocket.

A strand of wheat-colored hair came free and trailed down, tickling her cheek. She brushed it back as she stood up.

The gate opened and Beth turned to greet whoever was there. She froze, her heart stopping.

Logan Tanner stood looking at her from just inside the fence. His gaze moved slowly from her eyes, down over her breasts and soiled apron, and back up again. He walked toward her. Her heart pounded harder and faster and she pressed a hand to her breast.

He stopped in front of her and smiled slightly, his eyes enigmatic. "You've got dirt on your face, Miss Tyrell."

Chapter Seven

BETH QUICKLY REMOVED her gloves and stuffed them into her other apron pocket. Flustered by Logan's intent scrutiny, she wiped her face to clean off the smudge of dirt and said, "I thought you'd left town, Mr. Tanner."

"Something you were no doubt hoping I would do after our last meeting," he answered, smiling wryly. "But no, I had business in San Jose. Now I've returned to stay until my business here is settled."

She frowned, wanting to ask him what business he meant, but didn't dare.

"Is your father gunning for me yet?"

"Pardon me?" she stammered, shocked.

"I'd think he'd want me dead after the way I manhandled you."

Her face went hot at his reminder of the episode at the river, and she tried not to look at his finely shaped, firm, curving mouth. She could almost feel that ruthless, punishing kiss and the way he had forced her mouth open. "I wish you wouldn't refer to it again, Mr. Tanner," she murmured. "I told you then I wouldn't mention it to my father, and I haven't. What good would it do for you two to argue over what happened?"

"Oh, I think it might come to more than that." His blue eyes darkened and glowed in an odd, half-excited way that made her uneasy.

Logan stepped closer. She drew back sharply, eyes going very wide. He clenched his hand. "Just think of it, Miss Tyrell. If your father called me out, you might never have to worry about me coming close to you again."

Her face paled. Surely he didn't want that kind of trouble?

Moving away from her, he glanced around at her beautiful garden. "Have you seen your Avery lately?"

Her chin tipped. "No, and he is not *my* Avery."

Logan looked back across his shoulder at her and laughed mockingly.

She had to ask. "Are you here to do harm to someone?"

The laughter died in his eyes. "You don't want to know anything about me or why I'm here."

Her lips parted slightly. "Could you possibly put whatever your business is aside and just forget it altogether?"

A muscle worked in his jaw as he regarded her in silence. "Do you think I could change my gunslinging ways?"

Her heart raced at his derision. "Yes. If you wanted."

He laughed again, coldly. "Once this is done, I plan to do just that."

What was *this?* "Were you hired here by someone?"

"You are full of personal questions today, aren't you?" he drawled.

She wanted to look away from that hard, unyielding face but couldn't. "I think it's terribly important," she said frankly. "Violence turned against anyone only comes back on yourself."

"And who taught you that bit of wisdom? Your father?" he asked sarcastically.

She frowned. "I'm sorry he asked you to leave town the way he did," she apologized with quiet sincerity.

He stared at her, half-bemused, and then looked away sharply. Main Street stretched before him. He let out his breath. "I never expected to meet someone like you."

Something inside her bloomed warm and soft as she sensed his vulnerability. She acted upon it instinctively. "Would you care for some lemonade and cookies, Mr. Tanner?"

"Good God!"

She laughed, her hazel eyes lighting up. "You look almost frightened, Mr. Tanner."

His face became tight and withdrawn. He looked into her eyes, his own growing a deep indigo blue.

Beth realized that she wanted very much for him to stay and visit. It frightened her just how much she did want it. He was dangerous, unpredictable, not like anyone she had ever known. Perhaps that was part of his attraction, that and the blatant masculinity he exuded that she had mistakenly thought repelled her when he'd kissed her by the river.

Her heart thumped hard and she felt breathless. She had never felt these things before, not with Avery when she had thought she loved him, not with Adam Buchanan. It was a heady feeling, headier than the fine wine Adam had served her. She had felt these stirrings the first day she saw Logan Tanner. They had grown since then, each time she saw him. It felt as though fingers were strumming her nerve endings, as though a hearth fire burned in her breast. All of it was a painful kind of pleasure coming warmly from deep in her body.

Could she feel all these things and not have him know just by looking at her in the way he was? His blue eyes pierced her and made her ache.

"People are going to take you to pieces, Beth," he said.

His use of her name sent a soft thrill through her. "Why?"

"You're ingenuous."

"But not a fool," she added, smiling.

He frowned. "No, not a fool. A dreamer, and that's worse."

She tilted her head. "Why did you come here today, Logan?"

"Sounds nice the way you say my name. It's not a curse on *your* lips." He turned toward the gate. She followed him at a sedate distance. He left it open. She closed it gently behind him. After mounting his roan, he tipped his hat back and looked down at her.

"You didn't answer me," she reminded him.

He gave a soft, self-mocking laugh that had no pleasure in it. "Damned if I know."

She watched him walk the horse toward the center of town.

Logan seemed to avoid her after that. She saw him several times during her errands about town, but he never looked at her.

Entering the general store a week later, Beth saw him standing at the counter. Faith was obviously flustered, her movements jerky, her cheeks pale as she took his order. She turned and dug the scoop into the tobacco bin and measured out a small pouch before tying it and setting it on the counter for him.

"Good morning, Faith," Beth said, and saw Logan's back stiffen. He straightened and glanced back at her. She smiled at him. "Good morning, Mr. Tanner."

His eyes went dark, and she felt his swift, all-encompassing perusal of her from her face down to her skirt hem and back up again. A muscle locked in his jaw as he gave her a slight nod that could have been taken for greeting or dismissal.

She frowned, searching his eyes, but he turned away and paid Faith in coin. As he glanced once more at her, she saw grim entreaty in his eyes before he walked past her out of the store. She stared after him, confused.

"How can you dare speak to that man, Beth? Don't you know the sort he is?" Faith shuddered. "I've never seen a man with such cold eyes before."

Beth had thought them overwarm. She looked back over her shoulder again and saw him striding across the street and going up the steps of the hotel.

She didn't see him again for several days. Then, while walking to her father's office with the noon meal on a covered tray, she sensed someone watching her. Glancing up, she saw Logan framed in one of the second-story windows of the hotel. He had pushed the curtain back and was looking down at her. A woman appeared and began to unbutton his dark shirt. He let the curtain fall back into place.

Beth walked on, her throat squeezing tight with hot pain.

The following Saturday, Adam took Beth with him on his rounds of the southside farms. They stopped at Susan and Charles's farm. Susan was glowing. Charles was pale and drawn. "Don't you think we should move her into town yet?"

"Nonsense," Susan said. "Who'd feed the chickens?" she teased.

"It's not funny," her husband growled.

Adam looked at Beth, his brown eyes sparkling. "Take him out for a walk, Beth, while I examine Susan."

Once they returned, Susan took Beth back into the kitchen to make coffee and put cookies on a platter. Beth had always liked plain-speaking Susan Cummings Whitsett. She was friendly, honest, and not given to cruel gossip.

Susan put cups and saucers on the tray. "Doc can't take his eyes off you, can he?"

Beth turned away. "We're just good friends."

"You have to watch out for those good friends. They sneak right up and become lovers."

Beth laughed. "I don't think so."

Susan's eyes widened in mock alarm. "Don't you like him? Everyone's talking about how much he thinks of you and how many times he's been seen sipping lemonade on your front porch."

Beth dimpled. "Yes, exactly. We talk and sip lemonade."

Susan chuckled. "Well, if you'd be just a little less shy, he might decide it was time to do something more."

"It's a bit soon for anything more," Beth insisted.

"Oh, Beth!"

They served the men refreshments and sat with them for a while. Charles took Adam outside to show him some new stock while Susan and Beth went back into the kitchen to clean up the dishes.

"Doc's very good-looking and the grandest person I know," Susan said. "Excluding Charles, of course."

Beth looked at her, her eyes merry. "Of course."

"I don't think it's a bit too soon for anything," Susan said, "unless you're not madly in love with him."

Beth liked Adam very much, but she wasn't filled with yearning for his touch nor in any great hurry to have him press her into a more serious relationship. They had been together more than a dozen times and the most he had done thus far was hold her hand. Beth liked that just fine.

The thought of Adam kissing her as Logan had was faintly repulsive; however, the thought of Logan kissing her filled her with an almost feverish anticipation.

Only last night she and Adam had been out walking and discussing his day. They had intended to go to her father's office for a visit. When they reached it, Beth saw Logan standing outside the hotel, leaning against the front pillar smoking. Her heart jumped. His eyes met hers only briefly as he took the cigarette out and flicked it into the street before turning away and reentering the hotel.

"Are you in love with him?" Susan asked.

"Who?" Beth's face was suddenly suffused with hot color.

Susan gave her an odd look. "Adam, for heaven's sake!"

Beth let out a shaky breath. "I like him very much."

"As much as you liked Avery?"

Beth glanced at her sharply. "Avery?"

Susan shrugged. "You must know everyone in town thinks you've never married because you're still in love with him."

"I never was really in love with him."

"You weren't?"

"I was young."

"What's age got to do with it? I was married to Charles only a few years after you and Avery were chasing about Kilkare Woods acting like the inseparables."

"Oh, Susan," Beth murmured, laughing.

"They also think he broke your heart when he went east to study and brought back that haughty wife of his. Can't say much for his taste in women," she grunted.

"You were just talking about *me* a moment ago!" Beth reprimanded.

"Well, that's different."

Beth dried a cup. "Edwina is very beautiful and she comes from a fine family."

"I could care less about her blue blood, though I suppose it matters to Avery's mother. It's you we were discussing. You're not going to get me off the trail that easily. Are you in love with Doc or Avery?"

"Why do I have to be in love with either one?"

"You're hopeless, you know that? How can you not fall in love with a man like Adam? He's so handsome. I just love the way he talks."

"You keep on about it, Susan, and I swear I'll tell Charles you just said that," Beth threatened, grinning.

"Don't you dare!" Susan exclaimed in mock horror. "Charles thinks he put blinders on me on our wedding day, but I can still notice a good-looking man."

Beth thought of Logan Tanner.

"Besides that, Doc has better breeding than Edwina Carlile," Susan giggled.

Beth laughed. "You're incorrigible."

Susan grinned and turned to one side to present her rotund profile. She patted herself proudly. "Look at this, Beth, whyever don't you marry Doc so you can start your own family?"

Beth blushed hotly. "Because I'm not in love with him."

"Haven't you any sense?"

"I don't think he's in love with me either." She turned away to put a saucer into the cupboard.

"He's well on his way to being in love with you if he isn't already, and he knows you would make him a perfect doctor's wife. You're patient, kind, persevering—"

"And dull?"

"You said that, I didn't. And it's not what I would've said. You're just . . . well, you don't know very much about certain things. For example, he was dying to hold your hand and you thought he was motioning for more coffee." She chuckled. "He'd like to kiss you, I bet, and you've probably fed him more macaroons."

Beth dimpled. "But I thought macaroons were what he was after."

"Oh, dear," Susan sighed. "Maybe you'd fall in love with him if you let him kiss you a few times."

"I'd rather do things the other way around."

"Beth, sometimes people fall in love after they're married and have . . . well . . . you know." A faint questioning frown crossed her brow. "Well, maybe you don't."

Beth saw by Susan's expression that she was about to launch into an explanation of things that should be left private. "I wonder where the men are?"

Susan gave her a pinch. "We can always go look for them if it's getting too hot for you in the kitchen."

They found the men by the corrals discussing horses. Adam took her hand. "We'd best head back for town," he said softly. They thanked the young couple for their refreshments. Adam accepted the basket of fresh eggs and apple pie for his medical services.

On the way back to Kilkare Woods, they talked about Charles's horses and the Whitsetts' coming baby. "Have you ever thought about having children, Beth?"

"Yes," she admitted. "Sometimes."

"I've watched you with them on Sundays. They love you."

"Maybe because I'm still half child myself." She smiled.

Adam drew the buggy to the side of the road and tied up the reins methodically.

"What is it? Has one of the horses picked up a stone?" she asked.

"No." He took her hands. "Marry me, Beth."

She gaped at him. "Oh, Adam," she said in dismay, and

lowered her head. "Susan was going on and on at me about marrying you. Was Charles browbeating you out by the corral, as well?"

He laughed softly and tilted her chin up. "No. It's been on my mind for weeks. I think we'd do very well together." Lowering his head, he kissed her very lightly.

She had seen the kiss coming and let him. Now, she felt embarrassed. Nothing had happened inside her at all. Adam might have been the town dullard for all the emotion that had been lit up inside. She remembered how different she had felt when Logan Tanner kissed her.

She was thinking so deeply about him that she didn't expect Adam's second kiss, which was profoundly different from his first. This time emotion did stir. She drew back, frowning.

"I won't press you for an answer right now," Adam said huskily, "but would you think about it?"

"Please, Adam, don't tell Papa," she said softly.

He smiled ruefully. "I know. Sometimes having a parent as an ally can be a decided disadvantage." His eyes crinkled teasingly. "Don't hold it against me, Beth. Alright?"

They talked of other things on the way back to town. Beth knew, however, that their relationship had taken an irreversible turn, and it saddened her. The time they spent together now wouldn't be casual companionship and easy camaraderie. She had seen in his eyes that he wanted her, and it filled her with distress because his desire wasn't returned. She had never wanted to hurt him.

Adam lifted her down by the gate and held her before him, searching her face. "Are you making a lunch for the auction?"

"Yes." It was a favorite fund-raising event each year. Single ladies made fancy picnic baskets on which the bachelors bid and thus enjoyed one another's company as well. Other fund-raising activities also filled the afternoon; bake sales, pie-eating contests, games, and races kept everyone busy. The entire town turned out, with very few exceptions.

"Put a pink ribbon on your basket so I'll know which one to buy."

Beth laughed. "That's cheating."

"My conscience won't bother me in the slightest as long as I have you for my companion." He grinned, unabashed.

When Beth's father came home that evening, she mentioned nothing of Adam's proposal. Her father didn't question her about the day, deep in some dark reverie of his own.

Chapter
Eight

"ARE YOU GOING to bid on the widow's picnic basket today, Papa?" Beth asked innocently, not looking at him as she prepared her own special lunch. She felt her father's sharp attention from where he sat, legs outstretched beneath the kitchen table, a mug of coffee in his hand.

"What do you know about me and Missus O'Keefe?"

She smiled back at him. "Just that when she has trouble now and then she sends someone lickety-split into town to fetch you."

His craggy face reddened and he grunted a noncommittal reply.

"She asked after you the other day when I saw her at the general store with her foreman. She wanted to know why you were so morose lately."

Her father stood up abruptly. "I didn't know you were so friendly with her. What was her foreman doing with her?" He replenished his mug with coffee and slammed the pot back on the woodstove.

"Buying supplies." Beth's lips parted in anger. "Why shouldn't I talk with her. I like her, and it seems you like her too, or you wouldn't—"

"Just do as I tell you," he said gruffly.

She felt affronted.

He softened his expression. "Some things you damn well don't understand yet."

"Papa, you're getting harder and harder to live with."

He sat in his chair again, stretching out his legs. "Well, until you get a husband, you're stuck with me." He watched her tie a pink ribbon to the handle of her wicker basket. "Why you putting that on it? Looks silly."

"Adam asked me to so he'd know which one to bid on," she admitted.

Frank grinned broadly. "I bet a month's wages he proposes to you today."

Her face went hot. "Maybe, maybe not. It won't really matter."

His good humor dissipated. "What do you mean, it won't matter?"

"I'm not in love with him."

"Damnit, you like him well enough. Let the rest come later."

"I want to love the man I marry, Papa. We've been over this before." She half expected him to explode in anger. He had been so unpredictable lately and given to inexplicable dark moods.

This time he surveyed her grimly. "Beth, sometimes loving someone the way you mean isn't the best way to choose a husband."

"You loved Mama, didn't you?"

"We're not discussing your mother," he snapped. "We're talking about you and Doc."

"You still haven't gotten over losing her, have you?"

He grimaced and stood abruptly, slamming his mug

down. "I loved her, yes. Maybe too damn much," he said, and left the kitchen.

What had happened to their closeness? He seemed to attack her most of the time now, with his ill temper and withdrawn moods. He wouldn't tell her what was wrong, and when she tried to persist and get him to talk, he left the house.

She heard the cottage door slam.

Some of her joy for the day went out of the house with her father.

Basket in hand, Beth set out for the church grounds alone. Just as she closed the front gate, Avery drew his carriage in. "Beth! How are you?" he greeted, smiling broadly.

"Fine." She saw Edwina sitting rigidly beside him, refusing even to look at her. Hannah was in the back seat and her expression was one of grim curiosity.

"Would you like a ride to the church? There's room beside Mother."

"No, thank you, Avery," Beth said, appalled. "I have an errand on the way."

"Then we'll see you when you get there." Avery tipped his hat and snapped the reins. Beth watched them ride away with a mingling of relief and concern.

Half the township was at the churchyard when Beth arrived. She took her basket to the ladies in charge of the auction. It was set among numerous others on a large table. The potato-sack races were under way, hilarious laughter filling the morning air as father-son teams fell and rolled over one another in a tangled heap in an effort to reach the finish line. Women looked over piles of embroidered pillowcases, dish towels, and fancy linens as well as knitted and crocheted blankets and patchwork quilts to be sold for the church. Pies were being set out for the pie-eating contest.

Children rushed to Beth, tugging at her skirts and letting her know everything they had been doing since they last saw her. She laughed, listening to each in turn. Once she crouched down to kiss a little boy's cut finger.

Feeling someone watching her, she glanced around. Logan Tanner stood at the far side of the church grounds, near the mulberry tree just outside the fence that bordered the cemetery.

"Beth!" Adam called, and she straightened quickly, holding Tammy Whiler's hand. She smiled at him as he strode toward her. "There you are," he exclaimed, taking her other hand. "I went by the cottage, but you were already gone. Where's your father?" People were watching them and whispering.

"I don't know," Beth said. "He left early."

"Well, he's probably at the sheriff's office. Don't worry about him. I'll take good care of you." He looped her arm through his possessively. Beth felt people staring and chuckling among themselves.

She glanced toward Logan. He was leaning indolently against the broad trunk, almost hidden in shadow.

"Is something wrong?" Adam asked.

She looked at him quickly. "Papa and I had words again this morning."

"I'm sorry."

Beth's heart thudded heavily as she still felt Logan watching her. Others also stared at her and Adam. She could feel their speculation. Being the center of attention embarrassed her. Adam, on the contrary, seemed to enjoy it, pausing to talk to everyone, his hand over hers as it rested on his forearm.

Beth kept thinking about Logan.

"I should help the ladies, Adam."

He finally let go of her, at which point Avery intercepted her. "Well, have you two set a date yet?"

Beth let out her breath sharply. "Are you playing big brother again, Avery? Your wife and mother look very warm over there in the sun. Why don't you get them something cool to drink?"

His eyes widened. "What's the matter?"

She shook her head, her gaze drawn surreptitiously to the man standing motionless in the shadows of the mulberry.

"Speaking of Edwina," Avery said, "she needs a dress for the square dance in two weeks, and cloak for fall. I'd like to bring her in tomorrow if that's convenient."

Beth blushed. "I don't think I have time at the moment, Avery. I'm sorry, but I've overextended myself. Perhaps Missus Abernathy could sew for Edwina this time."

Avery searched her face, his expression shrewd and growing angry. "What did she do to upset you?"

"Nothing!"

"I know you, Beth. You're so organized you could finish dresses for every woman in town and still make time for one more. So, it's got to be Edwina. What'd she do?"

"Avery, let's discuss it later."

Adam came over, rescuing her from further explanations. "I thought you were going to help the ladies." He shook hands with Avery and exchanged greetings.

"Come on out to the ranch this week, Doc. Mother's been complaining about her back again."

Beth turned her head to look toward the cemetery and felt immediate dread when she saw her father talking to Logan. She could tell even at a distance that her father was furious. His shoulders were set and his chin jutted out as he talked to the younger man, who hadn't changed position and did not seem to be responding.

Adam followed her gaze. "I wonder what Tanner's

doing here." She heard disapproval in his tone.

"I'll bring Edwina in tomorrow, Beth," Avery told her, and before she could protest, he walked away, a set look on his face as he headed for his wife. Edwina looked pale and drawn as she watched him approach. He said something to her and she shook her head, her eyes flashing at Beth in resentment.

Adam touched Beth. "What's wrong?"

Beth shook her head, wishing she were well away from the entire gathering. Her nerves felt stretched thin.

Reverend Tadish went up to the front platform that had been brought out. He clapped his hands to draw attention. "The auction of picnic baskets is about to start! If you ladies will please take your places at the front, we will begin."

The children were laughing and running among the adults gathering in groups. Men and women came forward, calling out remarks and teasing friends. Beth saw the widow gazing at her father. Adam grinned, and heat rose into Beth's cheeks as she lowered her eyes quickly from his.

The pastor lifted the first basket. "We'll start the bidding at ten cents," he called, looking hot and uncomfortable in his dark suit and starched collar. His wife, Sadie, stood by watching. "And keep in mind, gentlemen, that the proceeds will go to a good cause. So let's be generous in our bidding."

"Put your hand in your own pocket, Reverend!" someone shouted, and received laughter.

Reverend Tadish grinned. "I'd reach into yours, Howard Polk, if I didn't know you had sewn them tight for the occasion!"

Louder laughter came at that, and Howard raised his hand in defeat.

"Alright. Let's get going before half my congregation

starves," the pastor said. Bidding went up to a dollar and a half on the first basket. It was a good price. The highest price ever reached had been six dollars the year before for Chelsey MacIntosh's basket. She was there, now married to the ardent young cowboy who had bought it.

Two more baskets were sold. One belonged to the widow and was purchased by Beth's father. Beth saw that Missus O'Keefe looked pleased as he collected the basket and her from the front of the tables.

Half the baskets had been sold when Beth's was raised high. She saw Adam's glance in her direction, as did others. People began whispering again.

"There's a veritable feast in this one, gentlemen," Pastor Tadish informed the crowd after a peek beneath the cloth.

"Two dollars!" Adam shouted. Everyone laughed.

"Hold your horses, Doc." Tadish smiled. "I haven't even opened bidding yet."

Adam shrugged. Beth cringed. Two dollars was an extravagant opening bid, and she was embarrassed by the laughter, whispering, and speculative looks they were both receiving.

"Alright, Doc, now you can begin," the pastor said in mock severity.

"Two dollars!" Adam shouted again.

"Two and two bits," a young man called from the back, surrounded by friends laughing and prodding him. Beth knew him as one of Avery's ranch hands.

"Three," Adam called.

"Three and two bits," the cowhand returned, and held out his hand to another cowboy, who passed him more coins. Adam grimaced in mock threat seeing the trick being played on him.

"Come on, Doc, you can afford it!" someone called from the crowd.

"Four!" he called.

"Four and two bits," the cowhand said.

"Five!"

"Here!" someone shouted, pitching another coin through the air to the cowboy, who had almost given up bidding. "Doc better pay more than that for Beth Tyrell's basket!"

Her face went fiery red.

"Five and two bits."

"Six!" Adam returned, grinning broadly now, knowing the cowhand had finished.

"Ten." The voice was not loud, but it carried. Silence fell over the gathering. Beth's heart hammered as her head jerked up and she watched Logan walk forward slowly. People moved back out of his way. He stopped at the front of the crowd. Adam stared at him, all laughter gone.

"Eleven," Adam said belatedly, and glanced at Beth.

"Going once, going twice—" Pastor Tadish began quickly.

Logan looked straight at Adam, his eyes glittering. "Fifteen."

A faint rustle of alarm swept through the watching crowd.

Adam hesitated and cast a questing look around. Where was Frank? "Sixteen."

Beth saw her father approaching, face taut and dark. "Oh, God," she whispered, mortified.

"Twenty," Logan said in that same quiet, steely tone. The gasps were audible. Everyone stared. Frank stopped, his face thunderous. Adam's was white.

Logan looked up at the pastor. "I don't hear any further bids."

"Going, going, gone," Pastor Tadish said, and it sounded like last rites.

Logan strode forward, reached out and took the basket from the minister's hand, and crossed to stand in front of

Beth. "Miss Tyrell?" he said. She swallowed hard as he put his hand beneath her elbow and escorted her back through the parting crowd.

"You didn't like that spectacle much, did you?" he said softly.

"No," she managed.

Frank blocked them at the church gate. "Where do you think you're going with my daughter?"

Logan's fingers bit painfully into her arm. "Get out of my way, Tyrell."

"You're not taking her beyond this gate."

"Then why were you and your widow lady heading for the privacy of the apple orchard?" Logan taunted sardonically.

Frank's face went red and his eyes burned hot. He looked at Beth. "Go on back to the church." He knew the moment he'd said it that he had made everything worse. She stiffened.

"He bought the basket fair and square and I am going to have lunch with Mr. Tanner, Papa. Don't make any more of a scene than there has been already. Please."

"Let her go, Logan."

"Stand aside, Tyrell, or by God, I'll—"

"Don't!" Beth said in a soft tone that drew both men's attention. Her mouth trembled. "Just please stop it," she pleaded in a hoarse, cracking whisper, eyes closed. "Everyone is staring. . . ."

Seeing no other course, Frank stepped back. He gave Logan a dark, warning look before he let him pass.

Logan grinned baldly. "She'll be just fine," he said coldly, and escorted her out the gate. "I don't make war on women or children." His expression was derisive.

Beth glanced up at Logan's face as they walked down the hill together. His expression was inscrutable. "You needn't look at me like that," he muttered, eyes narrowing angrily. "You'll have less to fight off with me than with that drooling doctor of yours."

"Whatever do you mean?"

His hand tightened again as he drew her along. "You know exactly what I mean," he snarled.

"Where are we going?"

"That's up to you."

"Why don't we have our lunch on the front porch?"

He laughed cynically. "And be in plain sight of everyone in this damn town? No, thank you, ma'am." He looked down at her. "I was thinking of a certain place along the river."

"No," she said in alarm.

"Too many memories there? Maybe you're right." His gaze was dark and brooding as he stopped. "Someplace around here without any memories. Where have you and your Avery and that damn doctor *not* been?"

She was afraid she was going to cry after all.

His hand gentled. "I should have stayed out of it," he snapped, and she heard him let out his breath.

"Stayed out of what?"

He jerked his head back toward the church. "That!"

She lowered her head.

"Come on. There's a place south of town, up on a hill overlooking town," he said very softly.

She looked up at him again, surprised. He was talking about Jedediah Kilkare's hill. No one went there because of the superstitions surrounding it.

He searched her eyes grimly. "What's the matter? Don't you want to go anywhere with me?" he challenged, eyes glinting.

No one would go anywhere near that hill, and suddenly it was exactly where she wanted to be with Logan Tanner.

He caught her wrist. "You want to go back?"

She smiled. "No. The hill will be fine."

He frowned. "Why'd you look like that?"

"Just thinking."

"If you're afraid of me, we'll sit on your damn porch."

She smiled into his eyes. "No. I think we've both been stared at enough for one day."

They walked along the dusty road out of town and headed up the grassy slope. He had become silent.

"Why did you bid on my basket, Logan?"

"To be with you."

Her heart raced. "You could've seen me anytime you wanted just by stopping by the cottage, but you haven't even spoken a word to me since you came that one time."

His expression darkened at her challenge. "I thought better of it."

"Then what changed your mind today?"

"Today I didn't give a damn what people had to say about it." He gave a short, hard laugh. "And I wanted to see how deep your doctor's affections ran." He looked down at her again, eyes narrow. "Not deep enough, Beth."

"Twenty dollars is a great deal of money around here."

"He's too damn complacent."

She fell silent.

They reached the knoll and Logan set the basket down beneath the shade of an old oak. He faced her, arms akimbo, eyes fierce. "Something you'd better know from the start, Beth Tyrell. This isn't going anywhere. When I finish what I came to do, I'm leaving and I'm not coming back."

She frowned at his grim little speech and gave a soft, confused laugh. "Well, thank you for warning me ahead of time."

He frowned angrily.

"Feeling that way, Logan, it makes no sense at all that you bid on my basket."

He stiffened, gazing back toward town. "I saw the way

he was holding on to you like he owned you. I wasn't going to let him walk off with you in his back pocket." He looked at her again, his eyes flinty. "Was the pink ribbon his idea or yours?"

"His."

Logan didn't say anything else for a long while, and Beth sat down in confused silence, wondering at his mood. Why should it matter to him whom she was with, especially after what he had just said.

"I should have brought a blanket," he muttered, and sat down, a distance between them that was more than propriety demanded.

"Why? It's new spring grass. Softer than a down mattress."

He looked at her.

"Are you hungry?" she asked softly.

"Famished," he said huskily, his gaze moving slowly over her face.

She took the linen cloth from the basket, spread it, and began laying out the picnic lunch. Cheese, a small loaf of french bread, a small jar of watermelon-rind pickles, raspberry tarts, slices of roast beef, and a bottle of fine red wine that had cost her all of one dollar.

Logan took it first and glared at it.

"He brought wine once," she felt impelled to explain.

He made a low sound in his throat and thunked it down, looking at her enigmatically. After a moment he shrugged off his leather jacket, untied the thin, dark bowtie, and unbuttoned the top three buttons of his shirt, revealing dark, curling chest hair.

Beth stared, heart racing, stomach curling tightly. She forced her gaze away from him, alarmed by his virile presence and yet excited by it, too.

"Wouldn't you be more comfortable without your holster and gun?" she asked finally, looking at him again.

"No."

She smiled, eyes teasing gently. "No one will come up here."

"I'm sure they won't," he said darkly.

She shook her head. "You don't understand. This is Jedediah Kilkare's hill. It's haunted."

He gave her a look that implied she was mad.

"He was a trapper who came here fifty years ago," she explained. "He had an Indian wife and a partner in business. He found them . . . well, they . . ." He smiled provocatively and she blushed. "Anyway," she went on, lowering her eyes, "he killed them both and burned the cabin. After that, he wandered in these hills with his pet she-wolf. He must have died, but no one ever found his body, so they're convinced he's still up here somewhere. He couldn't be, of course. It was such a long time ago. But sometimes a wolf howls and there's a sound like a man crying."

Logan laughed. "Are you frightening yourself?"

"No, but it's a sad story, don't you think?"

"He should've killed them," he said indifferently, resting back on his side and looking at her. "Why don't you take your jacket off, too?"

"It is warm," she agreed, and unbuttoned the prim high-waisted jacket that matched her russet skirt. As she drew it back off her shoulders, she saw Logan's gaze move down her breasts pressing against the pale cream blouse. A muscle tightened and worked in his jaw, and he looked away slowly.

"Has he ever kissed you?"

"Pardon me?" she stammered, flushed.

He looked directly into her eyes. "Has that doctor ever kissed you?" he demanded.

She bit down on her lower lip, confused by such a personal interrogation. "That really isn't your business, Logan," she managed.

"Was it the same as when I kissed you?"

"Hardly. You grabbed me."

He laughed softly. "Well, I won't grab you like that again. I'll give you plenty of warning next time."

Her face heated up and she stared at him, worried.

He picked up the bottle of wine. "Were you having a maiden's dream of seducing him?" he asked grimly.

"Of course not."

"Two glasses and you'd be flat on your back, Beth."

She was mortified at the turn of conversation.

He sat up straight and worked the cork out. Looking at her pointedly, he poured the entire contents into the glass and heaved the bottle away before standing up and moving away from her. His shoulders were terse. He raked his fingers through his dark hair, then stopped and looked back at her, a muscle working in his jaw. "What're the chances of your father following us up here?"

"None. It's the last place in the world anyone would go."

He frowned. "Why didn't you tell me that in the first place?"

She stood up. "Because I wanted to be alone with you."

He stared at her, the muscle jerking again. "We can go in closer."

"No."

He swore softly. "Go lightly with me, Beth," he warned.

She stood and came toward him. "I don't understand."

He looked almost exasperated. "Don't you? Well, don't press it." He walked past her and nodded toward the lunch she had laid out. "We'd better eat."

She came back and sat down with him, her skirts spread

out around her. She held out the loaf of bread to him. He broke it in half and handed part of it back. He wore a knife as well as a gun, and he drew it out and cut wedges of cheese.

"Do you ever take your gun off, Logan?"

"When I make love to a woman."

Her cheeks turned scarlet as she remembered him standing in the hotel window, a woman unbuttoning his shirt.

"If I ever start unbuckling it, you run like hell," he said, mouth curving slightly.

Her eyes went wide until she realized he was only teasing her. "I'll remember that," she laughed softly.

They ate bread and cheese together in silence. She was intently aware of his scrutiny, and raised her eyes once to see his brooding look.

"How long have you and your father lived in Kilkare Woods?"

"Since I was three. I don't remember anything about where we were before, but Papa said we lived in Texas. Mama died there and Papa was too brokenhearted to stay in the same place without her, so we moved on."

Logan took one of her watermelon-rind pickles and tasted it. His brows lifted and he took another. "How'd your mother die?"

Beth frowned. "I don't really know."

"Texas is a long journey for a man and child."

She looked at him. "I don't press him about any of it. It seems to hurt him to talk about her. I think he still loves her."

Logan began eating sliced meat. He leaned back again. "I've heard about the famous gunfight," he drawled. "Your father shot down three men in the local saloon."

Beth paled. "It wasn't like that."

"No?"

"There was a feud going on between two ranches over a

stream that ran through both. It came to bloodshed. Papa and I arrived in town during the thick of it, I guess. When the shooting began, Papa just . . . ended it."

Logan laughed.

"He didn't kill anyone," she said defensively.

He just looked at her.

"The fighting stopped after that," she added.

"No doubt. Who'd dare go up against someone who could outdraw three men at once?"

"You're wrong about him, Logan," she told him softly. "Papa is a peace-loving man."

"Your bias makes you a poor judge of character."

She stiffened. "If you wish to speak ill of my father, don't do so to me, Mr. Tanner."

His mouth curved sardonically. "Yes, ma'am."

They fell silent. This time it was she who watched him openly. "Where are you from, Logan?"

"Points east and south."

She waited.

He gauged her expression grimly. "I've worked cattle a good deal of the time."

"You're very good with your gun, aren't you?"

His eyes narrowed and darkened. "Yes. Very." He shifted. "I've hired it out and made better money than by running stock for wealthy ranchers. Usually I was hired to prevent what you claim your father stopped here. When trouble started, I came in to finish it."

"By killing men?"

He bared his teeth. "Are you asking me how many notches are on my gun handle?" He withdrew it, leaned toward her, and dropped it in her lap.

She sat stock-still, staring down at it, horrified. "Take it away, Logan," she rasped. She closed her eyes tightly.

He left it. "Look at it."

"No!"

"Look at it!" he ordered in a low, burning voice.

She looked at him first, then his gun.

"No notches on the handle." He tapped his forehead. "All the marks are cut up here, laid in deep so they'll never be forgotten. Killing a man stays with you. Rots the heart right out of you after a while."

"Then why do you do it?"

"Sometimes killing's got to be done. Sometimes a man deserves to die. And using a gun is what I do best."

"You could learn something else," she said in earnest. "You said you used to work cattle. There are cattle ranches all around town. Avery owns one." She stopped at the dark change in his expression.

"Ah, yes, your Avery. Would you put in a good word for me?" he drawled incitingly. He leaned toward her and picked up the gun. His knuckles whitened for an instant and he slipped it expertly back into his holster.

"What made you the way you are, Logan?" she asked after a long, pulsating moment.

"A natural course of events," he said cynically.

"What events?"

"Leave it." He picked up another slice of beef and ate in silence.

"I can't," she admitted finally. "Why did you come here? Who hired you this time?"

His eyes were steely. "I'm here for myself this time. And I said *leave it!*"

Her eyes smarted.

"Damnit, don't cry." He threw the meat aside and stood in one fierce motion that made Beth draw in a startled breath and cower back.

He glared down at her bleakly. "Pack it up. I'm taking you back."

At that moment, Logan reminded her piercingly of Faraday Slate, the proud, bad boy distrusted and misunderstood by everyone except her father. Was it only beatings from a drunken father that had killed the trust and gentleness in the boy? And what past crimes done to Logan had created a man who exuded so much pent-up violence and lonely self-imposed exile?

A battle raged inside him. She could feel it as surely as if the same fever burned in her own blood. It didn't matter what the cause was. The outcome was death, his or someone else's.

And she couldn't let it happen.

She stood up. "I don't want to go back yet."

He glanced at her sharply, then moved away into the deeper shadows of the oak. She followed.

"Logan, you don't have to do *anything*."

His head was bowed and he rubbed the back of his neck in agitation. "It's the only way to put things right for me."

"But killing never puts things right. There has to be another way. If violence is the only way to solve things, what hope is there for any of us?"

He glared at her. "You don't know what the hell you're talking about."

"I know what I feel," she told him softly, and came close enough to touch his arm with her fingertips.

He stiffened. Turning slowly, he looked down into her eyes. "I had it all worked out, except for this."

"For what?"

He shook his head. "We'd better go back," he said hoarsely.

She felt reprimanded and her eyes burned. "Have I been so very forward?" she asked softly.

"Oh, Beth," he groaned, and caught hold of her.

Her heart stopped and then surged with quick, fluid heat as his mouth covered hers. Her stomach tightened and fluttered. He stepped closer, one hand slowly moving down from her hair to her shoulder. He raised his mouth; his breath quickened. "Why couldn't you be like other women?"

"Like the lady in the hotel window with you?" she whispered painfully, eyes closing as she felt his mouth glide against the pulsating vein in her throat.

"No!" he rasped. "No!" He cupped her face and kissed her again, hungrily.

She knew this was the way it was meant to feel. Her lips parted and she slid her arms tightly around his hard, narrow waist. He groaned deeply and forced her mouth open wider.

The first shock of the intimacy and demand of his passion passed as her own passion grew. He drew her closer and closer until their bodies were full length against one another. She could feel the hard rise and fall of his broad chest, the restless, restrained way he moved, his hands firm against her back, moving downward slowly, then stopping.

He dragged his mouth away. "Oh, Beth, you taste like heaven."

She felt the tremor in his hands as he cupped her head and lightly caressed her cheeks with his callused thumbs. Then he pulled her close again, his hands on her shoulders and back, playing the singing, pulsing beat deep into her body until she made a soft sound in her throat.

"Now we know, don't we?" he whispered against her lips, and he kissed her again, nibbling, drawing her lower lip gently between his teeth, parting her lips and exploring her mouth with his tongue. She could hardly breathe past the wild pounding of her heart. "I could take you anytime I want," he whispered. "And I *do* want, Beth." He pushed her back and gave her a gentle reproving shake.

She gazed up at him without subterfuge or hesitance in showing exactly what she felt. He withdrew completely then, his face hardening. "Pack it all up," he ordered again, and this time he meant it.

She did as he asked, dismayed that he wanted to end the afternoon so soon. He watched her, but didn't come close. Once he gazed off toward town, his face rigid.

She held the basket in both hands before her and waited for him to come near. He said nothing at all as they walked back to town, and she was too full of confused emotion to attempt any conversation.

Frank Tyrell was sitting on the front porch of the little white cottage at the edge of town. He saw them coming and came to the gate and opened it.

Seeing him there, Beth paused at the bend in the road and turned to Logan. She put her hand lightly on his arm. "Come to dinner tomorrow night, Logan," she said on impulse.

"No!" He was appalled. Looking past her to Tyrell standing at the gate and glaring at them in the road, he sneered.

"Please, Logan."

Logan still looked at Tyrell, and a deep anger boiled up inside him, a devil prodding him on. He laughed low. "Alright. What time?"

"Seven?"

"I'll be there." Still not looking at her, he took her arm and walked her straight up to the gate and stopped before the sheriff. "I brought her back all safe and sound."

Tyrell was looking her over carefully. "Are you alright, Beth?"

"Of course," she assured him in embarrassment. She could feel the tension and animosity between the two men, while she stood in the middle. She glanced up at Logan. "Thank you for the wonderful afternoon, Logan."

"It's a shame it wasn't longer," he said, implying it was she who had ended it rather than he. She wondered why he had done that.

"Go on in the house, honey. I want a word with Mr. Tanner."

"Papa—"

"Go in the house!"

Seeing she would only make matters worse by resistance, she went, but resentment was high and heavy in her breast. She entered the house and went to the front windows, drawing the curtains back slightly.

Her father stood almost nose to nose with Logan, snarling at him. He jerked his head in dismissal, but Logan smiled and said something back. His smile grew as her father's face darkened in anger. Logan stopped, shrugged, and laughed. Tipping his hat in a mocking manner, he sauntered away. When her father turned back toward the cottage, she saw how old he looked.

Chapter Nine

THE NEXT DAY, Beth canceled her two appointments and spent the day cleaning house and planning a fine dinner. She had had no opportunity to tell her father Logan was coming. When he returned home late that afternoon and slumped so wearily into his chair, she found it hard to tell him at all.

"You look very pretty tonight," he said, noticing her soft yellow percale dress with French lace. It was the finest she had made for herself, and she saved it for special occasions. "Is Adam coming for dinner?"

"No, Papa. Logan is."

He frowned, looking at her, his face going white. His eyes narrowed. "What did you say?" he demanded through tight lips.

She swallowed hard. "Logan is coming for dinner this evening. I invited him." She had never in her life heard him swear so fiercely, nor look so wild. "Papa, please," she whispered shakily, frightened. "Give Logan a chance. He—"

"Give him a chance to do what?" he ground out, glaring at her as though he hated her.

"He came to church."

"Not to hear about God, he didn't!"

"You might be wrong about him."

"I'm not wrong about Logan Tanner," he said through his teeth. "You've become a fool over a handsome face. You're walking right into something you don't understand. I told you to stay away from him! The man is..." He stopped, his mouth working. Standing abruptly, he raked a shaking hand through his hair in a gesture that reminded her of Logan himself. "Goddamn him! He comes right into my house!"

"He hasn't done anything wrong, Papa. Maybe he—"

"Not yet, he hasn't. But he'll stay until he gets his deed done. You can count on that." He caught hold of her shoulders. "You think a man like Tanner can change? Well, he can't! He has no compassion in him, no damn conscience. He's already dead inside, Beth, dead from all his killing."

She averted her face, closing her eyes in denial and pain.

"I said listen!"

She winced and let out a muted gasp at his roughness.

"A man like him, he doesn't marry a girl."

"Papa," she protested, seeing where he was going.

"I saw it in your eyes when he brought you back yesterday. Jesus, Mary, don't you think I know? He knows women, Beth, I won't deny him that. He's had plenty, in every town he's been in and in every town he'll hit after this one. You just don't understand what's happening!"

She pulled away. "Are you saying you don't trust me?"

"I trust you."

"With someone like Adam!"

"Adam is right for you!"

"You let me decide who's right for me," she told him, her eyes stinging.

His face tightened and his mouth drew down. "When Tanner comes to that door, I'm going to send him on his way. He's not welcome in this house."

She felt sick at the thought of such an insult. "You do that to him, Papa, after I invited him here, and before God, I'll never forgive you." Her voice broke.

He stared at her, unbelieving. "Beth!"

"I mean it."

He reached out to touch her, but she drew back from him, her eyes glistening in reproval and disappointment.

The mantel clock chimed seven. A knock came, startling them both. Frank glanced sharply at the door, his eyes narrow, his features tightening up with violent inner turmoil. Beth's face crumpled. She clutched at his arm. "Please. Don't do such a thing to him. How could you do it to anyone? He's a man, just like you, Papa. He's not dead inside any more than you are. He's not," she whispered. "Give him a chance, Papa."

Frank frowned heavily. He turned away. "Let him in," he said gruffly.

Logan leaned indolently against the doorjamb and smiled down at Beth.

"Come in, Logan," she said, dipping slightly as she opened the door wider. He looked like a successful rancher in his neat suit. She knew it should have been her father who answered the knock, but he stood with his back to the fire, staring at the man framed in the doorway.

Logan entered, looking down over her in open admiration.

Beth saw that he wasn't wearing his gun. His eyes glinted as they looked into hers, reminding her of his words the day before. She blushed.

Logan came in and stood in the middle of the parlor, his hands lightly resting on his hips as he looked at Frank. Frank stared back at him coldly. "Hello, Sheriff," Logan drawled, the faintest sardonic inflexion in the title.

If they had been dogs, they would have been growling and circling one another, waiting for an opening. Being men, they let their hatred and distrust glow hotly in their eyes.

"May I take your coat, Logan?" Beth asked softly, glancing worriedly at her father's rigid face.

"Thank you." He shrugged it off. He was wearing a clean fine linen shirt and thin black bow tie.

Still her father said nothing, and the silence grated on Beth's already fraying nerves. She looked at him pleadingly. He flatly ignored her. She moved between the two men, disheartened. "Please," she whispered. "Both of you, sit down."

Logan's face eased. He nodded briefly and took a place on the settee. Her father sat in his wing chair. His face pinched for an instant as though a sharp pain had gripped him. Then his expression smoothed out, showing nothing.

Beth looked at them, worried. "I should check on supper."

"Do that then," her father ordered.

"I'm afraid to leave the room," she admitted, giving them both an impatient look.

Logan smiled slightly, but she wasn't fooled. She recognized the look in his eyes. He was coiled inside, ready to strike.

She sat demurely on the edge of the settee, a space between her and Logan. She folded her hands in her lap.

"Alright, Beth," her father said heavily.

Uneasy still, she left them alone.

Dinner was a grim affair. Logan finished a thick slab of

baked ham, a portion of mixed garden vegetables, and a roasted potato. Her father picked at his meal, pushing food about on his plate and glancing repeatedly at Logan with unconcealed anger. Beth tried to eat, but her appetite had gone completely. Logan complimented her on her cooking. She cleared the dishes quietly and poured the two men coffee. They sipped in tense silence.

"Would either of you like a piece of apple pie?" she asked, doubting either had the appetite for it.

Logan smiled. "Yes."

As she went into the kitchen, she heard him say, "Nice little place you have here. How'd you manage to earn it on a sheriff's pay?"

She took up the pie and plates and went back in before her father could answer the inciting question. She looked at him and saw how stony and silent he was as he glared at Logan.

"As I said, a nice little place," Logan repeated, smiling in challenge.

Beth saw her father's hands tighten. She placed hers over one of his. "Would you like some brandy, Papa?"

"Yes."

She looked at Logan and shook her head slightly, eyes pleading with him. He frowned, his mouth tightening. She went back into the kitchen to get the bottle of brandy. She heard her father. "I'm not stupid. I know what you're trying to do." He stopped as soon as she came back again. He leaned back in his chair, his expression masked. Beth set the small glass in front of him. Rather than sip, he tossed it off with a jerk of his wrist. She stared. Logan's mouth curved mockingly.

"Papa, are you alright?" she asked, seeing the pinched look on his face again.

"Fine. Stop your fussing," he snarled.

Color poured hotly into her cheeks at his abrupt tone.

She blinked, shamed by his rudeness. Logan, his face rigid, a muscle working in his jaw, looked at her and then at her father. "I'd like some more coffee, Beth," he said softly.

"Yes, of course," she murmured, turning away quickly.

Logan glared at Frank Tyrell. "In your shoes, I'd probably feel the same, Sheriff," he said in a low, coldly menacing voice. "I might even feel pressed to do something about the situation. But if I didn't have the guts, I wouldn't take it out on a woman."

Frank's eyes glinted. "How long do you plan on hanging around?"

"As long as it takes."

"For what? For your money to run out? Then what? I doubt there's anyone in town that'll hire you on. Not even for your gun. I'm surprised you didn't wear it tonight. You look half-dressed without it."

Logan laughed low, undaunted. "I never wear guns when I'm courting."

Frank's hand fisted and he clenched his teeth. Beth came in again, and he watched Logan give her a bold, sensuous smile that brought color high into her cheeks. Then Logan looked at Frank again, daring him. "Why should I hang up my guns permanently?" Logan asked. "You haven't."

"Papa has a reason for wearing a gun, Logan," Beth put in quietly.

"So have I." He picked up his coffee cup and looked at Frank over the rim as he drank. Lowering the cup again, his hand steady, he smiled coldly. "And our reasons aren't far apart. I'm not less respectable for the vermin I deal with than you are for what you do, Sheriff."

"My gun's hired out to maintain the law."

Logan laughed mockingly. "But how did you get so fast

in the first place if you're such a peace-loving man?" His blue eyes glittered.

Frank glanced at Beth and said nothing.

Beth looked at them both, her face leached of color. What was Logan implying? "Perhaps if you two talked instead of snarled at one another, you might find some common ground," Beth said, half pleading. She should never have invited Logan to come, knowing how her father felt about him. It was her fault this was happening.

"You're right, Beth," Logan said, not looking at her, but leaning forward and staring into Tyrell's eyes. "We should talk about common ground."

Frank stood abruptly. Logan jerked back, his hand lowering instinctively. Beth's eyes went wide, her heart lodging in her throat. Frank's face twisted in contempt before he left the table. Logan stared at his back, his eyes dark and fierce. He stood as well.

"I may just decide to settle here."

Frank glanced back with a sneer. "And do what?"

"Buy some land."

"You? What would you do with land?"

Logan walked into the parlor and faced him. "Raise cattle."

Beth still stood at the table, her hand at her throat, watching them.

"Who's going to sell you land, Tanner? Who'll sell you cattle?" Frank laughed derisively.

Logan's eyebrow lifted. "There're ways and means, Sheriff."

Her father looked at Logan oddly, a deep pain mirrored in his eyes. He said nothing for a moment, then frowned heavily. "Where'd you learn to use your gun?" he asked quietly, his manner changed.

Logan stiffened, withdrew. "Texas. New Mexico. Nevada. You might say I gathered experience as I went."

"Has it brought you anything but grief?"

Logan's face went cold. "Satisfaction."

The mantel clock struck. Logan looked at it. "I'd better leave before I wear out my welcome." He looked back at Beth, still standing by the table. "Will you walk me to the gate?"

"You can see yourself out," Frank snarled.

Beth winced. "Of course, Logan," she told him softly, and gave her father a sad look.

Frank stared at them grimly as they walked to the door. She didn't take her shawl with her. Logan glanced back once. Frank's hand tightened into a first and he seemed to shake with rage.

"I don't think your papa approves of me," Logan said dryly after closing the door behind them.

"I'm sorry. He's never been so rude."

He heard the tremor in her voice. "Rude? He hates my guts." He shrugged. "Did you expect him to greet me with open arms?" He laughed softly, glancing back at the cottage.

"How can you laugh, Logan?" she asked, miserable.

"Ah, there's an amusing side to all this, little Beth, though you aren't in any position to appreciate it."

She shivered.

Logan draped his coat around her shoulders. She looked up at him and saw something tighten his expression.

They reached the gate. She opened it and looked away from him. Logan faced her squarely then. Eyes down, she started to remove his coat. He caught the lapels and held it firmly around her. His hands lowered so that he felt the soft swell of her breasts beneath his knuckles. He sensed her heart beating like a wild thing, his own quickening. He said nothing, but looked at her grimly. She moved restlessly, embarrassed. His hands tightened inexorably, not wanting to release her yet.

She looked up at him. "Logan—"

"Don't say a word, Beth," he whispered huskily. "I'd like nothing better than to kiss you right now, right here. But your father's standing there in the window watching us, and it's you that has to go back inside and face him."

Her mouth trembled and tears welled into her eyes. "I wish you had both tried just a little harder."

His hold slackened. "It's too late. I am what I am, and he is what he is. Water and oil." His hands dropped to his sides.

Beth removed his coat, folded the shoulders of it together, and handed it back to him carefully. He took the coat and slung it carelessly over his shoulder. "Good night," he said briskly, and strolled away.

Beth watched, a hard lump in her throat. When he reached the boardwalk and hadn't looked back at her once, she turned away.

As she came up the steps slowly, her father opened the door. He was staring after Logan, his eyes burning.

"You don't have to worry, Papa. He won't be back, I'm sure." Her voice broke softly. She passed him quickly.

Frank slammed the door behind her. "Don't expect me to apologize! Good God, Beth. I thought you had more sense than—"

Beth turned. "Than what, Papa? Logan was more of a gentleman than you were. I've never seen you so unforgivably rude or surly to anyone!"

"He isn't just anyone. He's slime. And if you think I was rude tonight, just let him cross that threshold again!"

Beth's face paled and then went red. "What would you do? Shoot him? What's the matter with you lately?" she cried, confused and hurt.

"I don't want my daughter having anything to do with a gunslinger! Is that so damn hard to get through your head? Save your kindness for someone who deserves it."

"You'd push me into Adam Buchanan's arms fast enough," she said in agitation. "Or any other man around these parts that might chance to knock at our door!"

"You're right! I would! Adam's different and you know it! There isn't a dark side to him. Tanner's soul is black as Hades."

"You don't even know him!"

"What do I have to know, except his reputation? You're not going to see him again."

Her head came up. "I'll see whom I please, when I please, Papa."

The fire died in her father's eyes. "Why him, Beth? You'll ruin your whole life if you let yourself love a man like that." His face was gray and lined. "Don't you see it for truth? He's just using you."

"To get back at you for telling him to leave town? Oh, Papa, that's not reason enough, is it?"

"Take my word for it," he grunted.

"I've got to clean up the dishes."

"Beth. For me. Please."

She looked up at him, tears coming then. "I love you. You know that well enough to use it as a weapon, don't you?" She pleaded with her eyes for his understanding. "Something happened inside me when I first saw Logan. I felt I'd known him before. Always. I don't know." She bit her lip. "Papa, common sense aside, if he does come to call on me again, I'll welcome him."

"Beth," his father said huskily, his face lined. He came close and held her tightly, stroking her back. "How did I ever beget you? What freak of nature did this?" He sighed. "There's too much gentleness in you. You trust people and love them and believe there's good in everyone, and, honey, it just isn't so."

She drew back, looking up at him. "Papa, you've read your Bible faithfully for as long as I can remember, and you haven't learned one thing."

His smile was cynical. "Life taught me more than the Good Book ever did." He smoothed her soft hair back from her temples and held her face in his cupped hands. "Such beauty you have. I made a mistake rearing you the way I did. I should've told you a few hard truths, let you see more of the world than I did. But I didn't, and I've left you wide open to a devil like Logan Tanner."

"No. There's good in him. I know there is, Papa."

"I'm telling you, just as sure as God created heaven and earth, Logan Tanner was created to bring misery to anyone that cares about him. He's filled up and overflowing with hatred, and nothing you can do will take it out of him. Nothing, Beth."

It was strange that both her father and Logan had said much the same thing about her, that she ws too trusting and would be hurt. But she believed in what she felt and had no other course before her but to live by it. "Violence begets violence, and gentleness will beget gentleness." She reached up and touched her father's face. "That's the truth I believe in, Papa. I thought you did, too."

Chapter Ten

BETH SAW MARY GALLOWAY the next morning. She was planning a trip to San Jose to visit her sister and wanted a nice traveling dress. Faith Halverson brought fidgety Terence by to be measured for a Sunday jacket and knickers since he had already outgrown the set Beth had made him on his last birthday.

At noon, Beth delivered mulligan stew to her father at the jail and made several errand stops along the way back to the cottage. She sewed for several hours and then went out into the vegetable garden, filled with late-afternoon sunlight, to thin carrots and radishes and harvest some tomatoes and zucchini for canning. Hefting the loaded basket to her hip, she turned back toward the cottage.

Logan sat on the back steps watching her, a faint smile playing on his lips. "Hello," he drawled, his expression teasing.

She smiled, her heart jumping. "Hello." She walked toward him and saw his gaze move down over her and back up again, a warm, sensual glow in his blue eyes. He had a very provocative way of looking at her. Did he know what that look did? She stopped in front of him. "You'll have to move so I can get by you."

His eyes narrowed. "No time to stop and talk? Or are you still angry with me about last night?"

She shook her head. "I wasn't angry. I was disappointed," she said frankly. She smiled faintly. "If you'll open the back door for me, I'll pour you some cider inside."

One brow lifted in surprise. He stood slowly, shifting his body in a way that made her stomach curl in awareness. Everything about him proclaimed masculinity. He took her basket, his gaze dark and velvety. "Sure you want me to come in, Beth?"

She wasn't sure what to answer, thinking of propriety.

He grinned roguishly. "Open the door, Beth."

She did. He passed her. She looked at the broad set of his shoulders as she followed him inside. He set the basket down and leaned indolently against the table, arms crossed, watching her skirt around him to get to the cabinet where the jug of cider sat.

"What did your father have to say after I left last night?" he drawled sardonically.

"He said I lacked common sense. I said he lacked manners."

Logan laughed. He reassessed her slowly and frowned. "Was he very angry with you?"

She held out a glass filled with cider. "Yes."

He took it and set it on the table. "Worried about your chances with the doc?"

She felt his tension as he looked at her carefully through narrowed dark eyes. She looked down at the glass in front of him. "Don't you want the cider?"

"I want *you*," he said quietly. "I thought I made that clear on the hill."

She put her hand on her breast. "You're very direct."

"You did invite me in." He moved around the table.

She edged back, her breath catching. "Logan! For conversation, not anything else."

He laughed. "Are you sure, Beth?"

She felt the heat coming up into her cheeks. He watched her mercilessly, his smile broadening even more at her embarrassment. Then his smile dimmed.

"I keep thinking about how it felt to hold you and kiss you," he said quietly. He felt the heat rising in him. It would take very little to put her off-balance. He softened, seeing her vulnerability. He came closer and said truthfully, "I came by to see that you were alright."

She frowned. "Logan, my father would never hurt me. He was angry and he said what he felt he had to say. That was the end of it."

"You think so? What would he say if he knew I was here with you now?"

Her heart pounded heavily at the caressive look in his eyes. "He wouldn't be happy about it," she admitted softly. He would be furious and there could even be trouble.

"Thinking differently now, aren't you?" he drawled coolly. "What would that good doctor have to say about it, too, hmmmm? He might even think you've been soiled." He ran one provocative finger down her smooth cheek and slid his hand around against the nape of her neck. He drew her forward inexorably and watched how her lips parted and trembled softly. Frightened, yes, but more. Frowning, he released her.

"What is it?" she asked softly.

A muscle jerked in his cheek. Without another word, he walked out the back door, letting it slam hard. She opened it again and stood on the landing. "Logan?"

He stopped midway down the steps and looked back up at her. Some hard, violent emotion burned hotly in his eyes. He shook his head, eyes veiled, and looked away.

"Did I do something wrong?" she asked, her hand on the railing. "Tell me. Can't we talk, Logan?"

He combed shaky fingers back through his dark hair. Coming to a decision, he swung around, caught hold of her wrist, and pulled her along behind him as he went down the steps.

She gasped and almost had to run to keep up with his long strides as he ducked beneath the low branches of the trees that ran along the border of the cottage property. He kept going, and she knew he was heading for the solitude of the hills. Her heart raced and she tried to catch her breath.

"Where are we going?" she managed.

"For a walk." The line of his jaw was like granite.

"A walk? Well, could we go a bit slower?" she gasped.

He glanced down at her and saw the difficulty she was having. He stopped and let her catch her breath, his hands beneath her elbows in support. He looked away. "I want to go somewhere we can talk without Papa walking in on us."

"Do you have to talk about him in such an unpleasant tone? He's protective of me, of course."

His eyes glittered. "And I'm not good enough for you, is that it?" He let out his breath and let go of her. "Well, he's probably right about that. There's not a man alive good enough for you. Not even that damn pompous doctor dangling from your line."

She searched his face. "Why are you so angry?"

He swung to face her again. "Because I've had a single

thing driving me for years, and now I'm wondering what I do when it's done!" He let his breath out. "Damn!" Head down, he moved away from her, staring off at nothing. He rubbed the back of his neck while his other hand rested lightly on the hip above his gun. He swore again, softly.

"Is it all so important?" she murmured.

He glared at her, his nerves jagged with desire. She was distorting his judgment. What he had come to do was more important than she was, and whatever it took to bring out the man he had come to kill, he would do it. He had prepared for this moment, lived for it too long just to put it aside over passing feelings for any woman.

But Beth Tyrell wasn't just any woman.

Seeing the torment in his eyes, Beth approached him. She wanted to touch him in more than a physical way, though she wanted that too. She wanted all his barriers to come down. She wanted to understand what had made him the way he was. She saw the dark, fierce glitter in his blue eyes that had now become steely and withdrawn. "What did this to you, Logan?"

He didn't touch her, but began to walk again, measuring his steps so she could easily keep pace with him if she chose to. She did.

"What was your family like?" she asked, glancing up at him.

"Small."

"Just you and your parents? No brothers and sisters?"

"Just me and my father."

"What happened to your mother?"

"She died in childbirth. Mine."

She bit her lip, frowning at his terseness. "Did you and your father get on together, Logan?"

He gave her an odd, half-accusing look. "Some."

"Where is he?"

"Dead."

She lowered her head. "I'm sorry. I'm hurting you by asking," she apologized.

He gritted his teeth. He didn't want to talk to her or have her talk to him. The less he knew her, the easier it was going to be when he left; and he would leave, right after he finished what he had come to do. He had to remember that. He had to keep remembering that.

She was no part of this, but it was going to hurt her nonetheless. She was in love with him. He knew enough of women to see it in her eyes, to feel it in her body when he touched her. It made him ache to think about taking her, laying her on her back in the warm spring grass and going into her body and making himself part of her.

But she wasn't like the women he had known before. She was a virgin. When they came apart after sex, she would want to become part of him, too, in a permanent, imprisoning way. What he felt wouldn't last. It couldn't. He would leave when he finished what he had come here to do, and she'd never forget. God knew she didn't deserve that kind of pain.

"What about *your* mother?" he demanded, wanting to draw all conversation away from him, not really caring about her answer. "Do you remember what she was like?"

"She died when I was very young. I don't remember her."

"Does your father talk about her?"

"No." She frowned slightly. "I've asked him about her. He told me once she was prettier than a sunset."

"How did she die?"

"Logan, I don't ask him much about her. It still seems to pain him somehow when he talks about her."

He glanced at her and softened. "Who taught you about all the woman things you do?"

She dimpled. "Papa received much help from all the

ladies in town. It was the schoolmistress, Sadie Martin, who taught me how to sew." She thought of the old woman who had been Boston bred, and how she'd taken her under her maternal wing from the first day at school. "She died four years ago," she added softly, eyes glistened. She looked away.

"Why didn't your father ever remarry?"

She shrugged. "Once he'd loved Mama the way he did, I guess he couldn't settle for anything else."

He gave a curt, cynical laugh. "But there've been women along the way."

He knew he had shocked her, as she answered shakily, "Well, women have been interested in Papa, yes, but he's never chosen to marry."

"I hear he sees a widow lady quite frequently."

"Missus O'Keefe. Yes. Her husband died a few years ago and she's been running a ranch on her own. Occasionally, she runs into difficulties and sends for Papa."

Logan could tell her what else the widow wanted. Tyrell might be in his fifties, but he was a vigorous man. "Why don't we sit down up there for a while?" he suggested as she followed him along the slope toward a grove of sycamores. She was flushed, and he knew she needed a rest. She dabbed her forehead with the back of her hand as she sat in the cooling shadows of the trees.

Logan leaned against a boulder, his gaze enigmatic as he studied her.

"What're you thinking?" she asked, smiling up at him curiously.

"That I'd like to unbutton that high-necked dress and strip the corset off you so you could breathe properly."

She gaped at him.

He straightened and walked toward her. "Beth, didn't your father ever tell you never to trust a man?" he needled, hunkering down and deliberately trailing his fingers along the curve of her cheek and down against the wildly pulsing vein in her throat. Looking at her and touching her affected him. If she knew anything, she would lower her eyes and see what she did to him. He waited. She didn't.

He knelt, knees spread, and rested his hands lightly against her shoulder. She looked frightened, but beneath it he knew her senses were awakened. She was trembling beneath his hand and probably didn't even know fully what was happening inside her. He thought of baring her back and covering her body with his.

Her eyes changed, softening. She lifted her hand and touched his face. A shock of feeling went through him like wildfire. He thought he had forever lost the ability to be surprised by anything, but as she touched him in the same way he had her, he froze, stunned.

"I like it when you touch me, Logan," she whispered guilelessly.

His heart hammered, squeezing at the same time with an emotion he had never felt before. It hurt. A devil rose in him in quick self-defense against what she did to him by her simple, innocent act. He lowered his hand boldly and heard the soft, shocked catch in her breath. "Still like it?" He applied torment to the peak of her breast and saw how wide her eyes went, darkening and pulling him in. "You don't have to answer. I can see how much you do."

Hurt built moistly in her hazel eyes. "Are you mocking me?"

He took his hand away abruptly and straightened. He turned away and shut his eyes tightly. "I suppose I am," he said, finding it difficult to keep his voice steady and cool.

"Why?"

How could he answer that when he wasn't sure himself? He wanted to shake her. "You shouldn't have come out here with me."

"You wanted me to come."

He turned back and looked at her. "Yes, but you could have said no. You should've guessed there would be consequences." He was casting blame on her and despised himself for it. How much choice had he really given her, grasping her the way he had and half dragging her along behind him? He had only wanted to get her clear of that cottage and her father and the small-minded town. He hadn't stopped to think about consequences either. Consequences had never mattered to him before. "What did you think might happen?" he snarled.

She lowered her head. "I thought you might kiss me again," she admitted softly.

His hand clenched, his body tensing with sudden, hot, demanding life. "And just stop there?" He saw the little shock go through her body at that. She looked up sharply at him with wide eyes. He laughed softly, but wasn't amused. How would it be to take her innocence? Could he forget about her once he had? Or would she haunt him when he was miles from this place, miles from her?

No other woman had affected him like this. He had made love to many in the towns he had passed through, but none of them had been innocent. Some had wanted money. Others had only wanted to be with him. He had never been in a position to encounter a lady. He had avoided them. Why hadn't he avoided this one? He had known what she was the moment he saw her, her skirt tangled in that damn picket gate.

The ache to experience making love to Beth built inside him, clawing at him. He would be her first, probably her last if he judged her correctly. It gave him a power he wasn't sure he wanted to wield, yet he almost felt driven to it.

She stood up slowly and rustled her skirts gently to free

them of leaves and grass. It was a purely feminine gesture, simple, uncomplex, without coyness or subterfuge, and it pierced Logan strangely.

In how many hotel rooms had he lain on his back naked and smoked a cigarette he'd rolled just after having sex with a woman he had met in a saloon? Body sated, he'd watch her dress through the haze of smoke that always made the woman look a little better afterward. How many corsets had he seen laced up tightly, buttons done up, skirts lightly fluffed before the woman accepted the money he gave whether she'd asked for it or not?

Looking at Beth, he felt unclean and ashamed for having touched her at all.

She took a few steps and looked back over her shoulder at him. "Will you please walk back with me, Logan?" When he hesitated, she held out her hand to him. He came close, but didn't take it.

Neither spoke as they retraced their way back. When they reached the garden behind the cottage, Beth looked up at him. "You never did have your cider," she murmured, hoping he wouldn't leave but sensing he was in a hurry to. What had she done wrong?

"I don't drink the stuff."

She tried to smile. "It wouldn't hurt you." She reached out to touch him lightly on the arm and he drew back sharply, his expression angry. She blinked.

The back door swung open and her father stood glaring down at them. "What in hell is going on?"

"We were out walking, Papa."

"I didn't think you'd be back, Tyrell," Logan challenged insolently.

"Go into the house, Beth."

"Please," she protested, frightened by the look in his eyes and his rigid stance on the landing. He was wearing his gun.

Logan put his hand against the small of her back and pushed her away from him. "Go inside. This is between me and your father."

Frank waited until the door closed behind her. He came down the steps slowly. Logan backed up and gave him room. His hands were down, his eyes glowing darkly.

Frank broke the cold, tense silence. "For God's sake," he said softly. "Don't involve Beth."

Logan gave a terse laugh. "What am I doing, Tyrell? Messing with your sweet little daughter?"

"Somewhere there's got to be a strand of decency left in you."

"Don't count on decency."

"She doesn't know anything about men like you."

Logan felt his muscles go stiff and forced himself to grin baldly. "She doesn't know anything about men. Not even her own father. How's the widow lady, Sheriff? Good in the sack?"

Frank reddened in rising anger but forced it down again. "Leave Beth alone. That's all I'm asking."

"Maybe it's time she was straightened out about a few things," Logan suggested, his temper rising sharply.

Frank stiffened, a red haze going across his eyes. He clenched his hands. The tightness in his chest grew heavy. He breathed deeply, fighting for control, knowing what would happen if he didn't, knowing the cost of it all. "You won't get what you want here. The man you're looking for died a long time ago. I already told you that."

Logan sneered. "I don't happen to believe you. He's still here. I'm getting closer all the time to bringing the stinking, dirty, rotten bastard out into the open."

"You don't understand any of it. Just let it go."

"Not until he's dead."

Frank watched the younger man stride toward the side of the house where there was a roadway toward Main

Street. As soon as he disappeared around the corner of the cottage, Frank put his hand against the rail, bracing himself. The pain in his chest would pass in a few minutes, just as it had before. He sat carefully and tried to roll a cigarette. His hand felt numb. It was shaking badly. He put the pouch and paper away immediately, swearing under his breath. He was getting too old for this job.

Raking his hands back through his gray hair, he held his head and breathed slowly. He had made a vow that he had to keep, but Logan Tanner was going to keep pushing and pushing. He was using Beth, and the only way to stop him was to give him what he was after, and that meant breaking his word.

A man was only worth his word.

Somehow there had to be a way out for them all, if he could only find it in time.

Chapter Eleven

ADAM CAME BY. As soon as Frank opened the door and saw the look on the young man's face, he knew Doc had heard about Logan's coming to the cottage for dinner. "Evening, Doc."

Beth glanced up sharply from where she was sitting on the settee. She had been sewing passementerie on Mary Galloway's traveling cape. Her look was beseeching.

Frank's mouth tightened. She had already made up her mind which man she preferred and he couldn't let her do it. He opened the front door wide. "Come on in and sit with Beth awhile."

As soon as Adam was in the door, Frank put on his own hat and buckled on his gun. He looked back at the two young people staring at one another, Beth embarrassed and sad, Adam angry and confused.

Frank left them alone.

Adam crossed the room and dropped his hat beside her

on the settee. "Is what I heard true? Was that Tanner fellow here for dinner?"

"Yes, Adam."

"My God! Why?"

"Because I wanted him here," she answered softly, raising her head to meet his angry accusations. He had no right to accuse, but she was empathetic to his feelings. She had never meant to hurt him. She was only following her heart and her instincts.

"You can't do this, Beth. Think of what everyone is saying. I've heard about how you always take the underdog beneath your wing, but this man is worse than the lowest white trash."

She stiffened at his condemnation. "You've no right to go on about anyone in such a manner, Adam."

"No right? I've the right of a man who loves you and asked you to marry him a few days ago. If you remember?"

"I said no."

"You said you'd think about it!"

"No, you told me to think about it. That's a different matter altogether from having a choice about it," she said, stung and angry now herself.

He stood over her, arms akimbo. "What does your father have to say about all this?"

"Very little."

"He doesn't like Tanner. In fact, I'd go it a bit stronger and say they have a healthy hatred for one another."

She lowered her head and was silent. What could she say? Adam was hurt and angry and that was her fault. But what could she have done differently?

He sat down and tipped her chin back up. She looked at him sadly. "He'll bring you grief, Beth. That kind of man wants only one thing from any woman. If you don't know what it is, I'll explain a few facts of life to you myself so that you do."

"Doc Wingate told me already," she said, attempting a smile.

"He'll take your innocence, and then ride off without looking back once."

She lowered her head and closed her eyes. Logan had already warned her that was what he would do. "Nothing will come of this," he had said in that cold, flat voice he could take on. He would finish whatever he had come to do and then leave.

But she could hope. She held desperately to the chance that he might change his mind about everything.

"What can I say to make you listen?" Adam rasped, taking her hands and holding them tightly. "I love you, Beth. Doesn't that mean anything to you?"

Her eyes filled up. "I'm so sorry, Adam."

It was the last thing he wanted to hear. He didn't let her go. Pride aside, he loved her. She was a remarkable young woman and he wanted to make her his wife. She was too good for Logan Tanner, and it filled him with impotent anger that she might foolishly spend herself on such a man. He had never thought her a fool.

"Would you change your mind if you could?" he demanded softly.

She looked at him. "No."

"The town is buzzing."

"I can't help that."

"But it hurts, doesn't it? You've never said an ill word against anyone and now find yourself the brunt of gossip. They've been talking since that gunfighter bought your picnic basket."

He was being deliberately cruel in his anger. She understood but couldn't condone it. She took her hands from his, folding them in her lap. "I have to follow my own heart."

Adam stood, picked up his hat, and went out the door.

After a long, still silence, Beth took up her sewing again.

Avery brought Edwina around the next morning to be fitted for the new dress. Beth looked at her and knew she had told him nothing about their last conversation. Dreading the scene that might come between husband and wife if she flatly refused, Beth acquiesced and told Avery they would need only half an hour. Surprised at the little time required, he nodded and left. Not once had he touched his wife.

Edwina said little. Her beautiful young face was pinched and her eyes shadowed. She selected a fashionable eastern-style dress, a pale peach fabric, lace trims, and pearl buttons, all with a minimum of words. "I'll leave the rest up to you," she said tonelessly. "You needn't worry about anything," she said, and her voice broke. She turned away sharply and shook her head.

The girl's distress disturbed Beth. Rather than the usual termagant she had become accustomed to dealing with, Edwina was now only a miserably unhappy young woman. Why?

"Edwina, would you care for some tea?"

Edwina stiffened. "I don't want anything from you." She walked to the door and opened it.

"Avery won't be back for you for another fifteen minutes."

"When he does come, tell him I've gone for a walk." Edwina looked back over her shoulder, a wealth of arrogance and dislike in her brown, shimmering eyes. "But then, I don't imagine he'll be in any great hurry to come looking for me." She went out, clicking the door shut behind her.

Avery came on time. He was furious when he learned Edwina had left. "I could use some of your coffee, Beth," he said, picking up a swatch of peach fabric, along with the dress pattern Edwina had chosen. He tossed them both onto the table again.

"No. I think you should go look for Edwina."

"She's just sulking again."

"Avery, what about?"

"Who the hell knows? She hasn't gotten on with Mother since we arrived. She gets angry over everything I say. She doesn't even want to come to town anymore." He shoved his hands into his front pockets in a frustrated, boyish gesture. "I'm thinking seriously of putting her on a train and sending her back east for a while. Maybe then she can sort things out and decide once and for all what it is she does want—me or Philadelphia."

"Oh, Avery," Beth whispered. "I don't think there's any doubt she loves you."

"Well, she's got a mighty strange way of showing it. What about that coffee, Beth? I'd like to sit and talk with you awhile, the way we used to."

She shook her head. "You go look for Edwina. She was very unhappy when she left. How would it look to her if you sat visiting with me?"

"Right now, I don't much care." He took up his hat, belying his hard words. "She's probably at the millinery looking at hats." He glanced back before he left. "Beth, she wasn't at all like this back east. I just don't understand her anymore."

Beth wrote down all of Edwina's instructions in detail and put them together in a small folder. She put it on the stack of others on her worktable.

She roasted potatoes, steamed some squash, and seared a thick steak for her father's lunch. There were no prisoners in the jail this week. Mac Slate was back with his family, and McAllister had gone back to the ranch where he worked as a cowboy. He'd be back in town in a few weeks after he was paid and probably would end up in her father's jail again for being drunk and disorderly at the saloon. John Bruster had ridden out to check into some rustling near Pine Ridge. He wouldn't be back for a day or two.

Frank glanced up as she carried the tray into his office. She had just missed Doc by a few minutes, and her father had been glad for the chance to talk with him in private. They had spent the morning talking about her. Buchanan was in love with her and didn't know whether to give up or keep courting her, hoping she'd come to her senses over Logan Tanner. Frank had told him he was sure it was only infatuation and that Tanner would be moving on. It was a lie, but he could hope. "You come on back," he'd told Adam, "and you just keep on coming back until you wear her down. Tanner will lose interest in her. She's a good girl, Doc. He'll want his pleasures, and when he takes them elsewhere, we'll make damn good and sure Beth knows about it. That'll shake her back to her senses quick enough." It was cruel, but short of watching her ruin her life, he couldn't see any other way.

Unless he gave Tanner exactly what he'd come for.

"Adam wants to take us to dinner at Rinaldi's little place this evening," he informed her.

"Still pushing, Papa?"

He glared at her. "The man's in love with you."

"Encouraging him will only hurt him worse."

"Or make things better when you see sense." He relented slightly as she turned away. "You told him how you felt, so he won't be coming around with any illusions; but the man doesn't want to give up on you, and I want you to give yourself time." He leaned back in his chair and kicked his feet up on the desk. "Besides, it'll keep gossip down if everyone sees Doc's still interested."

"What about Logan, Papa?"

He laughed shortly. "If he's really interested in you, he'll come around again. If he isn't, he won't. Simple as that." Frank hoped the man would try another tactic in trying to gain his objectives. And Frank would find a way to block that, too. Eventually, Tanner would have to acknowledge defeat and put it all behind him. Then he'd leave and they'd never see him again.

"I didn't mean that, Papa," Beth said. "I mean if you welcome Adam and treat him cordially, I'll expect the same manners toward Logan when he comes to call."

Frank's mouth tightened. "I can't promise that. If I saw a man walking into a bear trap, I'd have to warn him."

"You've warned me already, and I can see for myself what problems might lie ahead."

"There's no 'might' about it," he said darkly.

Seeing no use in prolonging the discussion, Beth turned to the door. "I'll see you back at the cottage."

"I won't be back until late. Me and Faraday got some talking to do tonight."

She glanced back, troubled. "Everything all right with Annie?"

"She's holding up her side of the marriage," he said, admitting to more of the situation than he had in the past. Maybe it was time she learned how bad things could be.

Beth left. A group of men was standing outside the saloon across the street. It looked to be a grim, agitated bunch, and she wondered what it was all about. She went along the boardwalk to Halverson's store and purchased tea. Faith was brisk and not given to talk. Beth left, hurt by her manner.

Logan was just going into the gunsmith's shop, and Beth's heart leaped at the sight of him. Either he hadn't seen her as she thought he had, or he was ignoring her. She kept walking, head high, her pace the same as usual. Her throat was tight.

After putting the tin of tea into the cabinet at home, she wasn't sure what to do. She didn't feel like working her garden or sewing or doing any of her usual household duties. She felt restless, pensive, yearning for something she couldn't put a name to.

Taking up her shawl, she went out the back door. Adam wouldn't be along for several hours and she felt like having a walk in the hills. She found herself retracing the same path she and Logan had followed. Sitting for a time beneath the sycamores, she plucked blades of grass and thought about him. She rose and went up to the tree-scattered knoll and gazed back toward town. Where was he now? What was he doing?

Turning away, she walked on.

She saw Logan's horse grazing in the dusky sunlight down near a meandering creek. Then she saw Logan.

He was drawing his gun. She put her hand to her lips, but realized that he was only practicing, not firing. He dropped the gun back into his holster and crouched slightly again, spreading his hands. He drew again, a swift flash of motion bringing the weapon up and out, aiming straight at some imaginery foe. She had never seen anyone draw so fast, not even at fair exhibitions.

Again and again he drew his gun, each time seeming incredibly faster. His body grew more and more tense, as though he drove himself on with some deep, burning rage.

She watched from the hill above him, mesmerized, terrified.

Logan drew again, one last time, and fired. A tin can bounced. He fired five more times as he walked slowly toward it, zinging it wildly into the air before it stopped. He stood still for a long moment, then shoved the gun back into leather and turned away, relaxed again. He strode to his horse, mounted, and swung it around, sending the high-strung, prancing stallion into a lunging gallop.

Beth stood motionless, watching him until he disappeared. Then she turned back for home.

Chapter Twelve

LOGAN LAY ON his back in his hotel room, staring up at the ceiling through a heavy haze of cigarette smoke. He was out of tobacco and papers and it was too late to buy more at the general store. He drew hard on his last one, the end glowing as it ate downward toward his mouth. He took it and smashed it into the tin tray on the commode and held the smoke in his lungs for a long moment before slowly exhaling it.

Nothing seemed to alleviate the tight knot in his belly. He had ridden hard through the hills and come back by way of the road when it became dark. The exercise hadn't helped. All he had accomplished was to lather his horse and cost himself extra coin to have the livery man stay late and walk the animal until he cooled down.

Logan had stayed in the bar, drinking and listening to some cowhands talk about rustlers at Pine Ridge. He had taken the bottle and sat down at a small table near the windows so he could look across the street at the sheriff's office. A lantern burned inside and Logan knew Tyrell was still there. He should have left for home hours ago.

Tina, one of the saloon girls, had come over. She sat on the edge of his table and bent over as she poured more whiskey into his glass. He could see her heavy breasts right down to the dusky, aroused tips. She smiled and asked him if there was anything he wanted. Raising his glass to her, he said no.

Now, in his bedroom, he wondered if perhaps Tina was exactly what he needed. She was lusty and experienced. She would know how to take the full, hard measure of a man and leave him exhausted enough to sleep. All he had to do was go out to the landing above the saloon and look down at her. One nod and she'd come up to him.

So what stopped him?

He sat up and raked his hands back through his hair, swearing softly. He stood angrily and paced restlessly to the window. Drawing the curtain aside, he looked across at Tyrell's office. He was still there, sleepless too. Logan could guess why.

Leaning back, Logan lifted the curtain a little more so he could see down the street to the little white cottage at the edge of town. The front window glowed there too, a warm beacon.

What was Beth doing now, at almost midnight? Sitting on that settee stitching some hem for one of the snooty ladies of town? Or was she ironing her father's shirts? Or canning the vegetables she grew in her garden out back? What did a lady do in the privacy of her own home?

He let the curtain drop back into place. All the women he had known spent their nights pouring whiskey in a saloon or lying sprawled in a stranger's bed.

He poured himself another shot of whiskey and slouched into the chair near the window. He lifted one foot and rested it on the end of the double bed and wondered what it would be like to share it with Beth. The knot in his belly grew harder and sank achingly into his groin. He tossed the drink off angrily.

He was ready to finish things. The waiting was what was gnawing at him. Maybe that was what was wrong with the whole plan. He had pushed and gotten nowhere. Maybe this inaction was intended to fray his sharpened nerves.

He got up and poured another whiskey.

Why had he stopped to assist Beth that day? Similar things had happened in the past and he had ridden on by. What was it about Beth that had pulled at him so strongly and made him want to be with her?

He had used her for leverage. Or had that only been an excuse to see her again? The whole plan bothered him now because of her.

He tossed the whiskey back again and poured another. He stared at the glass in his hand and wondered how many he had had. He looked at the half-empty bottle and wondered why in hell he couldn't even get drunk tonight. He slammed the glass down and paced back to the window.

Tyrell was strolling down the boardwalk toward home. Logan watched him through dark, narrowed eyes. Checking each shop door like a conscientious bastard, he thought. He remembered sitting at a table downstairs the first night he'd come into this town. He remembered seeing Tyrell walking toward him. He would never forget the look on his face when he'd told Tyrell his name.

He watched Beth come out onto the front porch. Logan's heart began pounding hard and fast as he looked at her. Damn! What was happening to him? He watched her come down the steps and say something to her father. Tyrell put his hand out to cup her cheek and she came forward, embracing him in the moonlight. They went up the steps together, Tyrell's arm around her shoulders.

Logan let the curtain fall back into place again. What

would happen to her when the thing was all over and done with? He couldn't let himself think about it. Or her.

He sat in the chair again and leaned his head back as he closed his eyes tightly. He thought of Beth and what it felt like to be with her. Never before had he wanted to get to know a woman. They had always served one single purpose. But Beth was different. Why? Every time he saw her, something moved inside him, gripped him, tore at him. He thought about the way she smiled, those dimples in her cheek, her eyes glowing from within. She was honest and open and so damn naive.

He remembered the first time he had kissed her, her body rigid with fear. He had shocked her into a near faint when he'd forced her mouth open to explore hers with his tongue. But the second time had been different. His heart hammered now just thinking about it. Arousal swept through him and he made a low, angry groan of frustration in the back of his throat. He stood up again, walked to the table, and picked up the glass of whiskey. Then, not wanting it, he heaved it violently against the wall.

He wanted her. That was what was wrong with him. He wanted *her!* He'd never felt this gut-wrenching need for one particular woman before, and he sure as hell didn't like it. It complicated everything.

Take her and be done with it. He thought of her gentle goodness, of the Christian way in which she had obviously been raised, and raked a hand back through his hair. She would want to get married.

His head came up slowly, his lips parting slightly. Why not? Grim resolve filled him. Maybe there was a way to have her and still finish what he had come to do. His heart thudded.

Stretching out on his bed again, he stared up at the ceiling, thinking it over. She would marry him. If she was at all hesitant at the idea, he knew exactly how to bring her around. Her naiveté would work for him. All he had to do was show her what it was like between a man and a woman. Once he had made love to her, she would be his.

He could take her away from Kilkare Woods.

No. Why? Better still if they stayed right here. Ah, yes. Even better.

Logan's eyes glittered as he felt the deep, convincing heat of the old hatred rising in his blood, renewing his purpose.

How much better this than what he had originally planned to do. Rather than the split second it took to shoot a man down, this revenge would go on and on and on.

And Beth Tyrell didn't have to know she was part of it.

Chapter Thirteen

IT WAS MONDAY morning and Beth was out back hanging wash. Her father had strung the lines for her early that morning, and she began by hanging all the underwear in the center so that it would all be hidden from view by the shirts, pants, dresses, skirts, and shirtwaists she hung around the outside of the circles of rope.

She was almost finished when someone grasped her waist from behind and planted a warm kiss on the curve of her neck. She gasped and pulled free, swinging around in fright.

Logan laughed down at her, standing with his hands on his lean hips. He grinned roguishly. "Morning, ma'am," he drawled, blue eyes dancing with deviltry.

Beth didn't even want to hide her joy at seeing him. She hadn't for days, though she had heard he had been seen out riding in the hills repeatedly. Everyone seemed interested in Logan's goings-on and there was always talk about him.

He was still wearing his gun.

He held out his hand. "Let's go for a walk."

"I'd like that very much, Logan, but I can't." She gestured toward the still-half-full wash basket.

"Forget about that."

"It'll only take a few minutes."

"You can do it later." He took her hand and pulled her close, kissing her temple, her cheek, her mouth as she gave a startled gasp. He loosened his hold and smiled down at her. "I've got something to show you."

"But—"

He pulled her close again and this time he kissed her deeply. When he raised his head finally, he saw the dazed look in her eyes. "Now quit arguing and come along with me."

His horse was just beyond the trees. He grasped her waist and lifted her so that she sat sideways on his saddle. Mounting behind her, he put his arm around her waist to keep her secure. She looked up at him and his hand tightened. Without intention, he lowered his head and kissed her again. She slanted her face and his heart thundered. He deepened the kiss. After a moment, he drew back with an effort, trying to think straight.

This wasn't the place to seduce her. They were in plain sight of anyone coming by the house from the main road. He'd take her up into the hills and not bring her back until everything was settled as he wanted.

"Where are we going, Logan?"

"You'll see."

She knew soon after. He was heading toward the hills where they had picnicked. Old Kilkare's haunted wood. Majestic oaks, pungently scented pines, and red-barked madrones hid them from the prying eyes of the townspeople. The peace was broken only by birdsong high overhead, the creak of Logan's saddle, and the clop of the roan's shod hooves.

The feel of Logan's hard body against hers, and the

musky, heady scent of his body, made Beth feel light-headed.

When he reached the crest of the hill where he had kissed her after the church auction, he stopped and dismounted. He lifted her from his horse and set her down slowly. The darkness of his eyes sent her pulse racing.

Innocent desire glowed in her face. His body was quick to respond to her unknowing appeal. He hadn't meant to kiss her again, not until after he'd talked to her, but the feel of her as she had brushed him when he lifted her down had made his blood pound. Her small hand rested shyly against his chest, a burning brand on his heart. Her lips parted softly in tension, and he covered her mouth with his own. He almost lost himself in the taste of her. He drew back, battening down his desire, and rested his hands on her shoulders. She was trembling, her eyes wide and dilated.

"What would you say if I made an offer on the land?" he asked, his voice heavy and shaken by her effect on him. "This hill and all the land around it." He leaned down and explored the delicate curve of her neck. She caught her breath softly. The sweet scent of her went to his head.

His touch left her weak and filled with tingling sensations and a heat that grew from the womanly core of her. He stepped back slightly, and she felt bereft until she gazed up into his darkened eyes. What had he said?

He took her hand, pulling her along with him. Sweeping his other hand in a wide gesture, he said, "Plenty of grass, water just down the hill, enough for a small herd to start. I could build a cabin right over there on the spot where we had our picnic." He glanced down at her to see her reaction.

"Oh, Logan," she whispered, and tears flooded her eyes as she smiled up at him. "You *are* staying," she said joyously.

His heart constricted. The first doubt about what he was

doing with her and why hit him square in the stomach.

"You'll have a much better life than you've ever had, Logan. I know it. You'll see. Whatever it is that's driven you will heal itself."

His face tightened. She thought he was putting his other life behind him. Wasn't that what he wanted her to think? Then why this hesitance, this ache in his gut when he looked into her trusting, glowing hazel eyes. He could drown in them if he let himself. He turned away, looking at the land instead of at her. What drove him would never heal until he finished what he had come to do.

"Does it matter to you that you'll live on a haunted hill?" she teased. Her gaiety was so spontaneous.

He had lived with ghosts all his life. He had no fear of the one more he would add. He watched her walk away from him. Her arms were spread in a gesture of exaltation. She was as open as any happy child. Why did she have to be so damn guileless?

"It's wonderful land, Logan," she told him. "Avery once thought of buying it, but his mother said no. Hannah Carlile does believe in ghosts. I think it's the one thing she is afraid of."

The mention of Avery Carlile set him on edge. He clenched his teeth, fighting down the rush of feeling that came whenever he thought of Beth and that smug rancher, with his prissy, spoiled wife who looked down her nose at Beth.

"I don't care a damn what Carlile or his mother thinks," he snarled.

Beth turned at his sternness.

"I want to know what you think, Beth," he said, walking toward her, a faint smile lifting one corner of his sensual mouth. He saw she didn't understand at all. She took nothing for granted.

"I used to be frightened of this place," she admitted.

"Avery brought me up here once when I was twelve—"

Logan caught hold of her shoulders, his fingers biting into her flesh. "I don't want to know anything about what went on between you and Carlile, or you and that damn doctor either." He saw her wince and loosened his hold on her. He hadn't meant to hurt her and was angry at his own loss of temper. What was the matter with him?

She looked up at him searchingly. Then her expression lit up with dawning surprise and a tenderness that made him uncomfortable.

"Logan," she said softly, touching his cheek, "you've no reason to be jealous."

He let go of her abruptly.

She was troubled by the grimness in his eyes. He was fighting some inner battle, and she could see the cost in the rigid muscles of his face and the emotion that flickered in his eyes before they became flinty with self-defense. A hard man, but vulnerable.

"I love you," she murmured, color staining her cheeks as she opened her heart. Would it only serve to embarrass him?

Implacable, he looked at her. "If you love me, you'll marry me."

It was a challenge rather than a gentle offer. She looked confused and hurt.

His heart twisted at the look on her face. "Why do you look ready to cry?" he demanded harshly.

"I don't know. It's the look in your eyes and the way you asked," she said frankly. She had seen no softening to indicate he cared deeply, only a hardness she couldn't comprehend. "Do you love me?"

Did he love her? Every muscle in his body stiffened at the question. "Asking you to marry me should tell you what I feel," he said.

"Is it so hard to say?"

He turned away, unable to hold her look. "I did this all wrong," he said, running a hand back through his hair. He gave a sharp sigh. "I've never even thought of marrying before."

"I'm honored that you would ask me," she murmured huskily.

He looked back at her and saw how her mouth trembled and her eyes welled up with tears. His heart pounded hard and slow, laced with pain. "Marry me, Beth."

"How could I not, Logan?"

The hard heaviness melted inside him. Her tender smile and the light in her eyes filled him with feelings he couldn't begin to analyze—and didn't want to. He pulled her close. God, what was it she did to him with a few words and a look?

"I want to marry you as soon as possible," he told her roughly.

She laughed, and drew her head back to look up at him with eyes shining. "In a few weeks it'll be May—"

"Not May. Now. Tomorrow. The end of the week. I don't want to wait a few weeks."

Her eyes clouded. "But there's Papa to consider. We'll have to make him understand."

"To hell with your father," he said before he could stop himself.

"Logan!" she protested softly. "I know you two haven't gotten on together, but—"

He cut her off. "You know what he's going to say, Beth. He won't change his mind, not until *after* we're married. Then what choice will he have."

She hesitated, her face pale. "I can't marry you under those circumstances. I love him, too. He's my father. I don't want to hurt him."

He cupped her face. "And what am I to you?" He saw the burden he placed on her but he wouldn't give in. It was what he wanted, to make her choose and for him to be the chosen one. Only then could he set about putting his plan in motion. The inferno of hatred swelled and filled him with a sense of dark power. His triumph was so close he could almost taste it.

"Why do you look at me like that?" she asked. He looked through her, beyond her, to something else, something that frightened her. His eyes cleared though they remained dark and fathomless.

And where was Beth in all this? He had put her in the middle. But he couldn't allow himself to think of that now.

"I want you," he rasped, and it was true. His whole body was on fire for her. He kissed her savagely, wanting to possess all of her and to leave nothing for Tyrell. Her slender form stiffened slightly and she made a muted sound of protest. Her hand pressed for freedom. The dark moment passed and he was flooded with remorse. "I didn't mean to frighten you again," he said thickly. Her mouth was swollen and her eyes enormous. He reminded himself again that she was not like any woman he had known before.

Beth was an innocent—innocent of how deep a man's physical desire could run. He had to slow down. He needed to find the gentleness in himself, if there was any left after the life he had led. She had never known a man's sometimes violent need for coupling. The experience would devastate her. Yet her ability to respond was there in the warmth of her skin, the way her mouth opened to him, and the sinuous movement of her body when he caressed her waist. He knew instinctively that she was capable of real, abandoned passion.

"We'll work everything out," he murmured against her lips. Her soft, gasping breaths mingled with his own deeper ones as he kissed her again, tenderly devouring the sweetness of her mouth. He was shaking and couldn't stop.

Too long without a woman, he thought ruefully, but he had wanted no other after seeing her at the picket fence the first day he rode into town.

Logan caught her up in his arms. Her arms went around his neck, her fingers combing into the thick softness of his dark hair as he carried her up the hill. He set her down beneath the cooling shadows of the ancient oak, then stepped away.

Beth watched him, her heart beating fast. His eyes never left hers as he slowly bent and untied the leather strap around his thigh and then unbuckled his gun belt. Straightening, he wrapped the wide belt around the gun itself and set it into the crotch of the tree for safekeeping. "Come here, Beth." His smile beckoned.

Her lips parted softly and color mounted high in her cheeks. She bit her lip, her hazel eyes wide and darkened. "Logan," she said huskily, and shook her head.

She was every inch the shy virgin. He ached to make her his. He came to her and tipped her chin gently. "Don't be afraid of me." Lowering his head, he kissed her, working her mouth languidly. He kissed the smooth curve of her cheek and ear. "My sweet Beth, lie with me on the grass for a while."

"I shouldn't," she whispered tremulously.

"You want to," he murmured against her lips, his hands moving gently against her waist. "Do what you want for once, Beth."

She was breathless, her head going back as his mouth explored the sensitive column of her throat. He cupped her breasts. Heat poured through her as he spread his hands over their fullness. "Lie with me," he said again, his voice low and thick. "I need you." His voice sounded so raw she was lost.

The grass was soft and fragrant. Her breathing was constricted, her tension growing with the heat of her body. She was shaking violently.

Logan saw her uncertainty and felt a pang of remorse. Smothering it, he slowly removed the pins from her hair. He loved the feel of her hair in his hands and spread it against the grass, then plucked a golden poppy to tuck in the silken blond waves. He moved closer. "Your warmth draws me. It has since the first. I could lose myself in you, Beth."

He drugged her senses and drowned her protests with slow warm kisses. She was still hesitant, and he knew not to rush her. Her body was taut as a bowstring. Too much too soon and she would take flight from him. But how he longed to tear off all her constricting clothing to get to her. How he wanted to go into her and give release to the hot ache in his belly and heart. *Did he love her?* If this was love, it hurt like hell. Yet he was helpless in the face of it, and that very powerlessness drove him all the more toward his purpose.

Raising himself slightly, he looked down at her. Her eyes were dark and luminous, her lips swollen pink. Smiling, he pulled at the high-collared dress, watching her reaction. She swallowed, cheeks blooming, and closed her eyes. He unbuttoned one button, then another, lightly brushing his fingertips against the pale satin skin revealed. She bit her lip and opened her eyes. He tried to slow his breathing as he spread his hand wide against her belly.

"Do you have an ache for me here, Beth? I do for you." He unbuttoned his own shirt impatiently and took her hand. It jerked slightly as he laid it flat against his hard chest covered with dark hair. He held it there. "Don't be afraid." He tutored her until he knew she wouldn't take her hand away, then removed his own, cupping her hip and kneading her in a sensual massage that brought a dazed look to her face. She raised her other hand and stroked his rib cage and the smooth skin of his back, then glided down and around to his stomach. He tensed, his breath stopping, as her fingertips shyly explored the waistband of his pants. She went no further, and after a long moment the torment was too great. Groaning, he took her mouth hungrily and opened the rest of her dress with blind skill. He pulled free the ribbons of her camisole and corset. She moaned softly. He took his mouth from hers and lowered his head. She jerked as his mouth lightly brushed her breast.

"Logan," she said thickly, half in protest, stunned by the powerful sensations stirring in her belly.

He drew back, looking at the perfect, tender shape of her breasts as they rose and fell with her quickened breathing. Embarrassed, she tried to cover herself. He caught her hand. "You're beautiful," he murmured, smiling at her flushed face.

"I don't think this is . . . proper," she murmured, shaken.

He chuckled, amused. "What's proper? After I marry you, there won't be a place on your perfect body that I won't admire and touch . . . or kiss." He lowered his head again, opening his mouth over the small hardened bud. Her body arched sharply. He cupped the rich, satiny smoothness of her breast, kneading it gently, and drew the nipple into his mouth. Her sob of pleasure made his heart thunder. His flesh was hard, aching hotly. God, how he wanted her.

Rolling onto his back, he brought her with him, pulling her head down and slanting his mouth across her again in a fierce, demanding kiss. His hands moved downward, pressing her into him, cupping her buttocks and rubbing her hips against his tumescence.

Her muscles tensed and he knew he had gone too quickly. His own passion was raging out of control now. Dragging his mouth away, he rolled her over again. All he could hear was his own labored breathing and the racing hot blood in his brain. His need for her burned inside him. He wanted to go into her now and make her belong to him. He'd forgotten all his well-founded reasons, his plans. Nothing mattered but to make love to her.

"Logan . . ." she gasped, as he drew her skirt up.

She was wearing open drawers, one fashion Logan heartily approved of. Her muscles went rigid. "No, Beth," he groaned. "This is the way it's supposed to be. You're mine. Let me touch you." But she was a virgin and understandably frightened. Her soft protesting movements tore at his heart, but he knew she wanted him, too. Her inexperience made her a poor opponent to his own needs and will.

"Feel what you to do me," he whispered against her mouth, taking her hand and placing it over his heart. "I can hardly breathe for wanting you. Beth," he groaned, nuzzling her throat, then raised his head to kiss her again before saying against her lips, "don't make me stop now. Do you know what it'll do to me?"

She searched his eyes, and he saw how hers melted and warmed, a tender smile lighting them from within. Her muscles relaxed slowly and he slid his hand between her legs.

Warm silken skin and maidenhair. His heart thundered. He slid one arm beneath her shoulders, holding her close against him as he gently cupped her and began the voluptuous stroking that would bring a mindless need. She drew a soft breath, then held it. When she released it, she moaned, her face turning into his shoulder, her body shuddering. The soft sounds she uttered drove his passion higher. Her body shook, tensing even more, rising, ever rising. Carefully, trying not to hurt her, he entered her with one finger. Her hips arched and she gave a soft cry.

Fear shot through him at the feel of her tight flesh. What did he know of virgins? Blood and pain the first time was all he had ever heard. Pain and no pleasure. "Beth," he said hoarsely, shaking violently with his own needs. "Is this hurting you?" Suddenly, it mattered to him more than anything that he give her pleasure, more pleasure than she had ever experienced in her life, and he was afraid he'd fail.

"No," she moaned. "Oh, Logan . . . I feel so . . ." Her breath caught as he eased another finger inside her.

He raised himself above her. "Pull up your skirts," he whispered against her mouth, and she obeyed. He opened his pants, his turgid flesh springing free. Lowering his body, he guided himself to her. She gave a soft gasp of surprise. His heart pounded like a fist against the wall of his chest. Purposefully and slowly, he pressed into her.

She stiffened, her eyes going wide. "I'm sorry," he whispered. "I don't want it to hurt you, but it's going to. . . ." She cried out softly. He stroked her hair and kissed her eyes and mouth, but he didn't stop until he was fully inside her. Pain knotted in his loins as he remained still.

She made a soft sound. His throat squeezed hot and tight. "Shhhh, don't cry," he pleaded raggedly. He gave her a moment longer, then eased back and entered again. He was afraid of hurting her more, but his need had grown too demanding to stop now. Used to lustful women who almost raped a man when they were aroused, Logan was afraid of this uninitiated girl. She was an angel in his arms. She made him feel things he had never felt before, things he fought against. Looking at her and touching her set his body on fire, and no matter how hard he tried to defy it, she filled him with a tenderness and protectiveness that were alien to him.

Logan felt a flooding of protective tenderness so strong he hurt. She should have had a gold band on her finger and a feather bed beneath her back the first time, but it was too late to think of that now. Her nubile body was stretched and taut, ready for him. Only the fullness of his possession could give her the release her body craved now under his lovemaking.

Logan had brought many women to crisis. He had been taught how by whores. Reason had mated with passion before; experience and practice had brought ecstatic pleasure. Logan knew well how to use his mouth and hands and body to bring a woman her full measure of sexual pleasure. Yet past experience clouded and disappeared as this innocent girl taught Logan of surrender.

Beth opened her body to him, flowering. She whispered her love for him and stroked his cheek as though he were the one to be gentled of his fears. She opened her heart and her mind and soul to him as well, making a precious gift of herself. When the crisis came for both of them, it rocked the very foundations of Logan's miserable life.

He couldn't speak.

"I love you," she murmured against his damp temple.

The words reverberated through his brain. Something hard inside him melted. Fear gripped him. He held her closer. "Beth," he rasped, raising his head. "I never want to let you go."

He had never seen that look in a woman's eyes. Tenderness. Warmth. Love as he had never seen it. *Trust.*

Smiling, she kissed him.

He would have to find some other way to finish what he had come to do. But how? Anything he did now would touch her.

Her natural shyness returned as she adjusted her loosened clothing before him. Logan smiled at her teasingly while trying to obliterate the thoughts that were spoiling this moment. He wanted to think of nothing but her and couldn't. The other thing preyed on his mind.

Beth had never been more beautiful to him than she was

in her disheveled state, her cheeks flushed as she laughed
self-consciously at her own clumsiness. Satiation from his
lovemaking had left her weak and shaky. He wanted to
make love to her all over again. He ached with wanting
her, but next time, he was going to make sure she was his
wife and had the bed she deserved rather than take her in
an open field.

"When Papa sees how happy I am, he'll have to accept
you're the man I love."

Logan stiffened. The mention of Tyrell cut into him and
reminded him of everything. "It won't matter one way or
another."

Beth's bright smile died.

"I'll explain it to him," he said, the old hatred rising
hotly inside him. "He'll understand clear enough. You stay
out of it, Beth. This is between me and your father."

Her eyes widened in dismay. "He's a good man, Logan.
And fair."

He didn't say anything to that, but his bronzed face was
like stone. He put his gun on again.

Lifting her onto his horse, he saw her worried, distress-
ful look. Mistaking it, he smiled. "I'll talk to the preacher
about marrying us right away. I'm not going to leave you
after today." He mounted behind her and slipped his arm
around her, drawing her back against him. He cupped her
breast firmly. "The sooner you're my wife, the better I'll
like it," he said hoarsely. Maybe he'd take her away from
Kilkare Woods after all. He thought of stopping the horse
and taking her down again, but had to content himself with
cupping her breast and drawing her tightly back against his
chest as they slowly rode the long way back to town. She
leaned into him, her head back against his shoulder, her
hand on his thigh.

A gentleness opened up inside him. "I'll try to make

you happy, Beth. I swear." But would he? Could he?

As they neared town, he dismounted and lifted her down. "I think it would look better if we were walking and I was leading my horse." What had happened on that hill was only meant for Tyrell to know and no one else.

As they came around the last bend, Logan sensed trouble. He had a sixth sense about such things and felt it even before he saw the town stretched out before them. Glancing uneasily at Beth, he felt assailed with doubt suddenly.

They had reached the front gate, and Logan was starting to say something just to see her smile that special way again, when Frank Tyrell's voice roared at him from down the street.

"Tanner!"

Logan swung around.

Beth turned as well, startled by her father's fury. She felt Logan's hand bite into her arm. "Go inside," he ordered sharply.

She stared at her father striding toward them. People were coming out of shops, standing in bunches down the street. "You son-of-a-bitch!" he shouted. Logan shoved Beth away roughly as Tyrell came on, shouting curses. She stumbled back against the gate. Tyrell lunged forward and swung. Logan dodged.

"Papa!"

"You bastard!" Frank boomed, going for Logan again.

"Back off!" Logan roared, putting his hands out wide and stepping well away from Beth.

"Don't!" she cried.

"You did it!" Tyrell accused hotly, his face mottled. "You haven't even got her back and it's all over town what you've been doing!"

"Papa!" Beth started to step forward.

"Stay back, damnit!" Logan shouted at her, his eyes never leaving her father.

People were gathering in the street, staring. Adam was running toward the cottage. "Frank!"

Frank turned to Beth, and Logan stepped forward. "Avery's wife saw you! Kissing him like a harlot, she said to me right in Halverson's store. She said you rode off with him toward the hills. You, of all people! Damn you for a blind fool, Beth!"

"Shut up, Tyrell!"

"Didn't I tell you? I tried to warn you, but you wouldn't listen. You wouldn't listen!"

"Shut up!" Logan snarled, grabbing his arm.

"He used you to get to me!" Frank yelled, shaking him off. He caught hold of Beth and shook her. "Do you understand now? Do you?" He let go of her abruptly and pounded his chest with his fist. "Me! That's who he came for, and I swore I'd never kill a man again!"

Beth's face went chalk white. She looked at Logan. It was all there in his face. Everything. "Oh, God," she said weakly.

Logan stared at her. "Beth, listen to me. . . ."

She closed her eyes and felt all the warmth drain out of her.

Frank turned sharply and swung with all his strength, hitting Logan in the jaw and sending him backward to the dust. He stood over him, fists white. "Alright, you've finally got what you wanted! It's what you came for, isn't it? What you've been waiting for all your miserable, rotten, worthless life."

Logan pushed himself up and rubbed his jaw. He stood carefully and gave Tyrell a cold smile while brushing himself off. "Sure it's what you want?"

Frank shook with barely restrained rage. "I'm going to

kill you, Logan. Just the way I did your father."

Logan's face went rigid. "Which end of the street do you want?"

Tyrell jerked his head.

Logan walked down the street toward the far end of town.

Chapter Fourteen

ADAM WAS THERE, a supportive hand beneath Beth's arm. Her face was white but otherwise registered no emotion whatsoever.

"You'd better take her inside, Adam," Frank said grimly, unable to look at her. He should never have let it go this far. He should have gone against Logan the moment he dragged Beth into it. Now, it was too late. The damage was done to her.

He turned and began walking into the middle of Main Street. He shouted for everyone to get inside, but they already understood what was happening and were retreating.

"You've got to come inside, Beth," Adam said, drawing her inside the gate.

She looked blankly back over her shoulder at the two men in the street facing one another from opposite ends of town. "No."

"Beth, we're going inside," Adam told her firmly.

"You've got to stop them, Adam," she said hoarsely. "Logan will kill him."

"We can't do anything, Beth. This has been brewing for years. Frank knew he'd come someday."

She turned on him. "You knew about all this?"

He frowned heavily. "Your father told me a few days ago that Logan holds an old grudge against him." He saw her hurt, accusing look and rushed on. "What could I say, Beth? How could I tell you? Would you have believed me under the circumstances?"

"It's got to stop," she said, looking away toward her father and Logan.

"Come inside!" As he turned slightly, she pulled sharply away and darted back through the gate out into the street.

Picking up her skirts, Beth ran. "Papa, don't!" She reached him before Adam could stop her and grabbed desperately at her father's sleeve. "Don't!" she pleaded, trying to catch her breath, tears streaming down her face. "Please! No!"

"I've got no choice now. Get out of the street." He shoved her away.

She clung to him again. "He'll kill you. You haven't used your gun in years. I've seen how fast he draws, out by the . . ."

Adam dragged her back. She fought loose and clung tighter to her father. "No! It'll be my fault if he kills you!"

Her father's hands dug painfully into her arms, shaking her. "It's not your fault! None of it! He would've found another way! I should've gone against him sooner and saved you the humiliation." He shoved her toward Adam. "Take care of her. Get her away from here, Doc!"

Beth looked down the street and saw Logan standing there waiting. She shook her head and put her hand out in supplication. Adam caught hold of her and half dragged her toward the alleyway between the Polks' butcher shop and Maddie Jeffrey's house. "Stop them!" she sobbed. "Adam!"

"I can't. Nor can you!"

She tried to twist free. He yanked her tighter, holding her back against the wall.

"Logan!" she screamed. Adam slammed his hand over her mouth.

"You're not going to beg him!" The sounds she made as she struggled against him assaulted his heart. "Hush, Beth!"

"What're you waiting for, Logan?" Tyrell shouted derisively. "This is what you've been waiting for, isn't it? Go for it!"

Logan walked toward him slowly, not stopping until they were twenty feet from one another.

"Draw, you bastard!" Frank ordered.

"It never bothered you to kill a man in cold blood before, Frank."

Frank stiffened. "He drew first."

"You drove him to the wall and waited for an easy kill. He was a rancher. *You* had been a gunfighter. It was murder. Plain and simple murder! You knew it then. You know it now!"

Beth heard the burning hatred in Logan's cold voice. She knew what he was doing now. He was trying to smear her father's reputation before the town that respected him. Then he would draw and fire. She tried to fight free, but Adam was stronger than she had ever imagined.

"He took the only thing ever mattered to me!" Frank shouted, white with rage. "Like a damn thief in the night!"

"My father stole nothing from you, you lying bastard!"

"You were ten when it all happened. What did you know! Your father was a calculating, cheating son-of-a-bitch! He deserved exactly what he got!" Frank moved a step forward as he spoke, jaw jutting, fingers twitching over his gun.

Still Logan didn't go for his. The smile on his face

drove Frank into near frenzy. "What're you waiting for?"

Logan's cold smile broadened, mocking his fury. He looked Frank up and down contemptuously and laughed.

Driven, Tyrell went for his gun. It was a mistake.

Before he'd cleared leather, Logan's gun was out and aimed squarely at his heart. Frank stared at it, amazed, and waited for it to issue its jolting death. How many times would Logan pull the trigger? Why did Beth have to see this?

"It's been too long since you used your gun, Frank," Logan drawled, his cold smile flattening out, his blue eyes glowing darkly. "Too slow. Pathetic. You should have hung it up long ago." He walked forward a few steps, the gun never wavering.

Beads of sweat broke out on Frank's forehead, but he didn't move.

"Remember how it really was, Frank?" Logan said through his teeth. "You were as fast then as I am now, maybe faster. My father barely moved his hand before you shot him the first time. But it wasn't enough, was it?"

Beth's heart hammered and her head felt light. She thought she was going to be sick.

"You shot him five more times before he hit the ground. Then you walked over to his body and spit on him."

Frank raised his eyes from the barrel of the gun to Logan's eyes. "I'd spit on him again."

Logan's gun blasted.

Beth sagged against the wall, breath drawn tight and high in her throat, her eyes wide.

The bullet came within an inch of Frank's foot. He didn't move. The next shot drew blood from a graze along his thigh. He flinched, but stayed where he was, gritting his teeth.

Logan raised his gun so it was shoulder high and aimed it squarely between Frank Tyrell's eyes. "Say your prayers,

Sheriff," he said with a sneer. He wanted to kill him so badly his hand started to shake slightly.

All Frank could think of was Beth coming out of that alleyway in a minute and seeing him in the dust, his brains blasted out. His face tightened. "Logan, for God's sake," he said softly.

Logan didn't move. He was breathing heavily. He could feel sweat on the back of his neck. Hatred poured through his body. Slowly, he tipped the barrel up and brought his arm down. He slid the gun back into his holster.

Neither man moved.

"No contest." Again Logan sneered. "You're just an old man, Tyrell. Go on home and take your daughter with you." He turned and started to walk away.

A red haze came before Frank's eyes at the mention of Beth. He lunged. Logan turned sharply and blocked the first blow. He parried another and another. He gave a contemptuous laugh. "Go home!"

Frank swung again, but halted. He staggered, a searing pain spreading across his chest. Clutching himself, he tried to breathe. His face turned gray. Sweat poured and his knees started to buckle.

"Oh, Jesus," Adam said, releasing Beth. "Frank!"

Startled, Logan caught hold of Frank Tyrell as he fell forward, gasping.

Beth ran into the street, passing Adam who strode grimly toward the two men. She reached her father first and fell to her knees beside him. "Papa, what is it?"

"It's his heart," Adam said, bending down.

People were pouring back into the street and coming toward them. "Move back!" Adam ordered as a crowd began to gather. "Give him breathing space!" But everyone pressed forward tightly to stare. Their whispers came from all around Beth.

"Move back," Logan said, and swept the group with a

hard-eyed look. Everyone edged back.

"Why didn't you kill me, Logan?" Frank rasped, staring up at him as he stood there, his hands resting lightly on his hips.

"Will you shut up, Frank?" Adam ordered tautly, his face showing worry as he unbuttoned Frank's collar.

Faraday Slate shoved through the crowd. "Frank!"

"Answer me, will you?" Tyrell demanded, trying to sit up. Beth put her hands against his shoulders, urging him to be still.

"Papa, please."

He pushed her away. Adam shoved him down roughly. "Lie still—or are you trying to kill yourself?"

"You didn't know what was going on," Frank said to Logan. "You were just a damn kid! You hung around me more than your own father. Do you remember that, too, Logan? He never had time for you, did he? Do you know why?"

Beth tried to stop him, but he shoved her back again and stared up at Logan, whose face was as hard and unyielding as granite, his blue eyes burning like a devil's.

"I did kill John Tanner," he said. "I did push him into that fight," he admitted in a cracking voice. "If he hadn't gone into the street, I'd have found another way to kill him. Maybe with my own bare hands," he ground out hoarsely, eyes filling with angry, bitter tears. "I . . ."

"Frank, shut up, for God's sake," Adam shouted at him.

"I . . . caught him in bed with my wife," Frank gasped. Panting, he sank back.

Beth felt as though she'd been struck. She stared at her father's agonized face. Then she looked up at Logan. Something flickered in his eyes and then he masked his feelings. Looking into his expressionless face, Beth felt something break inside her.

"Are you satisfied now, Logan?" she managed. "Have

you gotten what you wanted?"

Logan's jaw tightened, but he said nothing. After a moment, he turned and strode away, the crowd moving back and staring after him. He went up the steps of the hotel as if nothing had happened at all.

Beth lowered her head, her mouth trembling. "I'm sorry, Papa," she whispered, and closed her eyes. "I'm so sorry. . . ."

Frank wanted to take her hand, but his arm was hurting him so fiercely he couldn't raise it.

"Let's get him to the cottage," Adam ordered, standing and motioning to several men to lift Frank and carry him. Beth followed behind, the focus of every pair of eyes in town. Vicious tongues were already wagging at her back.

Edwina Carlile stood on the fringe of the crowd, white-faced and crying silently.

"He's resting quietly now, Beth," Adam said, putting his hand on her bent shoulders. She looked up at him from red-rimmed eyes and a strained white face. "I think he's going to be alright. He's going to be bedridden for a couple of months."

"Can I see him now?"

"It'd be best to leave him alone now." One look at her was bound to stir Frank's emotional state, and that wouldn't do at this critical stage. "Missus Michaels is watching over him."

"I want to see him, Adam."

He sat down on the settee beside her and took her hands. "Your father can't tolerate any more excitement, and your present state isn't something to set his mind at rest."

She drew in a sobbing breath and lowered her head again, her shoulders shaking. "You must despise me," she managed.

"Why? Because you're human and you made a mistake?" He leaned back, pulling her toward him, holding her in a firm, comforting embrace. "Cry it all out."

She did so for a long time. "What people must be saying . . ." she whispered hoarsely.

"It'll all blow over in a few months' time. Don't let it worry you so much, Beth. When Tanner's gone, people will forget."

"I won't."

He tipped her chin, frowning. She gave a shuddering sigh and drew away. "Don't ask me, Adam," she whispered, seeing he wanted to know all. "Please."

His heart sank. The coldhearted bastard, he thought grimly.

She stood and moved away from him. Even though she was trembling from physical and emotional exhaustion, she knew she wouldn't be able to sleep.

"You need a stiff shot of brandy," Adam said, pouring some.

"I don't drink."

"Doctor's orders." He pressed it to her lips, and she looked at him beseechingly over the rim of the glass as she sipped. "I love you, Beth," he whispered. "Nothing's changed that." She drew back sharply, her hands covering her face again, and he knew he should have waited to say it. He set the glass aside. "You need sleep. Everything will look better in the morning."

She let her hands drop to her sides. "Yes, Adam," she whispered, knowing that to argue meant he would only stay with her longer, and he had already been up all night with her father. Dawn's light glowed through the front windows.

Morning was here already and nothing looked better. Nothing was going to be better ever again.

Chapter
Fifteen

FRANK LOOKED AT his daughter's pale, shadowed face and her valiant effort to smile as she bustled about his bedroom, tidying things and taking fresh linens from his armoire in preparation of changing the bed for him. "Sit down, honey. I want to talk to you."

She turned away quickly. "I can't right now, Papa. I've a cake in the oven for you, and John had to arrest McAllister last night, so I thought I'd take stew and dumplings along to the jail."

"Sit down. I want to tell you about your mother." It had been over two weeks, and things couldn't go on this way.

Her mouth trembled as she faced him again. He saw how dark her eyes were, tears welling. She shook her head. "You don't have to tell me anything, Papa. Really, you don't."

"It's time you know."

"It'll only upset you to talk about her. It always has, and you know what Adam said about your getting upset."

"I've had a good enough rest," he snapped, hating the confinement imposed on him. "I'm fit enough to talk, damnit! And if I'm going to die so soon, I want you to know before I do what in hell happened all those years ago!"

Seeing he was exciting himself, Beth sat.

Frank patted the bed. "Come here. You're too far away in that chair," he said more calmly.

Her mouth quivered as she came and sat on the edge of his bed. "Don't talk of dying," she whispered shakily.

He took her hand and squeezed it. "I am not going to die. I'm too damned ornery." He sighed, resting his back against his pillow again. He felt drained already and he hadn't even begun.

"It can wait, Papa."

He squeezed her hand again. "I'm going to talk, Beth, and I want you to just sit and listen and not interrupt." He took a deep breath. "I've never lied to you, but I've never told you all the truth, either. So it's just as bad as a lie, I guess."

She put her hand over his and lowered her head.

"I farmed for a while, after I married your mother. Before that I was just like Logan. Maybe worse. I didn't have any family. My pa ran off when I was a baby and my mother died when I was thirteen. I fell in with a gang of outlaws. Acted as their horseboy at their hideout. Currying their horses; mucking out their stable. They taught me how to get by with a gun. I was wild and reckless, and when I was old enough and fast enough, I rode with them."

He stopped and was silent for a while. "I was running when I came to Texas. I had a lawman's bullet in my leg and it was festering. I was real sick when your mother's folks found me in their field. They let Louise tend me." He closed his eyes, a grimace of pain tightening his face. "When I opened my eyes and saw her, I thought I was in heaven. She came to love me too, but not in the same way."

He paused again, deep in his memories, his eyes lighting and then darkening in remembered pain.

"I was something new to her. I wanted her, and when I was well, I took her. She was a good girl and her inexperience worked in my favor. I married her. I even made her happy for a while. Farming is hard work and I was used to an easier way, but I stayed honest and hung up my guns because I had her, and she was all I wanted. Then you came along and I had two of you to love."

His hand tightened. "Tanner had the section next to us. He ran a few head of cattle. He was a good-looking man like Logan, and he helped me out some. Or that's what I thought he was doing. He didn't have much time for Logan, so the boy dogged my steps. Like Faraday. He was a wild kid, but good. He was just lonely." His face twisted and he looked away.

"I was going to town for supplies, but the wagon's axle broke and I had to walk back for tools to fix it. Tanner's horse was tied up outside the house. I walked in and found them in bed together. You heard the rest from Logan."

"What about Mama?" Beth asked quietly.

Frank didn't speak for a moment, his mouth working and a deep grief grabbing at him. "It was Tanner she loved. Not me. I hated him for it, and killed him because of it." His face was very pale, his mouth tight. His dark eyes mirrored the agony he had suffered at his young wife's betrayal and his act of revenge.

"She was married to you, Papa."

"Yes, but that doesn't change things, Beth," he told her hoarsely, tears in his eyes as he looked at her. "She couldn't ever love me the way I loved her. It was all there waiting for him." His face was bleak. "A storm hit the day I killed Tanner. Your mother ran out into it. It was two days before I found her, and by then she was sick with fever. She blamed herself for everything. When I killed him, I killed something inside her, too. She just didn't care anymore."

"Not even about me," Beth murmured.

He couldn't deny that either. He remembered Beth crying for her mother and Louise just turning her face away as though she wanted no part of him, not even the child he'd sired.

"I changed when I left Texas. I didn't want my old life or what had happened to touch you. I guess I just didn't run far enough."

"I don't think he'll bother you again," Beth told him soothingly, not wanting even to speak Logan's name. It hurt too much.

"Is Logan still in town?"

She winced inwardly and shook her head. "Adam said he left the day after."

Frank sighed heavily.

She patted his rough, brown hand. "You've told me now, Papa. Rest." She leaned over and kissed him on the cheek. She saw moisture in his bleak eyes. He had paid dearly for what he had done. She understood so many things now. Certain looks that had crossed his face when she'd asked about her mother, the things he had said about Logan, his preoccupation with the Bible. He had been atoning all these years for what he had done.

And Logan had come to make him suffer.

Frank cupped her pale cheek and searched her eyes. "Do you still love him?"

"I don't feel much of anything anymore, Papa."

"You feel pain. I can see how much of that you feel."

Beth forced a smile and took his hand again. "It'll go away in time. And what's a flower without rain?" She stood. "I'll bring your supper in after a bit. I think I should take a tray down to the jail first so Mister McAllister won't drive John mad rattling his tin cup against the bars," she said, trying for a little humor.

Frank gave a small laugh, but it lacked conviction.

Beth didn't tell her father how people in town were treating her. It would only make matters worse for him. She bore the cold stares and whispers as she walked and the shunning when she entered shops. Faith served her in silence, took her money, but never spoke. Once Terence had started to tell her something and been slapped.

Reverend Tadish had come by a few days after the gunfight and regretfully asked her not to take it too badly but some of the good women of the church didn't want Beth teaching their children Sunday school lessons anymore. That had hurt more than everything else, not having the children around her.

Adam stood by her. He came by every night to check on her father and sit with her even when she had nothing to say. "It'll all pass, Beth. You'll see," he kept assuring her.

She didn't have much sewing to do anymore. Most of the women had canceled their orders and she was afraid even to mention to Faith Halverson the jacket and knickers she had completed. She kept seeing poor little Terence's face when his mother had boxed his ears.

Adam came by again that evening. She heard him talking to her father and she came into the parlor from the kitchen. She intended to peek in and say hello, but froze as she overheard part of their conversation.

"Say that again," Frank said in surprise.

Adam crossed his legs and leaned back in the chair. "Tanner came back, alright. He's staying at the hotel again."

Beth fled to the kitchen.

"Word has it now that he's bought some land," Adam continued.

"What? Where?" Frank demanded, sitting up slightly.

"Kilkare's old stomping grounds. The hill plus about three hundred acres around it."

"Well, I'll be damned."

"Does he worry you, Frank?"

Frank rested back again, thinking about Logan. "No. I think it's finished between us," he said, pensive.

"What about Beth? Is it finished with her?" Adam asked grimly, sitting forward and clasping his hands between his uncrossed legs.

"Can't say, Doc. She doesn't talk about any of it. She just goes about her work like nothing happened."

"That's what worries me," Adam admitted. "Since that first day she seems to have sealed herself off from feeling much of anything."

Frank frowned heavily, eyes dull. "How's the town treating her?"

Adam couldn't tell him, so he shrugged. "She's getting by alright. Beth is a strong girl for all her gentleness. You know that as well as I do. Everything is going to be fine."

Frank wasn't fooled. He thought to himself that Logan had almost as much to answer for now as he did.

Adam talked with Beth in the kitchen for a while, then left when she began to seem remote.

Nothing changed. Days passed. Beth scrubbed the floors and polished them for the third time in five days. She cleaned cupboards that had already been cleaned, finished canning all the vegetables she had picked. She washed all her father's clothes and hung them out, then spent the night ironing them because she couldn't sleep. She did the mending, and made a new pillow for the settee with scraps of material left from other projects.

What was she going to do with all those bolts of material she had ordered? All that money wasted . . .

She went to church by herself on Sunday. When she sat

down, the Polks got up and moved. She went to the back of the church and sat in the last pew and kept her head down throughout the service. She went straight home, her eyes burning and the lump in her throat throttling her. Adam caught up with her, but she couldn't utter one word and just shook her head and closed the gate before he could enter. She ran up the steps into the house.

Adam came to dinner that evening. When her father came out to join them, he ordered him back to bed, "Don't push it, Frank."

"Alright, alright."

Beth brought him a tray then went back to sit with Adam. She avoided discussing people's treatment of her by discussing the cloth.

"Why don't you make yourself some new dresses with the material?" Adam suggested. "It's better than leaving it there in the armoire. Make something really fine. I'll order some magazines from the East and you can do up the latest fashions."

Beth laughed softly. "What would everyone say if I strutted about in fine new feathers, Adam?"

Behind her smile, he saw the deep hurt in her eyes. "Why should you worry about what they say? They haven't been the least concerned about your feelings!" he told her angrily.

She shook her head. "It would be like rubbing salt in. And it'd only make matters worse. Besides," she said, and lowered her head, "I wouldn't feel right about it myself."

He put his hand over hers. "You think of yourself as the fallen woman, don't you?"

"I try not to think about any of it at all," she admitted.

He checked on her father before leaving.

"I don't know how we're going to pay you, Doc," Frank said.

"Shut up, you old fool," Adam said kindly, and left,

wondering how they were going to get by. He knew one way they could manage, but it was too early yet even to approach the subject with Beth.

She worked in her flower garden the next morning. She didn't look down the main street of town, but concentrated only on the flowers around her and on her weeding and clipping and the cutting of blooms for a bouquet for the mantel and another for her father's room.

There were no prisoners in the jail, and since John took his meals at the hotel, even that meager source of income was gone. She tried not to worry. The Lord would provide.

She left the cottage for errands. She needed a chicken and some flour, and some fine yellow silk thread for another pillow she was embroidering during the quiet evenings in her father's room.

"I shouldn't be long, Papa."

"Buy me some tobacco and a bottle of whiskey, will you, honey?"

She bent and kissed him on the forehead. "You know what Adam said about that."

"To hell with what Doc said. I'm dying for a shot of whiskey and a good smoke."

"I'm sorry, Papa. It's not good for you."

He swore heartily when she left.

She'd been gone about five minutes when the front door opened. "Beth? You forget something? Hey, damnit! At least bring back a little bottle of wine!"

His bedroom door swung open. Logan Tanner stood there, looking at him.

Frank pushed himself up, staring back at the tall, lean young man gazing at him enigmatically. "What're you doing here?" Frank growled.

Logan leaned against the doorframe and crossed his arms over his broad chest. "I came to see how you were, Frank."

"I'm alive." He looked Logan over. "Still wearing your gun, I see."

"Too late to change now, don't you think?" Logan drawled.

"I thought our business was finished," Frank said, frowning heavily.

"It is."

"Then why're you here?" Frank demanded.

Logan's eyes narrowed and a muscle worked in his bronzed, square jaw. "Were you telling the truth?" he asked roughly, and Frank recognized the burning question in Logan's eyes.

"Did I ever lie to you before, Logan? Think back to when you were a boy, and you can answer that for yourself."

Logan's mouth tightened. "Why didn't you tell me the first night I came here?"

Frank saw something in Logan's face in spite of the young man's effort to hide it. He leaned back slowly against the pillows and studied him. "Sit down if it's talking you want."

Logan did, but he looked uneasy despite his relaxed manner and placid, veiled expression.

"What do you really want to know, Logan?" Frank asked carefully.

"All of it."

Frank told him everything he had told Beth, but also other things he could never have admitted to her, things about what it was like to ride with an outlaw gang that robbed and killed to live, how living like that deadened a man's soul. "I'd only been out of that life for a few years when it all happened."

Logan's face was taut. "That's your excuse? You shot him six times, Tyrell. *Six times!* And then you spit on his dead body in front of the whole Goddamn town. One shot between his eyes would have been enough."

"Not for the way I was feeling."

"How did you feel?" Logan sneered. "I want to hear about that, too."

"I loved her," Frank said hoarsely. *"I loved her,* damn you! There's no excuse for what I did to your father, but when I walked into *my* house and heard them in *my* bed . . ." He closed his eyes tightly and ground his teeth at the memory. "I stood in the doorway. There she was, naked under him, writhing, and him rutting on her like a . . . Jesus! She was making those soft little sounds a woman makes when she's taking her pleasure . . ." He let out his breath sharply and opened his eyes to obliterate the memory. He looked up at Logan with tormented eyes. "I went crazy, and I wasn't right again until after she died."

Logan's face was stiff and pale. He stood up and went to the bedroom window and looked out, the muscle in his cheek working.

Frank sighed. "She asked one thing of me before she died—that I swear to her I'd never kill again, that I'd never stand against a man in a street for any reason."

"Well, you broke your word," Logan said flatly, dropping the curtain back into place. He turned.

"I haven't killed anyone since your father."

Logan gave a humorless laugh. "You shot down three men in the saloon the first night you were in this town."

"I didn't kill one of them, Logan. I could have, easy. I shot one in the shoulder, another in the leg, and the third in his gun hand. But I didn't kill them. I've kept the peace in Kilkare Woods for damn near eighteen years. It wasn't always the quiet little town you rode into."

"So I've heard."

The two men looked at one another.

Logan let out his breath very slowly and lowered his head, rubbing the back of his neck wearily as he rested his right hand on his hip above his gun. When he raised his head again, Frank saw the new lines around the younger man's eyes and mouth. More tension showed in his bleak eyes. But some of that boy he remembered from all those years ago was still in the hard man standing in his bedroom.

"I hear you bought land."

"Some."

"Why?"

Logan didn't answer. "Mind if I smoke?"

"Roll one for me."

Logan's mouth curled with humor. "What'll that doc say about that?"

"To hell with what he'll say. Beth won't buy me any tobacco either." He saw the slightest jerk in Logan's features at the mention of her name.

Logan rolled two cigarettes. Frank watched. They smoked in silence, Logan stretched out in the chair again, Frank sitting up in bed. Frank half smiled, the cigarette bobbing as he spoke through tight lips. "I taught you how to roll 'em right, didn't I? You used to watch me and try it. Spilled a damn lot of my good tobacco back then." His eyes narrowed slightly as he watched Logan's emotionless face. What was he thinking behind those veiled blue eyes?

"You asked me questions; now I got a right to ask you a few," Frank said in a hard voice.

Logan looked at him with cold eyes through a haze of smoke. "Guess that's fair enough," he drawled.

"You used to eat at my table, Logan," Frank reminded him. "You remember how little Beth used to want to climb up on your lap all the time. It embarrassed you like hell, but you liked it too. You—"

"You said you wanted to ask me something. What?" Logan demanded, eyes blazing.

Frank sat up abruptly and snatched the cigarette out of

his mouth. "Did you care about her at all, Logan?" he demanded harshly. "Did you ever once stop to think what you were doing to her? What you've done?"

They both heard footsteps on the front stairs. The front door opened. Frank took a couple of deep breaths and relaxed back against the pillows. He looked at his cigarette, then around for somewhere to extinguish it. Finding nothing, he gave a faint shrug and put it between his lips again.

Logan sat rigidly in the chair. "Jesus Christ," he breathed.

Frank turned and stared at him just as Beth opened the door, smiling. "Everything alright, Papa?" She froze, staring at Logan.

Frank looked at them carefully. His daughter's face emptied of color, then went fiery red, then white again. Her eyes were huge and dark with shock and pain.

Logan stood slowly and looked down at her. He took the cigarette out of his mouth and lowered his hand. Frank saw it shake and had the answer to all his questions.

"Get out," she said in a choked whisper, and backed out of the room.

"It's alright, honey," Frank assured her.

She looked as though she were suffocating. "It is?"

"Relax, Beth. I'm leaving," Logan said in a constricted tone. He started out of the room.

"Logan!" Frank said, and when Logan turned he gave Frank one slow nod.

As soon as Logan and Beth left her father's bedroom, she closed the door. "You leave him alone," she managed thickly.

"It's finished," Logan said without expression.

"After all you did to get at him, do you expect me to believe you?"

"Your father does."

"You stay away from him!"

"Beth . . ."

She yanked open the front door.

He looked down at her for a long moment, then left.

She went into her father's room again, took his cigarette from him, and marched back into the parlor to throw it away in the fireplace. She came back into his room again and jerked the window open. Then she turned and looked at him once before going out.

Frank closed his eyes and sagged back against the pillow, feeling the heavy, aching lump in his chest.

Chapter Sixteen

WHEN BETH SAW Avery lift Edwina down at her gate and then jump up to drive off, she could scarcely believe it! The young woman stared after him. Turning slowly, she opened the front gate, then started up the raked pathway.

Beth yanked the front door open and came out onto the porch. She stood at the top of the stairs with her hands on her hips. "What do you think you're doing here, Edwina?"

Edwina's mouth gave a nervous quiver before she lifted her chin. "I've come for my fitting, of course."

"Oh, no. I'm never sewing another thing for you. If your clothes fall off your back this winter, I still won't!" She breathed in shakily. "How could you think ever to come here?"

Edwina glanced uneasily over her shoulder. "Couldn't we go inside and discuss this civilly? People are going to wonder what's going on."

"They'll know what's going on! They'll know I don't want you inside my home."

"You could use the work, couldn't you?" Edwina said nastily, and started up the steps.

Short of knocking her off them, there was little Beth could do but stand her ground. "Go away, Edwina."

Brown eyes clashed with hazel ones. Edwina lowered hers. "I'm sorry about your father."

Beth stared incredulously.

Edwina's chin came up. "I didn't mean to hurt him."

"What did you think would happen when you stood in the general store and announced what you did? Did you think my father would just shrug the whole thing off and not do something?"

"I didn't mean to hurt *him!*" Edwina repeated doggedly, her hand whitening on her parasol.

Beth let out her breath, eyes stinging. "No. I'm sure you didn't. You only wanted to hurt me. You just never stopped to think what you were doing to anyone else. You've never in your life thought about anyone but yourself!"

Edwina glared up at her, eyes glistening with tears. "Haven't I? Haven't I really?" The bitter anger paled her pinched face and made her shake. "Avery didn't believe you could do such a thing!" she cried mockingly, throwing her head back derisively. "His perfect Beth! But I saw you with that gunfighter. Right back there!" She pointed to the side of the house toward the trees with the tip of her lacy parasol. "Oh, how I wish Avery had seen you then, too!"

Beth turned away and walked inside the cottage, intending to close the door. Edwina shoved her way in.

"Get out of here, Edwina!" Beth ordered.

"You think I haven't known all along what was going on?" Edwina said, voice rising almost hysterically. "You and Avery! Forever you and Avery! That's all I've heard about since the day Avery decided to come back here. And Hannah! I'm sure she wishes now that she had let her precious son marry a practical girl like you instead of me!"

"Are you mad? Hannah Carlile—"

"—sent him east to get him away from you!" Edwina cried out for her, tears welling up in her eyes. "She sent him away because he was in love with you and you weren't good enough for him! And you're not! But he's always been in love with you!"

"That's not true!"

"Oh, yes, it is! And you've never married anyone else because you're still in love with him. But that doesn't stop you from fooling around with other men, does it?"

"You say anything like that to me again and I'll slap your vicious little face!"

"He railed at me all the way back to the ranch," Edwina went on, pacing like a crazed cat. "He said I had to be lying, that you'd never behave like that. He thinks you're some sainted virgin or something!" She glared back at Beth through tear-filled eyes.

"So what does that make me?" Edwina continued. "A harlot? He loved me when we were back east. He couldn't wait to have me. He made love to me in the garden behind our home a week before the wedding." Her mouth trembled. "Now he hardly kisses me anymore." Her chin jutted forward, her face streaked and agonized. "He used to kiss me exactly the way that man was kissing you! Now he wants to send me back to Philadelphia!" Her face crumpled.

Beth softened. "Edwina, Avery doesn't love me at all," she said in a slow, firm voice. "If you've hated me so much, why have you had me sew your clothes for you?"

"You think I come here because I want to?" Edwina laughed bitterly. "You think I'd ever come if I could find some way out of it?"

"What're you saying? There are other ladies in Kilkare Woods who do fine dressmaking."

"Avery insists I come to you. 'Beth needs the money,'" she mimicked. "'We've got to do something for her,'" she went on, her lips trembling, her eyes spilling moisture. "He wanted to make sure you were well taken care of, so he sent me in every few weeks for another new dress! Do you think I need or want all those things? My parents had enough money to see that I had a trousseau! But Avery *insisted!* 'Go have her make you another dress, Wina. Beth needs the money.'"

Beth put a hand to her forehead.

"All he could talk about on the train coming out here was how much he looked forward to seeing you again. He'd go on about how you walked together and fished together and talked together for hours and hours. He hardly ever talks to me at all since we came out here. He's always riding his horse!" She sank down onto the settee and put her face in her hands, sobbing.

Beth sagged into her father's chair and stared at the miserable young woman with new, painful insight.

"He doesn't love me at all anymore. Maybe he never did," Edwina cried brokenly.

"Edwina," Beth said softly, and leaned forward. "Edwina, listen to me," she said gently. "Avery never loved me. We were very special friends, yes, but even that's changed. We've grown up. We don't talk anymore. We hardly ever see one another except to say hello at church on Sundays. We met once at the river where we used to go as children," Beth admitted, and Edwina's head came up sharply, her eyes filled with knowing accusation. "He told me he loves you," Beth said, "but he said you were so unhappy here, that you missed your home. He doesn't have any idea of the real reason why you can't adjust."

Edwina frowned. "He said he loves me?"

"Yes." Beth smiled. "Very much." She shook her head

ruefully. "Edwina, he thought I was pining for him and he was feeling guilty for me being a spinster. But it wasn't that way at all. I care a great deal about Avery, and I missed him terribly when he went away, but I was never in love with him. I was just waiting for . . . the right man." Logan's image pierced her with pain and she frowned, looking down at her hands.

"I almost believe you," Edwina murmured in a tear-husky voice. "But maybe that's because I want to so very much."

Beth forced herself to look up again. "You can believe it, Edwina. If only you'd just been honest with him," she said shakily, "he'd have told you himself."

Edwina's shoulders shook. "I love him so much, and every time he mentioned your name or made me come here for another dress or talked with you after church . . ." She looked away. "He'll never forgive me for what I've done."

Beth clenched cold hands in her lap and tried to speak clearly. "It's alright, Edwina. All that really happened was that the truth was brought out into the open."

Edwina looked at her again, searching her face. She bit her lip and shook her head. "That's not all I managed to do to you, is it?" she said sadly. "Or your father."

Beth raised her head. "I'm going to choose to look at it this other way."

Edwina's face crumpled. She stood up, her mouth working as she tried to say something. She couldn't. She turned to go, then turned back again.

Beth crossed the small room and put her arms around her. Edwina stiffened at the light, comforting hug, then pulled away and opened the door and left quickly. Beth went to the doorway and saw Edwina running across the road toward the shadow of the trees.

Avery came a half hour later.

When Beth opened the door, she let out her breath in exasperation. "Avery Carlile, I have a few things to say to you. Come inside."

His eyes widened. He stepped in and looked around for his wife. "Where's Wina?" His eyes darkened angrily. "What happened now? Did she say something to you?"

"Edwina is walking up in the hills just over the road," Beth told him. "And yes, she said some things to me, things that she should have said months ago. Avery, you are an utter fool. Do you know that?"

"What're you talking about?"

"She thought you were in love with me!"

"What?"

"Well, what did you suppose she would think when you went on and on about our grand times together. The last thing a woman wants to hear about is another woman. And what do you mean by making her come here for all those dresses when she doesn't even want them?"

"But I thought—"

"We aren't starving, Avery," she told him, shaking her head. "In fact, we're getting by quite nicely." Or they had been.

"I just wanted to help you out," he said lamely.

"Some fine gesture, thank you. Or were you just trying to salve your conscience because you thought I was dying of love for you?" She laughed.

Avery blushed to the roots of his hair. "Well, I didn't know."

"I always thought you were so smart. Now I know you're just swellheaded." She dimpled, then grew more serious again. "Edwina thinks you want to send her back east because you don't love her anymore."

"Oh, God," he said, raking a hand through his hair.

"No wonder she's been so unhappy."

"I'd better go find her."

"In a moment," Beth told him, putting a detaining hand on his arm. "A few other things while we're about it. You'll have to do something about your mother, I think. Edwina didn't say anything against her, but—"

"I know," he muttered grimly.

"Whose side have you been taking?"

"Mostly Mother's," he admitted sheepishly.

"Because it's easier, probably. But Avery, the ranch belongs to you now, and Edwina is your wife. Your mother deserves respect and consideration, certainly, but your wife has the right to be lady of the house."

"I know what you're telling me, but what do I do about Mother?" he asked solemnly.

"Get her involved in community work so she won't try to run everything at the ranch. God knows, someone always needs help. And the running of your house should be Edwina's responsibility now, or a good part of it, at least. And I think she's more than capable, considering her background."

"She ought to be having a baby."

Beth blushed brightly. "Well . . . that's something you'll have to take up with her."

He laughed. Then his expression fell. "God, what a mess I've made of things." He let out his breath. "I'm damn sorry about what she said about you and that gunfighter."

Beth lowered her head. "That's another thing I want to tell you, Avery." She forced herself to look him in the eye. "She didn't lie about what she saw, and she said it the way she did only because . . . well, she didn't want you to go on seeing me as some sainted virgin to keep on a pedestal."

Avery said nothing for a long moment, then reached out and squeezed her shoulder. "If you were with him that way, Beth, it must have been because you love him," he said quietly.

"Everyone makes mistakes," she said softly. "I just happened to make a very big one." Her eyes glimmered. She smiled and put her hand on his forearm, squeezing him back affectionately. "You'd better go find Edwina. We don't want her making any more mistakes about whom you're in love with, now do we?"

She closed the door behind him and leaned back against it.

"Beth?" her father called.

She went into his bedroom to see if he needed something. He patted his bed. She sat down and took his hand.

"Quite a day you've had," he said, smiling.

She dimpled. "You've got some color in your face again. You must've enjoyed eavesdropping."

"Think they'll work it all out?"

"Yes."

He cupped her cheek and studied her. "Now you've fixed things for them, can you fix things for yourself?"

She lowered her head. "Do you need anything, Papa?"

"I need to see some light in your eyes again," he said solemnly, forcing her chin up.

"When you're better again, I'll be better too," she told him, and he knew it was best to leave it alone.

Chapter Seventeen

BETH RESTED HER head against the back of the porch swing, letting the rocking motion relax her. Her feet were curled up beneath her skirt, and the hem lightly swept the wooden porch floor. Adam was beside her, and she could feel him studying her as he kept the swing moving. He touched her face lightly.

"You look exhausted, Beth. Aren't you sleepy?"

"Hmmm, a little. I'm fine."

"No, you're not. You've got to slow down. The house is perfectly clean and I come and find you on your hands and knees scrubbing that floor again. Why?"

Her eyelids fluttered and she turned her head away. "I don't know, Adam." But she did. She had to keep busy to stop thinking. Nighttime was worse. Like now, when Adam's questions brought Logan to mind again. Pain went through her and dug in deeply.

"You'll make yourself sick if you go on like this. You've lost too much weight."

She looked at him and smiled. "Nonsense. Stop sounding like a doctor. I'll be fine."

"Everything's fine, is that it?" he said, putting his arm along the back of the swing. "Come here and lean against me."

She did. Her head rested against his solid shoulder and she heard him sigh. She felt safe with him, but nothing else, not even when his lips grazed her forehead in a light kiss.

"Beth, you're trying to put a brave face on everything. There's one surefire way to put an end to all the gossip, and that's for us to get married."

She drew back sharply and looked up at him. His eyes were intent as he looked at her. "You're very gallant, Adam—"

"Gallant? It's got nothing to do with being gallant. Don't you know that yet?"

She didn't want to hurt him more, so she allowed his kiss though it left her feeling nothing.

"Don't throw away all your happiness just because Tanner—"

Beth flinched at the mention of Logan's name. "Don't!" she said, and drew back.

"Alright. I'm sorry," Adam said grimly, having seen the look in her eyes before she turned away.

"It's nothing to do with that, Adam. I just can't marry you."

"Why not?"

Her hand plucked at her soft gingham skirt. Her mouth trembled as she tried to look at the evening starlight, swallowing the lump in her throat so she could speak. Words wouldn't come.

"I know he took your innocence," Adam said softly, seeing the tears trickle down her pale cheeks. "Beth, I wish it had been me, yes, but it wasn't and it doesn't matter. I still want you."

She looked at him. "How could you?"

"Because I love you."

She shook her head.

"Is it more?" he asked pointedly. "Are you afraid you're pregnant?"

She gasped softly. "I . . . I don't think so," she said, frightened and wondering why she hadn't considered it before.

Adam tipped her chin up. "Have you had your monthly yet?" What if she was carrying Tanner's child? What then?

"Adam, what a thing to ask!" she said, mortified with embarrassment.

"I'm a doctor, remember? Well?"

She lowered her eyes and couldn't look at him again. "Yes."

He relaxed, his worry leaving him. "Then you're not pregnant." He put his arm along the back of the swing again. "If we got married, that one time wouldn't matter because we'd have our whole lives together. We'd have children and a home. I'd teach you how to be my nurse so you could work with me. We'd have a good, full life together, Beth." He watched her carefully. She was so quiet and withdrawn. "Your father is worried about you. He feels helpless."

"So do I," she admitted, gazing out at the night again. "I'd be lying to say it doesn't hurt the way people treat me now. I don't think I'm any different inside now than I was before."

"You're not."

She looked at him sadly. "I won't marry you just to prevent gossip."

He leaned toward her. "Beth, I don't care what the reason is. Any will do. I want you to be my wife."

"Oh, Adam," she said shakily. She had so much affection and trust for this man. "Nothing's changed. Don't you see? I'm not in love with you."

"What did being in love get you, Beth?" he demanded. "A little practicality might be a good thing. What if your father can't work again? What if the town hires a new sheriff?"

Beth paled. "I've thought about it already."

"You wouldn't have to worry about it. That house on Elm is big enough for two families, and there's just me and Missus Michaels rattling around in it. You and I could have the whole upper floor to ourselves, and your father could be downstairs. Missus Michaels has the section behind the kitchen."

"Adam, are you telling me that Papa is never going to be better?" she said, her eyes searching his frantically.

He let out his breath. "No, but it's going to take a long time, and he's never going to be the way he was. He's going to have to be careful. He's not a young man anymore, you know. Someday, someone is going to have to take his place, and when that happens, the house goes."

She rested her head back against the swing again, her throat working. Her garden!

"Don't cry, Beth. Everything will be alright if we get married."

"I . . . I just can't think about it right now, Adam. Please."

He wanted to press her. He had already heard talk of some of the men in town wanting a new sheriff. An outlaw gang had robbed a bank not a hundred miles from Kilkare Woods, and they were all afraid the gang might be heading up this way. But looking at Beth, Adam knew he couldn't tell her that now. It was enough that she had heard him out.

"Think about it, Beth. I could make you happy."

"But could I make you happy, Adam?"

He drew her close again and stroked her hair. "Yes," he said huskily. "You do *like* me," he teased.

"Yes, I like you very, very much," she said sincerely. "I admire you and I respect you. I feel safe when you're here."

His heart pounded faster. "Then you could learn to love me, too, Beth, if you only gave yourself a chance."

Beth thought of Logan and felt her eyes burn. Why hadn't she looked at Adam the first day *he* came to town and felt that trembling warmth inside her, that sense of fate? Why not this kind man who really loved her?

She tried not to think of the ugly truth that had been behind the beautiful hours in the hills with Logan. It had all been a lie for him, but it had meant her very life. He had taken everything, not because he wanted it, but because it had been a means to an end for him.

Adam kissed her forehead again. "I'd better go," he whispered. "It's getting late and you need to rest."

She walked with him to the gate. He bent and kissed her cheek. "Good night," she said, and watched him walk away, his medical bag in his hand. He never seemed to be without it.

When she came inside, she found her father sitting in his chair before the fire. "What're you doing in here? You're supposed to be in bed," she reprimanded him.

"I've been in bed long enough," he growled. "Three and a half weeks of lying on my back is all I can take without putting a hole in my head."

"Papa, don't talk like that."

He set the Bible aside. "I'm weak, but I feel pretty good, so stop fussing. When an animal's sick, you get it up off the ground and walking. Same ought to be done for a man, don't you think?"

"I don't know," she said doubtfully. She turned and put

her shawl over the back of the settee.

"Did Adam ask you to marry him again?"

She glanced at him sharply.

"He told me about the first time he asked you. Why didn't you tell me?"

"Because I knew you'd start pushing, Papa."

"What'd you answer?" he demanded roughly.

She sighed and sat down. "I said I couldn't say now. I need time to think about it."

"Well, that's something better than no, I guess," he drawled. He watched her face closely. "You think he could make you happy?"

She spread her hands over her skirt. "I don't know," she said truthfully.

"Not the same as with Logan, huh?"

"Oh, God, don't," she said, lowering her eyes, her shoulders hunching. "Don't mention his name to me."

"You hardly spoke to me for two days after he came to talk to me."

She looked up, her face white, her eyes haunted. "Do you blame me?"

"Beth—"

"Leave it be, Papa, please," she said unsteadily.

"How can I when you can't?"

"I will," she said, her mouth quivering. "I will!"

"Maybe, but I doubt it." Frank sat in silence, his eyes dull. "I never wanted it to touch you."

"You couldn't help it. It's over now anyway," she said flatly, staring into the flames of the low fire. She raised her head and forced a smile. "Would you like your thimbleful of brandy? Adam said it was permitted."

"You know the answer to that." He watched her cross the room. She held herself like a lady. Not the brisk, efficient movements of some women he had watched, nor the forced dignity of others. She had a gentle, natural grace about the way she moved. He loved to watch her. He smiled as she handed him a small glass of brandy. She had dark shadows beneath her hazel eyes. "Adam could give you something to help you sleep."

"Maybe I'll ask," she said quietly, thinking how she would relish one good, dreamless night's sleep, one night without seeing Logan's face.

Beth was working in her flower garden the next morning when the gate clicked open. She glanced up, expecting Adam, and saw Logan standing there, just inside the fence. She sat back on her heels, staring up at him. Then she struggled quickly to her feet and brushed down her skirt.

"I want to talk to you, Beth," he said, and closed the gate behind him.

"I don't want to talk to you."

"Well then, you can just listen."

"You're still wearing your gun."

"Why should I take it off?"

"No reason. It becomes you." She turned and walked toward the cottage. She went up the steps and swung the door open. As she went in, she tried to slam it, but Logan caught the edge and held it open. She pushed, but without effort he held it slighly ajar. His eyes were dark.

"Go away!" she said breathlessly, her heart racing wildly. She hated herself for the feelings he could still rouse in her.

He shoved the door open and walked in. She backed up before him and stood in the middle of the room well away from him. He closed the door and locked it. Her eyes went wide.

"I don't want the good doctor walking in and interrupting our conversation," he said through tight lips. He was silent for a moment, a muscle jerking in his cheek as he studied her face. "You've nothing to fear from me, so stop looking like that," he said raggedly.

She put a trembling hand to her churning stomach. "Say what you have to say and then leave, please."

The muscle jerked in his cheek again. She couldn't see anything in his blue eyes as he stared at her, but she could feel his tension all the way across the room.

"I'm sorry I dragged you into it," he said flatly.

"It's a little late to be sorry about anything, but at least it's all over."

"Is it?"

She blinked. Her lips parted. "You told Papa it was," she said chokingly, "or were you just getting him off his guard so you could come at him in another way?"

He took a step toward her. "That's not what I meant."

She moved back, heart jumping.

He stopped. "I carried what I saw inside me for years, Beth."

"I don't doubt that," she said, her face pale.

His gaze fell from hers. "It's a terrible thing to carry. It eats you up with hatred. It makes a man . . . not see things clearly." He rubbed his neck and started to pace. He stopped at the fireplace and put his hand up to the mantel in a long, slow caress of the wood as he stared fixedly at the big hammered-tin pot she had filled with a wild, colorful array of flowers. His hand dropped back to his side, almost over his gun. He turned and looked at her.

"I could fix it all by marrying you," he told her, face expressionless, body rigid.

She stared out him. Did he really suppose it was that simple? She felt her eyes welling with tears and tried to stop the surge of emotion that choked her—grief, not joy. Just a few weeks ago she had been so happy! It was hard to believe so much had happened, so much had changed.

"No. I wouldn't want to be married to a man like you," she said in all truth.

His hand clenched. "Fair enough."

They stared at one another from across the room.

"Would you marry a man like Buchanan?" he asked, no inflection in his deep voice.

"I don't know."

His eyes darkened. "He'd like to marry you, wouldn't he?"

"It doesn't concern you, Logan."

He looked away and sighed heavily. "No, I guess it doesn't." He looked oddly vulnerable, but she knew that couldn't be so. He was too hard, too relentlessly cold to feel much of anything. Except hatred.

His hand clenched and unclenched, then went loose and still. He looked at her again. "I think it might make things better if we were on more friendly terms."

She looked at him incredulously. "Friendly terms?"

His mouth tightened. "When we meet, by chance, we should speak to one another," he clarified stiffly. "If people see us behaving normally, then they're less likely to believe what was said."

She frowned, confused.

He let out his breath sharply and paced the room again. "Look, Beth. They've known you your whole life. They know the way you are. You're a lady. You go to church every Sunday. You treat people the way you'd like to be treated. Well, if we don't act as if anything went on, they'll begin to believe nothing ever did."

"I see."

He looked at her grimly. "Will you?"

"If you speak to me in public, I won't shun you, Logan," she said simply, promising nothing more. She saw the tiny jerk in the muscles of his face. Silence fell again.

"I'll be coming to see your father now and then," he

informed her, and searched her eyes.

"Only good can come of that," she said. "You liked each other once."

His expression changed. "Beth . . ."

His soft, rough tone touched her deeply, and rather than admit it to herself, she went stiff and closed her eyes tightly, crushing down everything that tried to resurrect itself inside her. Her cheek muscles hurt from tension.

"That's all I had to say," he told her in a flat tone. She heard the door latch lift and opened her eyes again. He went out, closing the door behind him.

Twice in the next few days she did chance to meet Logan in public places. She wondered if he was putting her through this deliberately. He always tipped his hat to her, said hello, and then went about his business. The third time, he met her before the Polks' butcher shop. He said a few inane remarks about the weather while searching her eyes in an intent manner. Then he went his way again.

She was standing on the porch the next morning, using her watering can to douse the geraniums, when she saw him coming up the boardwalk. It was so easy to spot him. He was tall, with such a proud, manly bearing. He had a compelling aura about him that drew attention, especially women's.

Children ran toward the schoolhouse where the bell was ringing, sending out a warning that class was to begin. They darted around Logan. He laughed, stepping aside and turning to watch them race along the boardwalk.

Beth's heart squeezed tightly and she forced herself to concentrate on what she was doing rather than on her surreptitious perusal of Logan Tanner.

Logan crossed the dusty street, and she knew he was coming to the cottage. She set down the watering can as he opened the gate. "Good morning, Beth," he said as he rested his booted foot on the first step but came no further.

She nodded.

"Frank awake yet?"

The door clicked open behind Beth. "Sure am," Frank said, startling her. She glanced back at him standing in the doorway. "I could use a man's company for a while," he said, actually smiling. "Come on in."

Logan looked at her. She resigned herself to it. "I'll make some coffee." She went inside.

The men sat in the parlor, talking in low voices, while she worked in the kitchen. She brought the tray out and set it carefully on the small coffee table between them. Then she took her shawl from where it was folded over the end of the settee.

"Where you going, honey?" Frank asked, surprised.

"I have some errands," she said lamely, but didn't fool anyone. She felt both men looking at her as she quietly went out the door.

Chapter
Eighteen

EDWINA CAME BY with Avery to pick up the dress Beth had finished. She looked much different from the miserable, angry young woman who'd come before. There was soft color in her cheeks and a glow in her dark eyes. Avery looked different, too. The lines of strain were gone from his face.

Beth served them coffee and tea cakes, and they talked of changes at the ranch. Edwina was planning all the meals and handling the instructions for the house servants.

"Mother wasn't the least bit upset. She said it was about time." Avery laughed, but Beth saw in Edwina's look that it hadn't been as simple as all that. "We're buying her a smart little buggy so she can come back and forth to town. She's going to help Pastor Tadish."

"I think she's more interested in working with the mayor for a bigger schoolhouse," Edwina reminded him. "She has quite an organized mind."

Beth smiled in amusement. "And she'll be putting it to

good use." The town would probably have a new school inside a few years.

Edwina stood and walked about the room. She paused at the big bouquet of flowers on the mantel and touched several blooms. "Beth, you'll have to tell me how you manage to make roses grow so well."

It was the first time she had said "Beth" and it drew a thankful smile. "With horse manure." Beth dimpled. They all laughed together.

Beth saw them to the gate. Edwina paused and exchanged a secretive look with Avery before looking at Beth again. "I think I'd like a new dress for the fall harvest."

"Oh, no, you don't," Beth said. "We discussed that once before, didn't we?"

Edwina frowned. "I . . ."

Beth saw her embarrassment increasing and reached out to take her hand. "The money from this dress is plenty. We'll talk about another in the fall. For Christmas, perhaps?"

Edwina squeezed her hand before letting it go. Avery smiled as he lifted his wife up to the carriage seat. He turned back and gave Beth an intent, questioning look. "Everything going alright?"

"Just fine, Avery. Thank you both for coming."

After their visit, Beth felt better than she had in days, but no sooner had she had that thought than she opened the front door to a small delegation of townsmen headed by Howard Polk.

"Can we come in, Miss Tyrell?" He had always called her Beth in the past, and the formality put her on her guard.

"Of course, Mister Polk. What can I do for you, gentlemen?" she asked, as Polk was followed by Pastor Tadish, Matthew Galloway, and Daniel Claybeck, the president of Kilkare Woods' only bank.

"We'd like to see your father."

"I'm right here, Howard," Frank said, coming out of his room, frowning darkly. "Have a seat. Beth, how about some coffee?"

"How are you, Frank?" Matt asked, shaking hands with him. "You look better than the last time I saw you."

"I'm up and around," Frank said, glancing at the other men. Howard Polk looked belligerent, Pastor Tadish embarrassed, and Daniel Claybeck pale with worry. What in Hades was going on now?

Frank sat in his chair and wished he had some tobacco for a smoke. He had a bad feeling about this visit. They weren't here to ask after his health, he was sure.

Polk got right to the point. "Are you well enough to go back to work as sheriff?"

Frank laughed low. "I'd like to, but Doc says no, not for another couple of months at least."

"Then as mayor of this town, I'm asking—"

"I know what you are," Frank growled, seeing what was coming.

"Now, just a minute, Howard," Matt stepped in. "Hold up a little bit there—"

"We can't hold up any longer!" Polk insisted.

"There's been trouble, Frank," Pastor Tadish put in, his index finger running nervously around the inside of his clerical collar as though it were choking him.

"I know all about the trouble," Frank said, relaxing and half smiling. "I may be an invalid," he said mockingly, looking squarely at Polk, "but I'm well aware of what's going on. I know there's an outlaw gang working the area just south of here. I also know that several people were shot in a stage holdup. They hit Las Positas a week ago and Madrone a few days later. Last word was they were seen around Murry Township. So whoever is doing it, they seem to be moving toward us."

"So what do we do, Frank?" Matt asked grimly.

"We get ourselves a new sheriff who's worth something. That's what we do," Polk snapped, almost relishing the words. He and Frank Tyrell had been on bad terms for some time. It had to do with Jessica's speaking her mind about the Widow O'Keefe and the number of visits Frank Tyrell had made to her ranch on the pretext of looking out for rustlers. The only rustling going on, Jessica had said, was the woman's skirts when she stripped them off.

"Damnit, Howard," Matt snarled. "Frank's done a fine job for years and he gets laid up for a few weeks and you're all ready to—"

"Not a few weeks. A month already and another couple to go. And what do we all do in the meantime? Let these outlaws ride on into town and clean the bank vault? My life's savings are in there. So are yours. Now, if he can't do the job, we've got to get someone who can. We're wide open without a sheriff, and you know it!"

"Why'd it take you so long to come around with your glad tidings, Howard?" Frank drawled in a quiet way that brought all the men's immediate attention to his rigid face. "Were you getting up what little guts you have to come down here?"

Howard Polk flushed in rising anger.

"Frank, we don't want to do this," Daniel said, looking grayer and older than his fifty-eight years. He pushed his spectacles up on his nose with his thumb. "I wish we had another solution."

Frank sighed heavily. "Hell, Daniel, I know that. I been thinking on this whole thing for weeks."

"You sure you can't go back to work again?" Matt asked, standing with his hands shoved deeply into his pockets.

"Wish I could. I been going crazy around here without anything to do, but you need someone who can fight, and fight now. I'm not fool enough to think I can. Probably won't be able to again. So you're going to need someone who's good with a gun and has a good bit of sense along with it."

"Any suggestions?" Polk asked grudgingly.

Frank leaned far back in his chair. "Sure do."

"Well, who?"

"Well, now, how about you, Howard? Are you up to the job?" Frank said.

"Me?" Polk choked, paling. "I can't . . . I mean I'm not . . . " he stammered.

Frank laughed at him. "Well, at least you're man enough to know you're not man enough."

"Frank," Pastor Tadish said in soft reprimand, trying to prevent a mudslinging argument.

Polk's ruddy face had suffused with color. Frank dismissed him with a sneer.

"Now, Matt here is capable, but he's got enough to do looking out for things at his train station, and truth to say, he's not too quick with his gun."

Matt laughed.

"And Daniel's got brains," Frank said. "I doubt you've ever held a gun in your life, but you're damn fine with long words. Unfortunately, the men we're up against aren't the listening kind." He looked at the pastor. "And you're in a different business altogether, aren't you, Pastor?"

"So who do you suggest?" Daniel asked.

"Well, you've got yourselves a big problem and one choice, as far as I can see. And he's living at the hotel."

All four men started talking at once. "Tanner? You can't be serious?"

"I wouldn't hire that killer if my life depended on it!" Polk snorted.

"Your life may very well depend on it," Frank said quietly.

"After what that bastard did to you and . . . " Daniel started to say, and then his glance fell away.

"And Beth?" Frank supplied coldly.

"We didn't come to discuss your daughter's relationship with that gunfighter," Polk said.

Frank turned his head and glared at him. "You've already discussed it plenty in your shop, haven't you? It's not just steers you butcher, is it, Polk? Does it make you feel big?"

Polk lost all the color that had mounted into his face.

Pastor Tadish got up and stood between them. "Maybe we could wire for the marshal," he suggested.

Frank pulled his eyes away from Polk. "Doesn't change the situation," he said grimly. "You still need someone to be full-time sheriff. Logan's all you've got, and I think he would do a damn good job."

"How can you talk for the man after what he did?" Matt demanded, not trusting Tanner an inch.

"He had his reasons. You all heard them plain enough in the street that day. He didn't know everything. Now he does, and we've made our peace. You men give him a chance, and he'll keep yours."

"Well, I don't see that we've much choice," Daniel said unhappily, pushing his spectacles up his narrow nose again.

Matt resisted. "Well, I don't agree. There's got to be someone else. Tanner is nothing but a gunfighter."

Frank smiled. "Twenty-five years ago, Matt, I was exactly like Logan. Didn't know that, did you? It's not something I'm real proud of, but living that way helped me learn how to keep trouble out of Kilkare Woods for almost eighteen years." He looked around at them all. "The facts are that right now you need Logan Tanner no matter what he's done or been, just as you needed me when I first came here. You don't have to know a hell of a lot about him except he's smart, he can use a gun faster than any man I know, and if he gives you his word, you can count on him."

The men all talked at once again, but the consensus seemed to go along with Frank, who sat listening, eyes narrowed, mouth tight.

"We'll see what the man has to say," Polk declared.

"Are you going to approach him, Howard, as mayor of this fine, Christian town, or do you plan on taking a big delegation with you to back you up?" Frank drawled sardonically.

Beth came into the room with a tray. Howard Polk looked at her and back at Frank. "When you hand over your badge, you also lose this house," he announced as a parting shot before he marched to the front door. "I hope you haven't forgotten that was part of the agreement when you took the job."

Frank's hands tightened on the arms of his chair. "I wondered how long it'd take you to get to that. You're the type of rodent that rubs his nose in his own mess just so he has something to show when he faces everyone."

Polk slammed out.

The three men remained, all looking embarrassed. They glanced uneasily at Beth, frozen in the open kitchen doorway, the tray still in her hands. The cups were rattling and her face was drained of color.

"What's happened?" she asked in a strained voice.

Matt stood and glanced pointedly at the others. "We'd best go."

The others were only too willing to agree. Frank saw them to the door and closed it. He turned to face Beth. "Just set the tray down, honey," he said very softly. If she didn't, she was going to drop it and then mourn the loss of her pretty china cups and saucers as well as her home. He rubbed his face wearily, feeling old.

She left the tray on the dining room table and walked toward him.

"Sit down," he told her firmly.

She did, but she was perched on the very edge of the settee, her fingers woven whitely together. "What did Mr. Polk mean about you turning in your badge?"

There was no easy way to tell her. "I'm not sheriff of this town anymore. They're going to offer the job to Logan."

She stared at him, motionless. She made two small fists and thumped them against her thighs, her eyes closing. Biting down on her lower lip, she rocked slowly, her face convulsing.

Frank got up and poured her a glass of brandy. "Here. Drink this."

"Ohhh, Papa. . . ."

He slammed the glass down with a thunk that threatened to shatter it. Hunkering down in front of her, he grasped her small fists and pried them open so he could hold her hands in his big, roughened ones. "Listen to me, Beth. It had to happen."

"He even takes my home?"

"Logan's not taking it. The town's taking it. It never belonged to us. You knew that."

Her eyes filled up and spilled over. "You gave this town almost eighteen years of your life and they paid you next to nothing, Papa. You kept them all safe and their children safe, and this house is all we have. I've got a little bit of savings, but not enough to last us long. Where do we go? What do we do?"

"We'll work it all out," Frank told her. "Missus O'Henry has the boardinghouse."

Beth lowered her eyes. "She'd never allow me inside it. Not now, Papa. You know how she is."

Frank squeezed her hands and straightened. He turned away. "There's a lot you haven't been telling me, isn't there?"

She didn't answer.

He looked down at her bowed head. "Do you want to go away from this town? Live somewhere else?"

She smoothed her skirt with shaking hands.

"Beth?"

She shook her head. She stood up, still not looking at him. "I'm going for a walk, Papa."

He frowned heavily. "Why don't you just stay right here with me?" he said, her despondence worrying him. An old memory rose and gripped him with fear. How much could she take?

Beth raised her head and looked at him in understanding. She came close and hugged him. "I'm alright," she whispered. "You needn't worry. I just need . . . to think things over for myself."

She went down along the river where she and Avery had swum and tossed rocks and fished as children. She sat on the big flat rock and skipped one stone after another. At first all she could think of was her home being taken away from her by Logan. Then she began to sort things out. Perhaps she could make an offer to the City Council and buy the cottage. She had her savings, and perhaps they would agree to allow her time to pay off whatever debt remained.

But business had fallen away since her reputation had been ruined, and what she made now barely covered the usual expenses. Without her father's income to rely on, she didn't know how they would manage.

What could she do?

How much of all this worry could her father take without having it adversely affect his health?

She thought of her roses and bulbs and she wept, her head in her arms.

When she thought she'd finished crying, she came back through the ivy-shrouded path and started for home.

Adam intercepted her. It was the first time she had seen him without his black bag. He caught hold of her. "Beth, you've had me worried sick! Where have you been? Do you know how many hours you've been gone?"

"I didn't think about it. I'm sorry. Is Papa terribly worried?"

"He sent Faraday up into the hills looking for you, and asked me to come down here by the river." He held her shoulders, searching her pale face intently. "Listen to me. I've got the best solution in the world for all your problems."

She glanced up and shook her head, knowing what he would say. "Adam, no. . . ."

"I've been all by myself in that big house except for Missus Michaels. I need a wife. I need you." He cupped her face, his thumbs stroking her cold cheeks.

"Adam, if I married you now, everyone would be saying how I used you because Papa lost his badge and I lost my reputation," she said truthfully.

"I don't care what people would say."

"They wouldn't be too far wrong, Adam," she added grievingly. "I'm sorry, but—"

His eyes ignited. "Don't say it again. We've been all through that."

She looked away, eyes burning.

"I know you're not in love with me," he said more gently. "But I love you enough for both of us. Given time, you'll learn to love me. You have a strong affection for me now, don't you?"

"Yes."

"Do I repulse you?"

"No."

"We can talk easily about any number of things. All that's a good beginning, maybe better than being so caught up in emotion that common sense goes by the wayside."

Her cheeks flamed.

"And you've got to think of your father, Beth. What's he going to do now? He's too old for this kind of work. What else is there for him?"

Her mouth trembled and she put her hand to her forehead.

"You've got to make a decision now, Beth," Adam insisted. "What else is there to do? It's as though fate keeps pointing you to the way and you refuse to look at the road right in front of you. Beth, I want to take care of you and love you and make you happy again."

"Adam, please," she pleaded in protest.

He drew her forward and kissed her. Startled, she stood placidly in his arms, feeling his mouth move warmly on hers. He raised his lips from hers and held her more gently, nuzzling her hair. "It'll work if you give us a chance," he murmured, and she could feel how fast his heart beat beneath her palms. Yet, her own remained so unmoved. She felt no inner trembling excitement, no rushing of warm blood in her veins, no urgency of her body to become part of his. Yet she wasn't repulsed either.

Was he right?

Adam drew back. "Other marriages have begun with far less than ours will, Beth," he told her, deciding the matter for her. He knew she was too upset to think sensibly.

"How could I ever make you happy?" she asked.

"When you marry me, you'll make me the happiest man alive," he said thickly.

"But wouldn't you always wonder—"

His face stiffened. "It's over now. All that's in the past and we'll forget it ever happened."

"Over, Adam, but never forgotten," she said, lowering her head. "The relationship with Logan ended that day, but..." She looked up, eyes welling with tears again. "Oh, Adam..."

"Passion isn't love, Beth," he told her softly. "A solid foundation of friendship and common interests and shared laughter and learned trust has to come first before passion can really mean anything, and all those things we have." He kissed her gently. "The rest will come, I promise you." He wasn't totally without experience.

"I don't know what to say," she said wearily.

"Say yes."

She looked up at him solemnly. "It's all so complicated."

"No, it isn't. It's only complicated if you make it so. It's the easiest thing in the world to accept love." He held her shoulders and shook her slightly. "One word, that's all. Yes. Think about that big front yard at the end of Elm Street just waiting for your green thumb."

She laughed, but there was a deep ache beneath it. "We couldn't be married immediately," she said, giving in to the comfort of his caring.

His eyes glowed. "August, then. Six weeks away."

"But that's so soon."

"Forget the gossips. They'll talk whatever you do."

That was only too true, but the reminder had pierced her sharply. "August," she repeated. She felt no joy, not as she had when Logan had asked her to marry him.

"We'll speak with your father as soon as we get back," Adam said, taking her hand and putting it beneath his. "I don't imagine this will come as any great surprise to him, and he shouldn't have any objections." He chuckled. "He rather started the whole courtship himself, didn't he?"

"A bit of gentle prodding," she agreed. She looked up at Adam. "If you change your mind . . ."

"Never, Beth," he assured her, and he lifted her hand and kissed it as they walked together. "We're going to go right down Main Street. By the time we get to your cottage, the whole town is going to know everything just by looking at my face." He grinned. "I want the whole town to know I love you."

People did stare as they passed. Jessica Polk came out to stand on the boardwalk before the butcher shop. "Hello, Doctor Buchanan. How are you today?" she said after casting Beth a scathing look and then ignoring her entirely.

Adam smiled and patted Beth's hand, still curved on his arm. "Better than I've ever been, Missus Polk. By the way, that ham there in the window is just about the right size to settle up your bill with me. Why don't you have it sent down to the Tyrell cottage? We're celebrating this evening, aren't we, darling?" he said to Beth, ignoring the flaming color of humiliation that flooded Jessica's face at the mention of her overdue bill.

They walked on. "That was cruel, Adam," Beth said softly. "She's so very proud."

"I'd say it was only what she deserved after how she treated you the morning you came in for a chicken a few days ago."

Beth glanced toward the cottage. Her step faltered and she froze inside. Her father was standing outside the gate talking to Logan on horseback.

"It's alright, Beth," Adam said softly. "Just keep your head high and hang on to my arm. I'll do all the talking."

Frank saw them coming and told Logan. Logan turned and stared at them as they crossed the street.

Beth met those blue eyes boring into her. "Relax, Beth," Adam murmured as her fingers dug into his forearm. He put his hand over hers possessively and looked up at the big man in the saddle watching them. Logan looked at him, and Adam felt a touch of cold fear. Then Logan looked down at Adam's hand on Beth's.

"Are you alright, honey?" Frank asked.

"She's just fine, Frank," Adam answered for her. He glanced down at her and saw she was staring up at Logan. "She's agreed to marry me."

A muscle jerked in Logan's cheek, and for the barest second his eyes darkened.

No one uttered another word for several uncomfortable seconds. Frank stared at them both with open mouth, then looked up at Logan with an expression that could only be a warning. Adam looked at the two men, his hand firm over Beth's. He could feel her tremble violently.

"Congratulations," Logan drawled, and he tightened his legs and walked his roan stallion down Main Street.

Beth closed her eyes and felt her heart squeeze up into a tiny, hard ball of hot pain.

Frank looked at her. "You're sure this is what you want, Beth?"

Adam's mouth tightened.

"It's nothing against you, Doc," Frank said quickly. "It's just that it's a little soon after, well, hell, you know what I mean!"

"I can make her happy," Adam said angrily. "That's what you want, isn't it? All we need is your blessing, Frank, not your reservations."

Frank looked at Beth's pale, strained face. "Beth?"

"I know what I'm doing and this is what I want," she told him, meeting his eyes.

"Then you've both got my blessing."

"Good," Adam said, smiling more easily. "It's all settled, then." He kissed Beth's cheek. "I missed an appointment earlier when I came looking for you. Talbot Henderson's having some lung trouble again."

"What about the ham you're having sent?" she asked, smiling up at him weakly.

"You go ahead and have dinner without me. I'll be by when I can." He kissed her lightly. Beth blushed when she looked at her father's face. They were all still standing right in view of the main street of town, after all.

Adam grinned down at her.

Her father opened the gate pointedly.

Beth hesitated, watching Adam cross the street. Her gaze drifted to the man drawing his horse in at the hotel.

"Aren't you going to wave to your fiancé?" her father asked roughly, and Beth realized that Adam had raised his hand to her when he glanced back. She lifted her own to him and forced a bright smile.

Frank didn't say another word until she was inside the cottage and he had closed the door behind them. "All a little sudden, isn't it?"

"Not really. He asked before."

"And you've always said no or put him off. Why did you say yes this time, Beth? Because I'm out of a job and the town wants to take the house back?"

"Partly," she admitted, gazing up at him half-ashamed.

"What kind of answer is that?"

She flinched. "Papa, I care very much for Adam. I admire him and respect him. We can talk together and laugh together. I can trust him." Her eyes glimmered and her last words hung in the air with a deeper message.

"But are you in love with him?" Frank asked softly, arms at his sides.

"No."

"Does he know that?"

"Yes."

"And he won't object to sleeping with another man in his bed while he's making love to you?"

Beth's face went hot. "Papa!"

Frank sat heavily in his easy chair and leaned his head back. "Just a few weeks ago I was praying for just this to happen," he sighed. "Now I'm not so sure."

Beth clasped her hands and sat down on the edge of the settee while meeting his eyes in pleading. "Why do you have to change your mind now?"

"Because I think you're reacting to everything that's happened. You're sacrificing your happiness to put a roof over our heads."

She heard the pain and self-accusation in his words and shook her head. "Adam and I will be happy together," she assured him quietly.

He leaned forward intently. "When Adam waved to you, you didn't even see him. Why not? Because you were looking down the street at Logan, that's why! Isn't that the truth? What does that tell you, Beth?"

"That I'm a fool," she whispered, hanging her head.

"No," he said gruffly. "Never a fool. You're still in love with the man, and that's why you can't marry Doc!"

Her eyes sparkled. "How many times in the past have you yourself told me to put my childish dreams away? And now, when I do, you object. Adam said it, Papa. Passion isn't love."

"The two go arm in arm," Frank said, leaning back again, his expression grim.

Color came and went in Beth's face. "Not this time, Papa." She spread her hands, palms up, on her knees. "I still hurt inside from the way Logan used me. I don't think I'll ever get over that hurt as long as I live," she admitted brokenly. "Could I love a man like that still?"

"You could and you do," Frank said flatly.

"Then I'll just have to get over it."

"It isn't that simple. You don't just stop loving someone."

"I'm going to give my love to someone else," she said, a faint lift to her chin. "I wouldn't want to marry a man who could use someone to hurt someone else. That's what he did, Papa. He used me to hurt you. How could I ever laugh with him or trust him again after what he did? No." She shook her head, certain. "I'll be better off with Adam."

"Logan cares about you, Beth."

A shock of yearning so intense shot through her that her muscles tensed painfully. "He has a strange manner of showing it," she said solemnly. "Words are very cheap. What a person does is what speaks the truth of his nature. And Logan's actions were vile."

"But not without reasons. Damn deep, hard reasons."

Her eyes filled. "What harm did I ever do to him, Papa, but be born a Tyrell?"

He had no argument for that.

They sat in silence, neither looking at the other, both deep in their own thoughts. "I should begin supper," Beth said, standing up slowly.

"What if I could work out some arrangement with Logan so we could keep this place after he becomes sheriff?" Frank suggested. "Would you still go through with marrying Doc?"

"When I said yes, I was giving my word."

Frank leaned back heavily in his chair again and closed his eyes. He didn't need to ask any more.

Beth crossed the room and pushed the kitchen door ajar. She paused. "When you see Logan again, Papa, will you please ask him something for me?" she said softly without looking back.

"Anything you want, honey," Frank said gruffly.

"Ask him if it'd be alright if I dug up my bulbs," she managed in a quiet, broken voice before she went out of the room.

Frank could hear her muffled sobs for a long time afterward.

Chapter
Nineteen

FRANK WATCHED BETH while Adam visited with her. He
had no doubt she liked Doc very much, respected and even
admired him as she had said, but there was no glow in her
eyes when she looked at him. When she smiled, it wasn't
with the warm spontaneity he remembered her showing
Logan. Adam wanted to go out on the porch. Beth hesitated, and Frank could guess why. Adam wanted to kiss
her. It was obvious in the way he kept touching her.

They went outside and Frank could hear the creaking
noise of that damn swing. It slowed and stopped altogether.
He held his breath and leaned his head back, wincing. Beth
was going to make the same mistake her mother had. She
was going to marry one man and be in love with another.
He had to do something to prevent it from happening.

The swing began creaking again, and he could hear their
low voices. If Logan left town and never came back, they
might stand a chance to have a good marriage. But if he
stayed, it would all end in grief. Logan was too much like
he had been all those years ago with Beth's mother. Jeal-

ousy and love would drive him to bloodshed.

Beth came in at a little past nine. Adam said good night and left. She sat for a few minutes in the parlor, then excused herself to go to bed. Frank knew she was resigning herself to everything. It showed in her shadowed eyes and pale cheeks.

Her bulbs! What was Logan going to say about that? Frank wondered grimly. He was pretty sure, after seeing Logan's face when Beth had crossed the street with Adam Buchanan, just how deeply ran his feelings.

Frank waited until well past ten before quietly pulling on his worn leather coat and going out.

He stood outside on the porch, listening for Beth, but he hadn't disturbed her. He went down the front steps, cursing under his breath when one squeaked. It was a sad state of affairs when a man had to sneak out of a house because he was afraid of what his daughter would say.

Pausing outside the gate, Frank felt his pockets for his tobacco pouch, then cursed again under his breath. God, what he wouldn't do for a smoke. Doc wouldn't allow it. A tipple of whiskey and that was it. But how could a man get by on that? He was better off dead if he couldn't enjoy living.

He crossed the street, breathing in the cool, fresh night air thankfully. It was the first time in weeks he'd had a lungful outside the confines of the cottage or the front yard perfumed by Beth's flower garden. All that sweet scent was fine and dandy, but he craved the smell of smoke and whiskey.

Entering the saloon, Frank grimaced at the music coming from the piano. Picker was pounding it again with all the finesse of a blacksmith shaping a horseshoe. Some evenings he seemed to avenge himself on drunken listeners. When patrons grew tired of the noise, they threw empty bottles at him. McAllister especially. On Monday nights.

Logan was sitting at a back table, a bottle of whiskey in front of him. His shoulders were hunched as he lifted a full glass to his lips. He saw Frank and his face tightened.

Frank crossed the room, saying hellos to those who called out greetings to him. He winced as he watched Logan toss off the whiskey as if it were water. The bottle was half empty, but when Logan looked up, his blue eyes were stone cold sober. They met Frank's briefly before lowering to the glass still in his hand. He poured himself a refill.

"Logan, we've got to talk."

"Leave me the hell along, Frank. If I wanted company, I'd've invited you," Logan growled, not looking up again.

Frank drew a chair over and sat down. He rested his forearms on the table. "You've got to talk to Beth."

Logan didn't say anything, but a muscle clenched along his jaw.

"She's going to make a big mistake, Logan."

Still Logan said nothing.

"Tell her how you feel about her," Frank said gruffly.

Logan lifted his eyes and glared across the table. "Just how do I feel, Frank?" he asked derisively.

"Like someone's eating your guts out," he said grimly. "Don't think it's going to get any better. Every time you see her with Doc, it's going to get worse. And if she goes through with it and marries him, you'll think about them in the same—"

"Shut up!" Logan grated, his eyes dark, his body rigid.

Frank just looked at him for a long moment, then sighed heavily. He felt his pockets out of habit and swore. Logan took out his tobacco pouch and papers and tossed them on the table. "If you want a drink, get yourself a glass," he said tonelessly.

"I need a drink," Frank said, and signaled a girl. When she left he poured himself a modest measure. He nursed it for several minutes as they sat in glum silence.

"What're you going to do?" Frank finally said.

Logan finished his whiskey and set his glass down again. "About what?"

"The job you've been offered. Beth. Yourself."

"Haven't thought about it yet." He rolled the glass between his palms.

Frank tapped tobacco onto paper and rolled it, licked it, and sealed it. He stuck it in his mouth and felt his pockets again. He swore, the cigarette bobbing in his tight lips. Logan took out a match and dropped it on the table.

"Thanks," Frank muttered, and struck it with his thumbnail, leaning into it so the small flame reflected on his craggy face. He took a deep, grateful drag and eased back into the chair. "Well, you'd better think about it."

Logan poured himself another glass of whiskey.

"You going to accept the job?" Frank pressed.

"Haven't decided."

Frank knew Logan was deadening himself to everything. He didn't want to be plagued with thinking right now. But time was wasting, and Frank knew something had to happen. He leaned forward again. "Beth asked if she could please dig her bulbs up before we leave the cottage."

Logan slammed the glass down, sloshing whiskey over his hand. He scraped back his chair violently, breathing hard. Picker stopped playing the piano and looked back over his shoulder nervously. Taylor stopped wiping the bar. Cardplayers stared.

Logan grabbed the bottle of whiskey by its neck, his hand so white Frank was sure it would shatter. There was no doubt Logan was feeling something now. He bent down and said in a low, thick whisper, "If I do take that Goddamn job of yours, I won't take the house that goes with it! You tell her that!"

Others went uneasily about their own business, casting wary glances at the two men.

"Sit down, Logan," Frank told him quietly.

Logan stood rigidly above him.

"Better the noise down here than the quiet in your room," Frank added.

Logan slouched into his chair. "Leave it alone," he warned Frank darkly.

"It's not so simple as that," Frank muttered.

Logan's face tightened. "I'm not discussing Beth."

"They want to get married in August."

Logan's eyes blazed.

"She's not in love with him and you know it!" Frank snarled, leaning forward again.

Logan's expression became veiled. He poured more whiskey.

"For God's sake, Logan, go easy. What good's that going to do?"

Logan laughed low, without humor.

"You can't let her do it, Logan," Frank pleaded. "If you talk to her, she might change her mind."

A muscle locked in Logan's cheek. "No. I don't think so," he drawled slowly.

Frank swore softly and stood. "You let this happen, and you're more of a fool than I ever was." He stalked over to the bar and leaned his elbows on it, talking to Taylor.

Logan got up, took the bottle of whiskey and his glass, and headed for the stairs. Frank glanced across at him and frowned.

Tina blocked Logan's way. She smiled. "Turning in early, Logan?"

He gave her a mocking half smile, stepped around her, and went slowly up the stairs.

Frank watched grimly as Tina followed him. Logan wasn't going to solve anything that way either.

Logan had no sooner closed his door than Tina opened it and sauntered in, closing it again.

He watched her through narrowed eyes. "I don't remember inviting you up here."

"I invited myself. You look in need of female company." She took the whiskey bottle from him and set it on the commode.

"You'll have more luck downstairs."

"Oh, I don't know," she said seductively, and began unbuttoning his shirt. She glided her hands in and combed her fingers into the dark, curling mat of chest hair. He moved away from her and went to the window. Drawing the curtain back a little, he looked out on the quiet street below.

Tina sat on his bed and loosened the front of her dress so that it hung open, displaying her large breasts. "I can help you forget all your troubles, Logan."

"I don't think so," he said flatly, letting the curtain drop back into place and facing her.

She pouted. Leaning back on her elbows, she arched her back slowly and moved her shoulders so that her breasts jiggled. "How do you know if you won't let me try?"

He looked at her coldly and came around the bed again to pour himself another drink. Why couldn't he get so drunk he'd pass out? Then he wouldn't think or feel anything.

Tina lay back and extended her hand and trailed her finger down the button-fly of his pants. "Why don't you take your gun off and lie down beside me?"

He gave her a sardonic look. "I only take my gun off when I'm courting."

Her eyes cleared and held his. "Did you take it off with Beth Tyrell?"

"Get out of here," he snarled through his teeth. He moved away from her again.

"People like you and me get by just fine," she said. "It's got to do with how many men you've shot and how many I've laid."

"I said get out of here!" His eyes were dark and hot.

She stood up very slowly. "Alright, Logan, but before I go, I've got something to say to you." She pulled the front of her saloon dress together and tied the ribbons. "Now, I admit I'm not much, but I've got feelings about certain things still. You can do anything you want with me and ride away without looking back once or feeling guilty and I won't care. But if you're thinking of going after Beth Tyrell again, I'd like to change your mind."

Logan's hand clenched and his face went stony.

"I know I'm not good enough even to say her name, but I'm going to this once," she said. "I heard what you did and why you did it. Now me, I can understand that kind of hatred. But she couldn't understand it in a million years, Logan, because it's just not in that girl to hurt anyone for any reason." She came a step closer. "You know something? She's the only lady in this whole damn town that ever smiled and talked to me. She did it right in Halverson's store in front of two ladies who wouldn't even look at me. She's done everyone in this town a good turn sometime, and now they won't even let their children look at her when she passes."

Logan turned away and shut his eyes, his fist up against the wall, his shoulders hunched.

"Word has it now that Doc wants to marry her," Tina went on solemnly. "Now, here you are getting drunk, and Frank comes in to argue with you about something. I don't know what you're thinking, but I'm asking you to leave that poor girl alone. She didn't deserve what you did to her." She came closer. "She's got a chance now of a good man and a good home and children. God knows, Beth Tyrell deserves all of that if anyone does."

"No one knows better than I do, Tina."

"Then leave her alone."

After a moment, she turned away and went to the door. She glanced back at him as he leaned his shoulder against the window frame, his hand holding the curtain out slightly as he looked down the dark street outside.

"You got yourself good and caught in your own trap, didn't you, Logan?"

He said nothing.

"Well, if you need a little comfort, you just nod in my direction. I may not even charge you." She went out the door and closed it softly behind her.

Chapter Twenty

"McAllister's back in jail," Frank said from behind the town newspaper.

Beth glanced up from sewing her pale apricot wedding dress. Adam had been furious with her when she flatly refused to wear white for the ceremony, but had finally given in when she looked close to tears after his tirade.

"Why don't you make him some stew and dumplings tomorrow?"

Beth lowered her eyes. "I don't think so, Papa. Meals are being sent over now from Rinaldi's Restaurant." Logan was now sheriff.

Frank lowered his paper. "Logan told me McAllister asked expressly for your stew and dumplings. He's been running his tin cup on the bars."

"Do prisoners have their say in what they're served?" she countered, still not looking up.

"Some do. He's an old friend, Beth, not just a prisoner."

"Alright, Papa," she said quietly.

Frank looked at her solemnly. It would be the first time she'd faced Logan since Adam had walked her home from the river and stated his plans. If she needed prodding, he would do it. God knew, Logan wasn't going to make a move. When he wasn't on the job, he was on his property. "Logan's building a cabin up on Kilkare's hill," he said casually.

Beth glanced up but didn't respond. She bit down on her lip and tried to concentrate on her shadow embroidery.

At a little past nine, Faraday Slate came by. "I gotta talk to Frank," he told Beth, his young face pinched. "It's important, Miss Beth."

"Come in, Faraday."

"No, ma'am. I gotta talk to him private."

Frank came over. "What is it, Faraday?"

"It's my pa."

Frank took his leather coat down from the hook by the door and put on his hat. "Are we going far?"

"No, sir. Just right outside. You don't need your gun."

Beth frowned as they went out. She followed them onto the porch and watched them stand and talk quietly outside the gate. Faraday was talking fast and was obviously very upset. Her father's head came up once in surprise; then he listened intently and nodded his head, a hand on the boy's shoulder. He glanced up. "I'm going to the sheriff's office, Beth."

He didn't return until late. "Everything alright, Papa?" she asked when he came in. He grunted. "Is Mr. Slate back in jail again?"

"He oughta be hung, but no. He's gone."

"Gone?"

"Rode out. Seems he joined company with that Ramos bunch that hit the stage line a few days ago." He raked a hand back through his gray hair after taking off his hat and putting it on the hook again. If there was anything those men needed to know about the layout of Kilkare Woods, Slate could tell them. Damn traitorous bastard. Seemed Slate had been behind the rustling out at Pine Ridge as well.

"Is his wife alright?" Beth asked, standing up and helping him off with his coat.

He grunted again. "Doesn't know when she's been blessed."

"I'll go round and see her tomorrow, Papa."

Frank sat down in his chair. "I'm too tired to even take my boots off. I must be getting old."

Beth came over and lifted his foot. She slapped the toe of his boot and pried it off for him. Then she removed the other. She bent and kissed him on the forehead. She drew back slightly and gave him a reproving look. "You smell like you've been smoking." She smiled. "And I'd bet you even had a couple shots of whiskey."

He gave her a sheepish smile. "You'd win."

"Did you put Faraday up to getting you this evening?"

He shook his head. "No." He was spent. A walk down to the sheriff's office and back and a few hours of man talk and he was exhausted. Another few months of getting his health back and maybe he could manage again, but he wasn't going to be a heck of a lot of help if trouble hit before then. And it seemed fair to certain it would. "Adam come by this evening?"

"He's on his way to the Whitsetts to deliver a baby," she said with a smile.

Frank grinned. "How's Charles?"

Her dimples showed. "He looked a little frantic when he arrived here."

He chuckled and pushed himself up. "I'm going to bed," he announced. He glanced back at her before he closed his bedroom door. "Don't forget that stew for

McAllister. He's counting on you. Said he wouldn't come out of that cell until you fed him proper."

Beth carried the tray down the next day, a few minutes before noon. Her heart was pounding faster the closer she came to the sheriff's office. She prayed Logan would be at the hotel having lunch. Balancing the tray on her hip, she started to open the door. Someone was opening it from the inside, and she uttered a startled gasp as the tray tipped. Logan's hand shot out and caught hold of it, his hard fingers brushing hers and sending heat up her arm.

He stared down at her. "What're you doing here?"

Her face flamed. "I . . . Papa said . . . McAllister . . ." she stammered, seeing he had neither expected her nor wanted her there.

"Miss Beth? That you?" McAllister shouted from the cells in back. "By heaven, I been waiting and waiting!"

Logan's brows drew down in a dark line. "You already had your breakfast, McAllister! Shut up back there!"

Tin sang against steel bars.

"Damnit," Logan muttered under his breath, exasperated.

Beth's mouth twitched. "I'm sorry, but Papa let him get away with it too long. He won't stop until he gets his stew."

Resigned, Logan opened the door wider. "You shouldn't be here."

She glanced back at him from halfway across the small sheriff's office. "Why not?"

He left the door wide open. "It's a jail. That's why not. A lady doesn't belong in a place like this."

She laughed in faint disbelief. "I used to do my school-work at that desk." She nodded to where his hat lay and went back into the cell block to slide the tray under grizzled old McAllister's door as he rubbed his hands together and thanked her profusely. "Ever tasted Miss Beth's stew and dumplings, Sheriff?" he called, his mouth full, as Beth returned to the office.

"Can't say I've had the pleasure," Logan drawled, looking down at her again. She raised her eyes and met his and he felt sharp pain go through him. He wanted desperately to reach out and drag her into his arms. "How are you, Beth?" he asked softly.

She didn't try to dissemble. "Getting by," she murmured, and looked away. She should leave, but she wanted to linger and talk to him.

"People talking to you?"

"A few." She glanced up at him. "Papa said you're building a place up on Kilkare's hill."

"That's right." He straightened and walked around the desk. He shoved some papers around because if he kept looking at her he was going to say or do something he'd regret. "I'll send the tray down to you when McAllister's finished licking the plates." His words came out curt and dismissing.

She made a soft, pained sound that brought his head up. She nodded once and went quickly out the door. He leaned both palms on the desk and closed his eyes tightly.

"Hey? Miss Beth?" McAllister hollered from the back. "How's about another big helping?"

"She's gone, McAllister."

"What'dya say, Sheriff?"

"I said *she's gone!*"

"Well, you don't have to get so damn mad 'bout it."

Logan took out his tobacco pouch and rolled himself a cigarette as he listened to the cowhand mutter in his cell. Someone was running on the boardwalk. Logan stood abruptly to see what was happening as Faraday Slate ran in. The boy stood trying to get his wind back while jabbing his finger toward the other end of town. "Seen 'em," he got out. "Eight of 'em down by the river. Had some Double C cattle."

"Head on down to the livery stable and have them saddle my horse," Logan ordered.

Faraday hightailed it out. Logan snatched up the keys and went into the back. "When you finish eating your stew, let yourself out," he told McAllister, and tossed the keys between the bars to the old cowhand. "Take the tray back to Beth and say thank you nicely, then give the keys to Frank."

"Trouble?"

"Rustlers."

"Which ranch?"

"Carlile's."

"I'll ride with you." McAllister grabbed up the keys and unlocked the door, swinging it open. He tossed the keys onto Logan's desk as they went out.

Logan knew John Bruster was in an upstairs hotel room and the two men headed there. "Livery stable, now!" Logan shouted through the door. He heard Bruster swear and a woman's voice say, "Just pull up your pants again, Johnny. You still got your boots on."

Faraday had two horses waiting when Logan and McAllister reached the stable. Faraday mounted one before a word could be said. Logan recognized the look on the boy's face. He wasn't going to be left behind. "You'll need me to show you where," he said.

Logan nodded. Fourteen was young, but the boy was proud, and he'd make sure the boy's head was down if there was shooting. Logan had another horse saddled for McAllister.

When they reached the river, there was no sign of the rustlers, but their trail led up toward the southeastern hills. The tracks indicated two riders had herded the cattle while six others had broken off into two separate groups. Logan grew uneasy.

Avery rode toward them. Logan didn't like him but knew it was for personal reasons concerning Beth rather than for any flaw in the man's character. Avery grinned broadly as he drew his horse in and around. "Those bastards ran like hell the minute they spotted us."

Logan's unease deepened. "Which way?"

"They split up." Avery frowned. "What's the matter, Tanner?"

"They're playing with us," he snarled, and swung his horse around sharply, spurring it into a hard gallop back toward town. Avery caught up.

"What in hell's going on?" he shouted above the thundering hooves of their animals. McAllister was close behind, flapping his hat wildly and shouting to keep his horse apace. Bruster, two of Avery's cowboys, and Faraday followed.

"There were eight. Six split off while the two ran with the cattle. I think those six doubled back and met up and are riding into town right now!"

Avery swore. "This way! It'll get us there quicker!"

Logan hoped Beth was inside the cottage or in the back tending her vegetable garden.

They heard gunfire as they rounded the last bend toward town. Logan whipped his horse faster, lunging out in front. A woman screamed and his heart stopped, but a flash of russet as he passed the cottage set his mind at ease.

People were running down the street. Horses were outside the bank as men poured outside and leaped to saddles. Two carried saddlebags. They spotted Logan and started firing again. Avery's horse screamed and went down, sending Avery over its head. Bruster barely missed riding him down.

His horse in full galloping stride, Logan drew his gun and fired. One of the men with a heavy saddlebag sagged sideways and fell from his horse. Another shouted and started to dismount to help him, but the others headed hell-bent for leather toward the other end of town. They separated, going up side streets.

The hesitation of the outlaw outside the bank was all Logan needed to reach him. He dove from his horse, taking the man off his. They hit the ground with a spine-jarring thud and Logan dragged him up.

"Tanner!"

Logan slammed his fist into the man's mouth as he recognized the opaque eyes. The outlaw dropped into the dust and lay still. Logan went across to the man he had shot. He was sprawled on his back, still clutching the saddlebag. His eyes were open, staring up, blood pooling around his head from the hole between his eyes. Logan pried the saddlebag loose and picked up the other. He flung them up the stairs to skid at Daniel Claybeck's feet.

"Anyone hurt?"

"Missus Polk fainted; otherwise everyone's alright, Sheriff," Daniel replied, pushing his spectacles up on his thin nose with a shaking hand. He bent and retrieved the saddlebags, trying not to look at the dead man in the street.

Logan dragged the half-conscious outlaw up by his shirt and shoved him toward the jail. "We thought you were dead," the man snarled back at him. Logan shoved him again, harder. "You'd better let me get on my horse and ride out unless you want more of what you got before, Tanner." This time, Logan swung him around and hit him again. Then he grabbed his arm and hauled him up over his shoulder and strode toward the office, his mouth set in a hard, white line.

He dumped the man onto a cell bunk and slammed the

barred door. He slammed the thick oak door that separated
the cells from the sheriff's office and then tried to slow
down the hot, rushing blood in his body by taking deep
gulps of air.

Half a dozen men were shoving their way into the sheriff's office, all talking at once. "It's all over. Go on home!"
Logan told them, but they were too excited and caught up
in it to hear.

"You going after the rest?"

"That was some fine shooting, Tanner. Clean between
the eyes!"

Frank Tyrell pushed his way through the throng and
studied Logan.

"They won't be back!" Someone laughed. "Got 'em
clean as a whistle as they came out the door, Frank!
Should've seen it! Scared them clear to kingdom come."

"Get out of here! The fun's all over!" Logan boomed,
his face dark with emotion. Frank stood by as the others
retreated, grumbling and casting confused, angry looks
back at Logan before he slammed the heavy door in their
faces.

"I'd say you did a fair day's work," Frank remarked,
glancing out the window and seeing the undertaker and two
men carry the body off the street.

Logan strode across the room and began shoving papers
around, looking for something. He swore.

"What's eating you, Logan?"

Logan jerked his head toward the door. "They love it,
don't they? Killing gets their blood up. Even the women.
Eyes glowing all hot." He swore again. "A quiet little
town, but it's no different than anyplace else."

"An affliction of the human race."

Logan found what he was looking for. "Have a look,"
he said grimly, and thrust the paper at Frank. Frank took it

and his brows rose. "He wasn't in that bunch," Logan told him, "but that's his kid brother I've got locked up back there."

"Jesus," Frank muttered, face paling. "We're in for more trouble."

"I'd guess a little," Logan said sardonically.

Frank glanced up. "How do you come by knowing him?"

Logan's laugh was short and cold. "I had a little run-in with him near Yuma about two years ago. A slight misunderstanding over how he dealt cards. His brother didn't like the way I publicly embarrassed a member of the family, so he and a couple of his friends ambushed me as I was leaving town. They thought I was dead when they left me there. I damn near was."

Frank looked at the dark, glittering blue eyes. He tossed the wanted poster and watched it drift back and forth to the desk. "What can we expect from Kane?"

"The unexpected," Logan said grimly. "He's crazy."

"You going after him?"

"No. Tried that before. He finds a rock and crawls under it and stays there until he's ready to come out. But I've got his pissant brother back there. This time I'll wait until he comes to me."

"What about the town?" Frank asked, frowning. "A lot of innocent people could get caught in the crossfire."

"You trying to suggest I turn that bastard back there loose? You've been out of it too long, Frank. He'd come back into this town with his brother just for the fun of shooting someone."

Frank sighed heavily. "You're going to have to get some men in on a plan then."

"As soon as I work one out," Logan said, rubbing the back of his neck.

Chapter
Twenty-one

BETH SAT WITH Adam in the back pew as Charles and Susan Whitsett stood at the front near the altar, their new son, Harding Whitsett, wrapped in a crocheted blue blanket and sleeping in Susan's arms. Pastor Tadish took the baby and said the words of baptism before putting water on the peaceful infant's head. Screams rent the quiet of the church.

"You'd think he was getting circumcised," Adam chuckled.

Charles winced as he stared down at his red-faced son, whose mouth was open as wide as it would go in howling rage. He fidgeted nervously and looked at Susan to do something as he ran a finger around his collar. Pastor gave the baby back to Susan. She held him close, soothing him, and the screaming subsided so that the unified response of members of the congregation could be heard. Soft laughter rippled through the church as the young couple took their seat in a front pew.

Adam took Beth's hand and smiled down at her. "We'll be standing up there in a few weeks getting married," he whispered.

She looked up at him and smiled. He kept looking at her and she frowned in question. He leaned close. "I'll handle pregnancy a little better than Charles." Hot color surged into her cheeks, and she lowered her head quickly.

Logan had come to church. He arrived a few minutes after the service began and sat down in the pew opposite Beth and Adam. He had glanced at them once and then not looked at them again. He didn't sing the hymns, nor bow his head for the prayers, but he wasn't wearing his gun. He had taken it off, rolled his belt around it, and set it on the pew beside him.

When services ended, Adam put his hand at her waist. "We'll go out this way," he said, nodding toward the side of the church rather than the center aisle. She knew he was keeping her as far from Logan as he could, and she acquiesced. Glancing back she saw her father had crossed the aisle to talk to Logan as people filed out of the church.

Outside, people took refreshments from the long, linen-covered tables. Logan came out. Several young women twittered together, casting interested looks in his direction. Rachel Whiler, Tammy's pretty sixteen-year-old sister, took a cup of coffee and some cookies to him while others giggled and watched. Cynthia Claybeck approached a moment later while casting her father a nervous look.

Logan grinned at the two young women and said something to them that made them blush and laugh. Beth looked away, feeling a sick pain in her chest. Time would come when it wouldn't bother her to see him charming other women. Time would come when she wouldn't remember at all how it had felt to be with him.

But how much time would pass before she could feel at peace with herself again?

Susan and Charles were surrounded by people, everyone wanting to get a close look at the baby and hold him. Susan kept him in her arms. Beth was nearby but didn't approach, not wanting to cause embarrassment to either of them. Adam had been drawn into conversation with Maddie Jeffrey, who told him about her aunt who was suffering from indigestion due to consuming too much rich red meat. Beth stood by, listening but not trying to enter the conversation. She felt Logan's presence at the gathering though he was more than twenty feet away. She kept her gaze carefully averted from him.

"I think he needs to be fed," Charles said as he and Susan came closer. Beth peeped at the baby and saw him sucking his fist, but stayed back.

"Charles, for heaven's sake, he's sleeping," Susan said, laughing. She walked to Adam. "See what you did, Adam?" she said, tilting the baby up proudly so he could get a clear look.

"He does look a lot better than the red, wrinkly bundle I last saw," Adam teased. "And don't go blaming me for handiwork your husband did, especially when he's standing right next to you."

Susan grinned. "Which reminds me. Thanks for keeping his body and soul together," she said, casting Charles a laughing look as he colored. "He fainted once, didn't he?"

"He did just fine." Adam smiled, patting Charles on the back. "And he'll do better with each baby."

"Lordy, I hope so," Susan sighed, her eyes merry. "For just a minute there in church when Harding started crying, I thought I was going to have to change *Charles's* pants," she whispered. Her amusement softened as she gazed back up at her glowering husband.

Neither had spoken to Beth.

Susan exchanged a look with Charles and he nodded. Susan stepped close to Beth. Beth looked at her and smiled shakily. "Hello, Susan." If Susan didn't answer, Beth was afraid she would cry right there before everyone. Susan leaned forward, and Beth's eyes went wide with alarm. "We want you to hold Harding first, Beth, before anyone else gets their hands on him." She held the baby out, a reassuring, warm look in her eyes as she met Beth's.

Stunned, Beth took the baby gently in her arms and pressed him close. She looked down at the precious sleeping face, with its rosy cheeks and tiny puckered rosebud mouth. Her throat squeezed tight and hot and her eyes filled up. She knew what Susan and Charles were doing. They were making a public statement of their continued friendship and belief in her. She could hear whispers rustling through the gathering as people stared. She glanced up, and the first face she saw was Logan's as he stared at her from across the space of green grass, the young women still surrounding him.

Almost blinded by tears, Beth gave the baby back to Susan. She tried to say something and couldn't. Adam put his hand against the small of her back and whispered something to her, but she didn't understand. Susan looked ready to cry herself. Beth put a trembling hand to her forehead and turned away. Head down, she wove her way quickly through the staring crowd and almost ran to the church gate.

"Beth!" Adam called, and she knew he was coming after her, but she wanted so desperately to be alone, to sort out her emotions. She darted between the Miller and Clarendon houses and cut across the back of the school yard toward the hills. She took the long way around to the river.

She sat on a flat rock for a long time, her head buried in her arms. She got up and walked along the bank. Stooping, she picked up a stone and tossed it. Concentric circles swirled outward and finally disappeared. The pain was like that. It had been an explosion inside her that first day, but gradually it would dull and dull and then ease out into calm again.

Someday she would see Logan without feeling as though her heart had been torn out of her. Someday she would be able to look at him, to smile and speak to him, and feel nothing but what she felt for any other man in town.

Someday she would love Adam.

She wept.

When she emerged finally from the grape ivy thicket, a man stood waiting for her. Her heart leaped, then slowed again as Adam came toward her. "Are you alright now?" he asked gently.

She wanted to cry all over again at the tender concern in his eyes. "Yes, Adam, thank you," she whispered, and lowered her gaze, unable to hold his.

He tipped her face up and kissed her. He drew her close. "I love you, Beth." He kissed her eyes and cheeks and lips again. She wanted to pull away. His hands tightened and moved down, drawing her against his body. She felt a sense of rising panic and fought it down.

What was wrong with her? This man would be her husband. He would want more than a few kisses. She would lie with him in bed, give herself to him, bear his children, grow old with him.

"Open your mouth, Beth," Adam groaned. "God, let me kiss you."

She tried to respond, but when he took her mouth, what her mind dictated, her body instinctively rejected. She pressed her hands against his shoulders and turned her face away. She could hear his heavy breathing, and rather than exciting her as it had with Logan, she felt repulsed and frightened by his passion for her.

"I won't force you," he said quietly, keeping her locked in the circle of his arms.

"I'm sorry," she cried softly, leaning against him again. Why couldn't she be attracted to him? He was handsome, well built, a wonderful, kind man. He was gentle, giving, compassionate, and he was as strong as Logan in different ways. Why did her body come to life at Logan's touch but remain cold at Adam's?

"Don't be sorry, Beth," Adam whispered, kissing her temple, kneading her tense shoulders. "It's going to be alright. It'll come. When we're married, I'll show you. A doctor knows a lot about a woman's body. I'll know how to make it wonderful for you."

Beth was mortified and uneasy at Adam's disclosure. What did he mean? That there was some magic place that he only had to touch to make her respond? With the proper physical stimulus, she would become passionate? If what he'd said was meant to reassure her, he had failed.

Adam sensed her distress. "I'm not talking about doing anything unnatural, Beth," he told her, tipping her chin again.

"I'm afraid to ask what you do mean," she admitted.

He laughed softly and kissed her again. "Trust me." He put his arm around her shoulders, drawing her close as they walked. She felt someone watching them and glanced up toward the hills. A man sat astride a restless horse beneath the shade of an old oak.

Logan!

How long had he been up there?

He turned the horse away and disappeared over the rise. Beth kept walking, the weight of Adam's arm on her shoulders. She hardly listened to what he was saying and had to force herself not to look back at the hill where Logan had been.

Shortly after Beth arrived home, the sky clouded over. By six that evening, it was raining. A drip started in Beth's small bedroom and she put a pan beneath it. Adam came for Sunday dinner. Missus Whiler came at eight saying little Tammy was ailing. Adam kissed Beth at the front door and left.

Her father was unusually quiet. He sat in his chair, staring at the rain streaking the windows, the Bible open in his lap. "It's a bad omen, isn't it?" he said once.

Beth sat on the settee, her legs curled up beneath her tan skirt as she worked on her wedding dress. Her father began to snore, his head thrown back against the chair, his mouth slightly ajar. She smiled, listening to him. She awakened him at nine.

"You should go to bed, Papa."

He laughed softly. "You mean I ought to get up from sleeping here and go and sleep in there?"

Beth heard the gate click and thought the wind and rain must have blown it open. She'd have to go out and relatch it so it wouldn't bang. Footsteps came up the stairs and she glanced around in surprise. She crossed the room, and when she opened the door she found a man standing on the threshold cloaked in a long buckskin cape, his hat pulled low over his face. Water still ran from his black, silver-banded hat. He pushed the hat up. Beth stared into blue eyes.

Frank came to the door to see why she was standing there. "Logan!" He drew Beth aside. "Let him in before he drowns."

Logan smiled wryly, shook himself like a dog, and shrugged off the cape as he stepped inside. "Thanks." Frank took the hat and cape and hung them on the hook. Logan shrugged out of his leather jacket. "Just checked everything out. It's quiet. No sign of trouble."

"Anything unexpected in the works, you think?" Frank asked in an odd tone Beth didn't understand. She looked at them both.

"I don't think so. Bruster and one of Carlile's men are down at the sheriff's office keeping an eye out."

"Why don't you make some hot coffee, Beth?" Frank suggested, seeing how she had moved uneasily away to stand before the fire. She was staring fixedly at the silver star glistening on Logan's chest, and he figured she was thinking about a whole lot of things she had best forget if she was going to be happy.

"Alright," she agreed, drawing her eyes away and looking at her father's worried face. She forced a smile. "It'll be but a minute."

She could hear the low rumble of their voices as she worked in the kitchen. She sliced beef and cheese and bread, reasoning that it was the proper thing to do. Logan looked thinner to her, and there were new lines about his eyes. It was wet and cold outside tonight, and he was doing the job her father had done for all those years. Papa had always been hungry when he came in and had welcomed something hot to drink to wash it down.

Logan was standing with his back to the fire, but he looked at her as she entered carrying the tray. Something about his eyes made her heart pound hard and fast. What was he thinking?

She set the tray on the narrow table in front of the settee and glanced at her father. He was looking up at Logan, then at her. His gaze dropped to the tray and his eyebrows shot up. She straightened, too embarrassed to hold his half-amazed, all-too-knowing gaze.

"She's made you something to eat, Logan."

Logan looked at her intently. "Thanks," he nodded, and came away from the fire. Beth sat down in the straight-backed chair as he sat to eat. He saw the pale apricot wedding dress on which she had been working. His face tightened and his eyes narrowed as he took it up. "Here," he said, and tossed it to her.

She gasped as it floated into a rumpled pile across her lap.

"Is that any way to treat a lady's wedding gown, Logan?" Frank reprimanded, secretly satisfied.

Logan ate the meal in silence and sipped the hot coffee. Frank looked at Beth perched on the edge of her chair, her fingers unconsciously plucking the apricot material.

Logan leaned back and tossed the napkin onto the tray. "That was good. I was half-starved. Thanks, Beth."

"You're welcome," she said flatly, staring down at her hands rather than looking at him.

Frank glanced at them grimly. Logan didn't look away from her, but sat in brooding silence, a muscle working in his cheek. "Frank, I'd like to talk to Beth—alone, if you don't mind," he said quietly.

Beth's eyes came up, wide and frightened.

"Alright," Frank drawled, and put his hands on his knees as he pushed himself up. "I'm tired anyway. Way past an old man's bedtime."

"Papa, please don't go."

"Good night, both of you," Frank said, lifting his hand slightly but not looking back at her. He went into his bedroom and closed the door firmly behind him.

Logan leaned back and rested his arms on the back of the settee as he looked at her. She stared back warily. He let out his breath very slowly and stood up. His gaze still holding hers, he bent and untied the leather strap around his hard thigh.

Beth's heart thundered.

He unbuckled the gun belt and wrapped it around his gun carefully, then walked to the fireplace and placed it on the mantel. He turned back and looked at her steadily. "We'll talk in the kitchen."

Her mouth was dry. She shook her head. "We can talk right here."

Logan's eyes blazed. "The kitchen and now, unless you'd like me to carry you there."

Beth stood up shakily, still unconsciously clutching her wedding gown. He nodded at it. "Leave that here or I'll stuff it into the wood stove."

"Logan . . ."

He walked toward her and her body tensed. She backed up a step. She put the dress down and he picked up the tray from the coffee table. "After you," he said softly.

She went into the kitchen and pressed back against the counter as she watched him set the tray down on the table. His presence had been overwhelming enough in the comfortable little parlor, but in here she felt trapped.

"I saw you down by the river with Buchanan this morning," he said, raising his head and looking at her.

"Yes. I know." She swallowed hard. "I saw you as we were coming back."

His face tightened. "When you ran out of the churchyard, I followed you," he admitted, coming slowly around the small table and leaning back against it as he looked at her. "Why did you run away?"

She clasped her shaking hands together and shook her head, her throat closing up.

"Why, Beth? People are starting to come round again."

Her eyes burned.

He left it and went on to what ate at him more. "You don't like him touching you, do you?"

"I . . ." She looked away from him. "I won't discuss Adam with you."

"Buchanan touches you and you freeze solid as a block of Sierra ice. I could see that all the way up the hill." The pain he had felt watching that doctor kiss her hit him again in the stomach. So did the rage. He clenched his hand. "It wasn't that way with us, Beth."

"Don't," she said in a hoarse whisper, her eyes over-bright.

"You'd like to think you can just forget all about it, put it behind you, pretend it didn't mean anything."

Her chin came up, her face very pale. "It meant something, Logan. It meant absolutely everything to me!" she said brokenly, eyes glimmering. "But it didn't mean anything at all to you except a means to an end. That's what hurts. I can forgive what you did, because I know now what happened all those years ago and what drove you, but I can't forget, Logan. I can't. I don't want you in my life anymore, not in any way."

"I'm in it whether you like it or not," he said grimly, aching for what he saw in her face. "I can't be plucked out and thrown away like a milkweed in your damn rose garden."

"I just want you to leave me alone," she whispered, mouth trembling. "Please, just go away. . . ."

"No," he said flatly, and straightened. "You don't love him, Beth."

"I can given time. I like him. I have great affection for him. I admire him and respect him. I can trust him." Why did it sound like such a meaningless litany to her ears?

Each thing she said was like a whip on Logan's back because he knew she was listing what she could no longer feel for him. Yet, he sensed a deeper truth, too. "It's not enough."

"It's been enough for others," she said firmly.

"You were waiting for something more."

She flinched. "What I found I can do without."

"But you're never going to forget how it was any more than you can forget me," he said harshly. "Beth, I was going to marry you. That was no lie," he said hoarsely.

She drew back. "But not for the reasons I thought," she

said. "You made love to me that day to make me *belong* to you, and you would have married me to get back at Papa. Those were your reasons, Logan."

He couldn't deny it and didn't. "It wouldn't have stayed that way for long," he said, and came close. When she backed away from him, he caught hold of her shoulders. Her muscles retracted at his touch, and he grew angry. "You think with a ring on your finger you'll be able to let Buchanan touch you without drying up inside?" he demanded harshly. "You think you're ever going to be happy with him?"

"I won't talk of this with you," she said, closing her eyes tightly and shaking her head. She balled her hands into tight fists, fighting the feelings stirring in her at Logan's closeness.

"I wonder how you're going to feel when he gets into bed with you and starts putting his hands where mine have been."

She gave him a stricken look and tried to pull free.

He held tight to her. "It won't be tender kisses in an open field then, will it, Beth?" She pushed at him, and he forced her back against the wall. "It'll be in earnest then. No high-necked dresses, corsets, tiers of petticoats, pantaloons. Just you. Naked. Under him!"

"Stop it!" she choked.

"Are you going to be as warm and willing with him as you were with me?" he demanded, relentless. "Or are you going to die a little inside every time he takes you?"

She was breathing fast and shallowly, her throat burning as she struggled frantically to free herself. Driven by his own emotions, Logan forced her chin up, flattening her body back with his own as he took her mouth. Her body contracted violently. He remembered piercingly the first time he had kissed her like this, and he didn't want the same panic and fear in her now. He wanted her to remember how it had been on Kilkare's hill when she'd surrendered herself to him. She was still his. Even if she married another man, it wouldn't change that.

Logan braced his forearms against the wall on either side of her head so she couldn't turn away. Easing his weight from her, he used his mouth instead to remind her of what they'd experienced once before. She felt so good. She tasted so good. He wanted her so much and had for so long that he thought he was going mad. Seeing her with Buchanan had almost driven him to violence.

He felt her body move and heard the softly moaned whimper just before she opened her mouth to him. He groaned and took what she offered, demanding more, his desire fueled by all the weeks he had been without her. He pressed against her again, rubbing seductively, and her body arched instinctively into him, turning his loins to fire and making his blood roar through his veins.

He'd made love to her like this before, manipulating her by his own experience. He knew he couldn't do it again. She deserved better. She deserved a choice. He wanted everything to last this time, not for the few minutes of ecstasy that going into her now would give them both, but for the rest of their lives. He wanted to wake up in the same bed with her every morning for the rest of his life.

Her body was trembling. He kissed her gently, slowly, trying to batten down the hard passion that burned in him. Raising his head, he looked down at her.

Her face was pale and distraught, and her wide, tear-glistening eyes looked up at him briefly before she turned her head away and closed them tightly.

"No!" he said raggedly. "Listen to me!" He forced her to look at him again. "You can't marry him! You're still in love with me. Doesn't what you're feeling now prove it?"

Her mouth quivered. "We don't suit one another. We never did."

He drew back sharply, angry, and spread his hands over her breasts, feeling how fast her heart was beating. "What's this then? Nothing?"

Her face convulsed.

He knew he was doing everything all wrong and didn't know how to right it. His own feelings were lacerated. Guilt had torn at him for taking her the way he had, premeditatedly and without marriage. Then guilt when he saw what the town did when they heard what had gone on. Seeing her with Buchanan had twisted his vitals. He wanted Beth so fiercely he felt he was fighting for his life.

"Beth," he whispered hoarsely.

She shook her head, her face tear-streaked. "You didn't want to feel anything for me, Logan. Be honest with yourself if not with me. You fought against any gentleness inside you. You fought against forgetting, or trying to learn another side of what happened all those years ago. You fought against putting it aside and going on with your life." Her voice broke, and she swallowed hard before going on.

"There were moments when you looked at me as though you hated me, and I could never understand why. Now I do. It was all mixed up with your father and mine. But all you ever really wanted was a way to feed your hatred, a way to keep it going on forever. That's why we would never work, Logan. You've lived your hate for too long. It's what kept you going, taught you what you know, made you what you are. That's what I can't abide. It's how you hung on to that and let it control your life. It's your guns and your violence. Even in this," she said, and cupped his face between her small hands. "You even bring violence to this. You make a war rage inside you."

He felt the tremor in her hands before she lowered them again. "What're you really saying, Beth?" he demanded. "If I hang up my gun you might consider me a possibility?"

His attack hurt, and she knew he didn't understand any

of it. She shook her head. "It doesn't matter anyway, Logan. It's too late. I've promised to marry Adam."

He forced her chin up. "You were going to marry me!"

"You didn't ask. You ordered. And we both know why."

He lowered his hand slowly. "All that's over and done with now."

"No, it isn't," she said softly, seeing she was going to have to say it all before he could ever understand. "Between you and Papa, yes, but not all the rest, Logan." She put her hand on his chest. "The other day when you killed that man, it didn't matter to you. You hardly looked at what you'd done. You just stepped over him and picked up the money bags and tossed them back to Mister Claybeck. You'd taken a human life, and that didn't even touch you."

She put her trembling hand over her eyes. "I keep thinking about you and the way you must have lived and how you're going to go on living." She lowered her hand and looked up at him. "As long as there are men like you around who live by their guns and for nothing but violence, there's never going to be any peace for the rest of us. Never! And since the choice is mine, I'd rather live with a man who saves lives than with one who takes them."

A heavy, strained silence fell between them.

She bit down on her lip, the tears still running down her pale cheeks. She swallowed hard and then said in all truth, "A part of me will always love you, Logan." She swallowed again. "But I don't think it's the best part."

He moved back and searched her face carefully. Then he left the kitchen.

She had seen what was in his eyes and drew an agonized breath before closing her own. Turning quickly, she went into the parlor after him. "Logan?" she said softly, aching inside and more confused and unhappy than she'd ever been before.

He stood at the fireplace, buckling his gun back on.

When he raised his head after tying the strap around his thigh, his expression was dark and defiant. What had been there before was gone. He strode to the door, shrugged on his leather coat, took down his hat and buckskin cape. "Thanks for the food and coffee."

He turned away, then came back again. "One thing," he said flatly. "You're going to live with him, but you're never going to love him no matter how hard you try. Not in the way you did me, Beth. You're going to pay for that and so am I, and so is Buchanan, him probably more so than either of us. And all that because of your brand of morality!"

He slammed out the door.

She went across slowly to the window and drew the curtain aside, feeling like the weeping night outside. She watched Logan swing the cape around his shoulders as he left the gate banging open behind him. He strode down the dark, wind- and rain-swept street, heading for the sheriff's office.

She wasn't wrong about him, but it didn't change anything at all. She wondered if it ever would.

Chapter
Twenty-two

"YOU'RE A HUNDRED miles away this morning," Adam remarked as he sat with Beth on the porch swing. "What are you thinking about, Beth?"

She shook her head. "Something I have to work out for myself," she murmured, glancing up at him sadly.

"A couple more weeks and we'll be married, then your problems become my problems," he reminded her, his expression an assessing one. "Are you worried about the plans to stop the outlaws if they come into town?"

She looked at him sharply. "Might they come back?"

Adam's brows flickered. "Well, your father and some of the men in town have met with Tanner to discuss a plan should the gang come to free Kane's brother from jail."

Beth looked away, disturbed. Why had her father mentioned nothing of all this? She had thought it was over.

"They probably won't come," Adam said, taking her hand.

Beth kept thinking about the guns firing and Logan

shooting that man right between the eyes. How many might be killed if that gang came back again? Logan? Her father? Some innocent bystander such as a child?

Adam leaned toward her and kissed her. Everything stopped moving inside her while his mouth played gently on hers. He drew back slowly and studied her. "Talk to me, Beth. What's bothering you?"

She clenched her hands in her lap and looked at them. "I think it might be a good idea if we postpone the wedding."

His face tightened. "Has Tanner been bothering you again?"

She sighed and looked away. "Oh, Adam, I'm just not sure of anything anymore, least of all myself."

"You were ready to marry me a few days ago. Did one conversation with Logan Tanner last night change your mind?"

He had every right to be angry and upset, and part of her wanted to say she would go ahead with the wedding. Yet another part of her plagued her about their life together. She couldn't forget what Logan had said before he walked out. Nor the way he had looked at her just before he left the kitchen. He was implacable and self-possessed, a gunfighter, and she had told him the truth. But even after that, she wondered if she could go ahead and marry Adam still feeling as she did for Logan.

"I don't know what to do anymore," she whispered thickly.

"What'd he say to you?"

"How did you even know he came by? Did Papa tell you?"

"Nothing happens in this town that I don't hear about. Jessica Polk told me this morning during her appointment that she saw Logan Tanner coming out of your cottage at well past ten." He suspected that was the reason she had come to the Elm Street office, and he had charged her outrageously because of it.

"Warning you about what you were getting into, I guess," Beth said sadly.

"I want to know what Tanner said to you."

She looked at him, clear-eyed. "I don't discuss you with him, and I won't discuss him with you."

"There's a difference here, damnit. You're going to marry me!"

His imperious manner made Beth bristle, but understanding smoothed her annoyance.

"He came to change your mind," Adam accused harshly. "And he did, didn't he? I'm curious what kind of tactics he used on you."

"Adam!" She stared at him. "I haven't changed my mind," she said carefully. "I'm just worried that . . ." That what? That she'd never forget what it was like to be kissed and held by Logan? That she did freeze up inside when Adam touched her? That she felt she was betraying both men at the same time? It made no sense. She should be thinking only of Adam now, and Logan shouldn't come into her thinking at all. But he did. Just as he had said, he was in her life whether she wanted him to be or not.

Why had it ever happened the way it had?

"Worried about what?" Adam pressed.

"That you're never going to be sure of me because of what I shared with him," she said truthfully, and saw him wince. "Worried that I'm never going to be able to have your complete trust or make you happy because of that."

"Is that what he said?"

"Please," she whispered. "Leave him out of this."

Adam stood, causing the porch swing to lurch. He went to the rail, his hands gripping it as he stared down the main street of town. "Damn him," he muttered, and wished the man would get on his roan stallion and ride out of this town for good. Adam knew Beth was confused. He knew she was far more than that.

Every time he was with her, he saw it in her eyes, felt it when he kissed her. When he held her, he felt something inside her retreating from him. All of that would go away given time and intimacy and a life together—and if that damn gunfighter would stay away from her and leave her in peace.

Adam turned. "Do you have errands this morning?"

She nodded slowly. "I need eggs and some oxtail for soup."

"I'll go to Maddie Jeffrey's and the Polks' with you." He held out his hand.

They talked little. Adam carried her basket in one hand while weaving his fingers firmly with hers with his other. Possession is nine-tenths of the law in this land, he thought wryly, and then thought on that again. Maybe he should stop acting the perfect gentleman and show her how he really felt about her.

When they returned to the cottage, Adam came inside and set her basket down. He drew her into his arms decisively. She stiffened, her eyes going wide.

He kissed her, then drew back, drawing her even closer.

"Adam—"

"Relax your muscles, Beth. God, we're going to be man and wife. . . ."

When he kissed her again, she willed herself to relax her body against his. It was enough to encourage him further. She felt his arms tighten, pressing her breasts against his chest. He slanted his mouth hungrily across hers and she tensed. He cupped her head. "Don't clench your teeth," he groaned, taking her mouth again.

She kept thinking of Logan's words: "You'll die a little inside every time he takes you."

She let Adam part her lips and tried to kiss him back as he wanted.

"It'll be in earnest then, just you as God made you. Are you going to be warm and willing . . . ?" Logan had attacked.

Adam's hands moved down her back to her waist, then lower. He caressed the back of her hips suggestively, pressing them closer to his. She could feel his desire ascending, her own descending. She kept reminding herself that she was going to marry him, but it didn't help. She felt him take pins from her hair and the weight of it loosening the rest. Panic set in. She dragged her mouth away. "No, Adam, please . . ."

"I only want to feel it down your back." He raked his fingers into it and drew her head back so he could look at her. She was frightened. He closed his eyes and kissed her again, determined to make her feel more.

Beth's heart thundered, but not with wanting him.

He drew back again, breathing hard. "I ought to give you more time," he said raggedly against her temple. "I ought to let you work everything out first so you're sure this is right." He kissed her again, then put his mouth to her throat. "You're confused, I know." He kneaded taut muscles. "But I need you, Beth. I'm not a monk. I can't wait forever. None of this is going to sort itself out until we're married and can get on with our lives."

Was he right? Was she postponing the wedding only to nurse her doubts? She had none where Logan was concerned. She had been truthful with him when she said she couldn't marry a man who lived for violence, that she couldn't forget his face after he had killed that man in front of the bank. How could she ever have believed that she had touched him in any way that mattered, when he could cut a man down without a blink of his eyes, and then stand over the lifeless body without a single sign of remorse? And if she was certain of all this, she was a fool not to follow her common sense and marry Adam. Worse, she was cruel.

She believed in peace and in caring about others, and it was her heart that rode at the head of her confusion. She knew what Logan was, and still she had fallen in love with him. He would never change. He didn't want to change. He clung to his way of life. He was a man of violence, a man who had made violence and death the central part of his existence. He went against everything she held to be right and true, everything she struggled to live by, everything she tried to be.

And there was no confusion about that at all.

No, if she could be honest with herself, there was no confusion about what she must do.

"If thy right eye offend thee, pluck it out, and cast it from thee: for it is profitable for thee that one of thy members should perish, and not that thy whole body should be cast into hell," Christ had said.

And if it meant casting away her love for Logan, so too must she do that.

"We'll leave things as they are, Adam. We'll be married in August," she agreed softly.

He let out his breath joyously. "Now you're making sense!" He drew her firmly into his arms and kissed her the way he wanted to.

The front door clicked open and they broke apart, both embarrassed to be found in such a manner.

Frank entered and looked at them, shocked. He stopped, his expression going placid as he looked from Beth's flushed face to Adam's half-challenging one. "Good morning, Adam," he said coolly.

Adam drew Beth close. He leaned down. "You'd better go fix your hair," he whispered against her ear. Her hands flew to it. Appalled, she turned away quickly and left the room. Adam was gratified that she hadn't seen the man standing just behind Frank, nor the look on his hard, bronzed face.

Logan entered slowly. Buchanan met his eyes, his body instinctively tensing at the dark anger glowing from those glacial blue eyes. "Tanner." He nodded in acknowledgment. Logan said nothing. His face said it all.

How could gentle Beth ever have fallen in love with such a man? Adam wondered. He was a devil.

"No patients today, Adam?" Frank asked, stepping between the two men.

"Not until ten." Adam took out his pocket watch and snapped it open. "Getting near that now."

"I'll tell Beth," Frank said.

Adam frowned. Was Frank telling him to leave? Or was he trying to keep Logan from starting trouble right here in the parlor? Better to face the man down now over Beth than to let it go on. "I'll wait until she can see me to the gate," he said, snapping the watch closed and tucking it back into his vest pocket.

"You can see yourself to the gate," Logan growled.

Adam stood his ground. "I'll wait," he repeated, thinking she would need support when she came back and found Logan Tanner standing in the middle of her parlor.

He was right. Her eyes went wide and her face paled when she saw him. Adam would have been more pleased had her gaze touched him first rather than fixing on the other man. He came to her and took her hand. "I've got to get back, Beth," he murmured, regaining her attention.

"Yes, of course," she stammered, and glanced at Logan again before her gaze dropped from them all entirely.

"Walk with me to the gate," he ordered softly.

Logan barely gave them room to pass, but Frank closed the door behind them. He flicked the door curtain aside and glanced out at the couple going down the front steps. "I see you and Beth got a lot settled last night," he remarked, dropping it back into place grimly.

"Shut up!" Logan snarled, turning away. "Let's get to the business at hand."

Frank shrugged. "Suits me." He laid out the town map on the dining room table and they tried to discuss the plans concerning the outlaw gang, but Logan was distracted. He kept glancing toward the door.

"You're going to have to keep your mind on your business, Logan," Frank told him impatiently.

"What is my business?" Logan snapped, and raked a hand back through his thick, dark hair. He walked to the front window.

"When was Kane sighted?"

"Three days ago in Los Angeles," Logan said without interest. He was staring out the window through the sheer lace curtains. "Got a wire about it."

"Goddamn it, Logan. Get your head clear of Beth. You've got something else to deal with first. When that's finished, worry about your other problems if you're alive to handle them."

"Good advice," Logan said, turning away from the windows and coming back. But after a few minutes, Frank knew Logan wasn't concentrating on the map. His expression was turned inward. Frank had a sick feeling in the pit of his stomach where it was all going to end.

Beth opened the door and Logan straightened sharply. She kept her head down, not looking at either of them. Frank looked at Logan's face, then bowed his head grimly and rubbed the back of his neck. "Make us some coffee, Beth."

She left the room quite willingly. She almost fled. Logan took a step after her, then stopped short. He swore under his breath, turned away abruptly, and crossed the room. He snatched up his hat and headed for the front door. "We'll talk later," he grunted, and slammed out of the house.

Frank went into the kitchen. "Forget the coffee. He's gone."

Beth's hands lowered slowly from the coffee grinder and rested on the counter. She didn't look back at him or say anything.

"I said I would stay out of it," Frank said gruffly, "but I can't. Are you sure you know what you're doing marrying Doc?"

"Yes, Papa," she said softly.

"You're not in love with him, Beth. Any fool alive can see that."

"I love him in a way that will last longer."

"You look me in the eye and tell me that!"

She turned slowly and raised her head, her eyes overbright with moisture. Her mouth worked. She closed her eyes.

"Adam's a fine man," Frank said quietly. "And he loves you. He'd take good care of you, but what about how you feel about Logan?"

She put a hand over her eyes. "I don't want to talk about all this now, Papa," she said tremulously.

"You've got to!"

She flinched at his sharp tone, then lowered her hand and looked at him again. "He's no different now from what he was the day he rode into Kilkare Woods."

Frank slammed his fist on the counter and swore. "What do you want from him? He made a mistake."

"Papa, I don't want him to do anything. I just want him to leave me alone."

"You think that'll make any difference? If he left now and didn't come back for years, you'd still feel the same about him."

She turned away. "I don't feel anything."

He forced her around again. "That's the first bald-faced lie you've ever told me," he said grimly.

"Don't . . . Papa, please . . ."

"I've got to," he said thickly.

"You want me to be with a man who can feel no remorse at all when he kills someone?"

He let her go. "Is that it? Or just your current excuse? You listen to me," he growled. "What would you have had him do? That man had just led a gang of outlaws into our bank and stolen the life savings of half this town! He was trying to kill Logan. Now, you expect him to feel sorry for cutting down an animal like that? Was he supposed to ride up and turn his other cheek?"

When she tried to look away, he caught her shoulders. "There's something you'd better remember. I was just like Logan. No better, maybe worse."

"You changed."

"I changed," he growled. "But why? You think about that, too, and what made it happen. I killed a man in cold blood because I caught my wife in bed with him."

She drew a soft gasp. "Is that what you think is going to happen with me, too, Papa? That someday I'll be unfaithful to Adam with Logan?" She shook her head. "No! Never! I'm not like she was!"

"Don't you ever use that tone about her," he said, shaking her. "Your mother was human! Nothing more, nothing less. She didn't plan what happened between her and Tanner. It just happened. You're no damn different from any of the rest of the human race," he said, letting go of her. "You may not make her same mistake, but you're making your own. A worse one! You're marrying someone you don't love *knowing* you're in love with someone else. There's always going to be that part of you that belongs to Logan. You tell me who's the real cheat!"

Beth hung her head, her shoulders shaking.

He knew he should stop there, but he couldn't. He saw too much of what had happened before happening all over again. So he cut in deeper. "Something else you'd better consider. There's going to be trouble. Big trouble. Logan can handle what he has to if he's got his mind on what he has to do."

"Kill, Papa?" she cried shakily.

"He can't think straight because of you."

"If I could make him give up his gun, I would!"

"I don't want him to give up his gun, damnit! If he does that, this town is wide open and blood's going to spill. I just want him to be able to think! The man's raw because of you!"

"That's not fair!" she cried.

"You're not hearing what I'm telling you. I'll make it plain and simple so you understand. You're going to get Logan killed."

He knew he didn't have to say any more. He left her standing in the kitchen alone because he couldn't face the look in her eyes.

Chapter
Twenty-three

BETH THOUGHT OF little else but Logan all afternoon.
Adam sent word that he was going to Avery's ranch to set a
man's leg.

She served her father supper but could eat nothing herself. He raised his head several times and studied her
grimly. He regretted some of what he had said. Too much
truth could tear a person to pieces. He stood up. "I'm
going on down to the hotel for a whiskey and some talk,"
he told her.

She nodded, her eyes haunted.

Frank paused at the front door as he buckled on his gun
and put on his hat. He glanced back. "Something could
happen to him anyway, Beth."

"I know that, Papa," she said huskily.

The cottage was silent after he left. Beth sat for a long
time at the table. When she got up, she cleared the dishes
away, washed them, and put them away. She came back

into the parlor, but she didn't feel like working on anything, certainly not the wedding dress that still needed the
special last touches.

She wanted to talk to Logan.

He seldom left the sheriff's office now, and when he
did, it was to take his meals and sleep a few hours at the
hotel. Even if she did go to see him, she didn't know what
she could say to change anything, nor how she could face
going down that boardwalk through town, past all those
windows. Everyone would be talking and Adam would be
hurt again.

Yet, she couldn't bear to stay in the cottage. She took
her shawl up from the back of the settee and went out for a
walk. She knew exactly where she was going, heading
along the road out of town and up toward the hills.

It would be past dark when she got there, but it didn't
matter. She wasn't afraid of old Kilkare's ghost.

She saw Logan's cabin through the trees as she came up
the hill. He had built it not far from the old oak tree where
he had made love to her. She stopped and studied the
small, rough-built house. No lantern shone in the window;
no smoke curled from the rock chimney. Logan wasn't
here.

She entered out of deep curiosity. His home was spartan: a bed against one wall, a small table and straight-
backed chair, hooks on the wall, and a roughhewn cabinet
hammered to the right of an open-hearth fireplace. No rug
warmed the wooden floor. No curtains graced the small,
open-eyed windows.

Standing at one, she could see Kilkare Woods in the
distance. From Logan's window she could see the road
entering town and the side streets. Lanterns glowed in a
hundred windows and smoke curled up from a hundred
brick chimneys. From Logan's window, she could see her

father's cottage at the edge of town. A deep, wrenching sadness filled her.

"Oh, Logan . . ." she murmured to herself, closing her eyes.

She sat in the straight-backed chair and looked around again. It was a good beginning for him, and there was a certain rough beauty in this house. Maybe he would stay and work cattle and never hire out his gun again. She could always hope.

Darkness filled the small cabin and left only moonlight streaming through the windows. She heard a dog howling somewhere—or was it old Kilkare's she-wolf mourning him?

She rose and went to the fireplace, where she bent and worked to arrange kindling and branches. She struck a flame and blew until it caught, then added an oak log. Exploring the cabinet, she found coffee. Looking around, she realized there was no bucket, no water.

No well.

She felt the stillness inside herself. Taking down the small bean grinder on his shelf, she set it on the table. She sat down again and ground coffee beans slowly, just to fill the small cabin with the rich homey aroma.

Why did she feel like crying?

The door swung open slowly and Logan stood looking at her. Seeing light in his cabin window, he had looked in cautiously, his gun drawn. Seeing who was there, he felt disbelief.

"I didn't know who'd moved in," he said, entering and closing the door. He glanced at the glowing fire and smelled the ground coffee. He looked at her, sitting in his straight-backed chair, her head slightly bowed, the soft folds of her tan skirt flowing about her, the lace demure about her slender throat. The fire glow lighted her pale cheeks. He remembered her dimples when she had laughed for him or when she'd smiled. He remembered her face when he had gone into her body and taken everything she had to give.

And what had he given her back? What did she have now because of him?

His heart felt like a stone in his chest. "Why did you come?"

She spread her hands, palms up, and looked at him. No words came, though he sensed she wanted to say something.

He left his gun on but hung up his hat on a hook by the door.

"I shouldn't have just walked in," she apologized.

He looked away and shrugged. "It's a little late for a walk. What brought you?"

"I . . . I wanted to see what you'd built."

He looked around the interior of the cabin grimly. He had been so proud when he had finished it, the first thing he had built with his own two hands. Now he saw it the way she must, little more than a line shack, probably worse constructed than anything one of her friend Avery's cowhands could do. No, there was nothing here to impress a woman.

"So you see it," he dismissed with a derisive wave of his hand.

"It's a beginning for you, Logan."

"It's nothing!" he said harshly, and walked the few steps to the fire to kick the log far back. "Does Frank know you're here?"

"No."

He glanced back at her sharply. "No?" She shook her head and sat with her hands folded in her lap. The soft glow in her eyes made his heart race and life come back into him again. After feeling dead so long, the pain was unbearable. "Go home, Beth," he rasped.

Her face grew pale and strained.

Logan felt his insides, knotting up. "If you're worrying about your father, I've got things planned out so he and the rest will be in covered positions. As long as they use sense and keep their heads down, no one's going to get killed when the shooting starts . . . except those that should."

The dark flatness of his tone sent a chill through her. A toll of death. But whose?

"What about you?" she asked softly.

"What about me? I'll be doing my job."

"Don't let anything happen to you, please," she whispered brokenly.

Raw emotion fanned his temper. "Just what do you want, Beth? You can't have it all ways. A few nights ago you said clear enough that as long as there are men like me around, there'd be no peace for the rest of you. How better to get rid of us who live by our guns than by pitting us against one another?"

She stood shakily. "I never meant I wanted you hurt or killed."

"That's what it does mean!"

"No!" She stood and came close. "Just take your gun off and live another way, Logan. Just stop."

He saw she really believed it was that simple. The gulf stretched wide between them. "Everything has a price, Beth. Peace is bought at the cost of human life. That's the way it's always been. That's the way it's going to always be."

Her eyes welled with tears. "Your life?"

He drew his gun and held it out in the palm of his hand for her to see. "Someone has to do the fighting. I'll do it because using this is what I do best. Because of what I am. You want peace, you hire a gun to get it for you and keep it."

He clenched the gun handle, pointing the barrel away from her. "The townspeople hired me for one thing. They knew what trouble was coming and they knew the only way to deal with it. Men like Kane and his gang understand only one thing, and that's six feet of dirt over their faces." Driven by his own pain, he mocked her faith. "Even the good shepherd who tends his sheep has to kill the predators that prey on them. Isn't that right, Beth?"

She put her hand out and pressed the gun down. "And where does it all end for you, Logan?"

He holstered it. "Probably the same way it will for Kane," he said indifferently, turning his back on her. He drew a ragged breath. "I've been wrong all this time. I should've ridden past you that day. You belong with someone like Doc, who's never held a gun in his hand, someone who knows death but has never caused it." He swore softly and turned to face her again. "You don't understand me, Beth. You don't understand anything about the way I've lived, and Jesus, God, I'm glad of it!"

He came close and cupped her face, his chest aching with what he felt for her, what he would always feel for her. "When it's over, I'm riding out. It'll be better that way. For you. For me. For that lucky damn son-of-a-bitch that's going to marry you," he said thickly. He let his hands drop to his sides.

"What about your land?" she asked, tears blinding her. "What about what you've started here for yourself?"

"What? This? I'm used to living in a fine hotel!" The mockery died. "What do I know about land or cattle? What do I know about anything but this?" He put his right hand over his gun.

"You could learn."

He gave a soft, disbelieving laugh. "Maybe someday, somewhere else." He opened the door. "I'll see you back safely."

He knew she was crying as they walked down the hill together. It was all he could do to keep himself from taking hold of her. He knew where that would end if he did, and then what would happen to her?

He clenched his right hand over and over. She had been right after all. She didn't belong with him. While knowing that, he could still sense what she was feeling as she walked beside him. She didn't want him to leave Kilkare Woods or old Kilkare's hill. God knew he didn't want to go, but he had to if she was ever going to be happy again.

As they came from the darkness of the hills toward the faint lantern light of town, he remembered the way she had been when he first saw her. Her eyes glowed. That glow wasn't in her eyes anymore, and it was his fault that it wasn't. It'd be even worse if he stayed.

When they reached the gate, Logan opened it for her.

She turned and put her hand out to touch him. "Logan," she whispered brokenly.

He heard everything in her voice. "Don't say anything, Beth. For God's sake, not one word." He left her standing there alone at the gate. Without looking back once, he strode away toward the hills.

Chapter
Twenty-four

FRANK LOOKED OVER the rim of his steaming coffee mug at Beth. "You look like hell this morning."

She smiled weakly and set his plate of scrambled eggs, bacon, and buttermilk biscuits down in front of him.

"Were you with Logan last night?"

She sat down slowly, too composed. "Yes."

"What happened?" he asked, setting his mug down heavily.

"He said that when it was over, he was leaving town."

"Did you ask him to?"

"No."

"What are you going to do about it?"

She just sat there, too still in herself. Frank frowned. "Eat something, Beth."

"I'm not hungry."

"Hungry or not, you've got to eat something. You're getting too thin. I've been expecting Adam to say something about it." He forked eggs into his mouth and watched her from across the table. Setting his fork down, he split the biscuit, buttered and jellied it, and put half on her plate. "What're you going to do about Adam?"

"Marry him."

He dropped his fork with a clatter. "How can you?"

"I gave my word." She looked at him beseechingly. "Before you say another word, I know you're right. And Logan's right. And Adam's right. And I'm right. Everyone is right, Papa. So"—she gave a soft cry, eyes welling with tears again—"there it is. Logan will leave and I'll marry Adam and maybe someday we can all be happy again." She stood, her mouth trembling. "I'll get you some more coffee."

He said no more when she came back.

Adam came at ten to escort her about town on her errands.

People were out talking in the warm morning sunlight. Faith Halverson was sweeping the boardwalk in front of her husband's store and calling across to Jessica Polk. Faraday was washing windows at the millinery. Beth's father was standing outside the hotel talking to several cowboys. Two wagons were being loaded down in front of the feed and grain. A buggy wheeled quickly down Main Street, a gray mare high-stepping.

"Beth, wait a minute, will you?" Avery called from the high seat. He stopped and leaped down, Edwina talking the reins and holding the horse steady.

"Don't you think you should park that thing, instead of just leaving it in the street?" Adam laughed.

"Have you told her anything yet?" Avery demanded.

"No."

"Good." Avery strode back to his wife and buggy, led the horse to a hitching rail, and tied it here. He lifted Edwina down. Taking her hand, he brought her up onto the boardwalk. Then he put his arm around her shoulders, hugging her against his side, grinning smugly. "Beth, we're going to have a baby."

Beth gasped. "That's wonderful!" she cried, laughing happily.

Edwina blushed. Avery bent and kissed her. "Avery! Not right here!"

"Why not? We're married!"

Adam was chuckling. "You planning on stopping by the newspaper office and publishing your news?"

"We're thinking about it." Avery grinned, unabashed.

Edwina laughed, eyes sparkling. "Why bother? Everyone's going to hear it from you in the next hour."

"Mother's damn happy about it," Avery told Beth. "Said it was about time."

"Well, you finally got things right, anyway," Adam needled suggestively.

"I'd say so. Now we've got the hang of it, it ought to be easier the second time. We're going to keep you in business, Doc."

Edwina was blushing. She moved away to talk to Beth as the two men discussed the new buggy and mare. Edwina smiled. "You know this means I'm going to need a whole new wardrobe, Beth."

Beth's dimples peeked through. "Oh, I'd say you have an excuse for a little indulgence this time."

Edwina laughed softly. "And a christening gown."

"I'd be honored."

Logan opened the door of the sheriff's office and came out. He looked down the boardwalk toward her. She felt her throat tighten painfully at the sight of him and forced her attention back to Edwina.

But Edwina had already noticed. She glanced over her shoulder at Logan, then looked at Beth again, frowning. "Beth . . ."

Beth put her hand out and took Edwina's. She shook her head, silencing her.

Logan crossed the street and went into the hotel.

Avery spotted friends in front of the saloon and hailed them. He grabbed Edwina's hand and brought her along with him.

"Doc!" Someone called. "Got a minute?"

Beth touched his arm. "Papa asked for tobacco, but I'm going to buy him peppermints. You go talk." As she turned away, she saw two riders draw up to a house at the south end of town. She didn't think she'd ever seen them before.

She went into the general store and bought a small bag of candy for her father. When she came out, she started to cross the street to meet Adam, but a slow-walking horse caught her attention, and the man sagging forward on it seemed ill or drunk. Somewhere in the distance, she thought she could hear horses coming at full gallop.

Beth put her hand up and stopped the horse. She came around the animal cautiously and put her hand on the man's arm. "Mr. Slate? Are you alright?"

He leaned forward very slowly and began to fall to one side. She uttered a gasp and tried to break his fall. She sank heavily, and he rolled onto his back on the ground. His face was distorted from a beating, and the front of his shirt was blood soaked. He stared up, dull-eyed, not breathing.

She screamed. "Someone help!" The horse shied and trotted off.

Adam was running for her. "Beth, get back!" Someone was shouting. The sound of galloping horses drew closer.

"Beth!" Adam shouted at her, trying to pull her up.

"He needs help!"

"He's dead!"

She froze, her head buzzing oddly, everything spotty as Adam dragged her up. Logan was there in front of her.

"Get her off the street!" he ordered. "Keep her down. Do you hear me, Buchanan? You keep her inside and safe. Now get going!" He shoved them toward a building and then gave a shrill whistle that raised the hair on Beth's head and made her want to cover her ears.

Everything was happening too fast. Adam was running her toward the boardwalk. She looked back and saw Logan's eyes blazing. "Stay down!"

"Logan!" she cried, shaking her head.

He ran toward her, seeing her frantic attempts to free herself. Grabbing her, he propelled her inside a building and shoved Adam inside with her. He slammed the door. She heard his running bootsteps as he headed away.

Adam pushed her further inside the building, which she realized belatedly was the O'Herlihys' bakery.

Mauve was hysterical. "They're going to shoot us! They're going to shoot us! What about my blueberry muffins?"

"Damn!" Adam muttered in frustration. "I need my bag. Someone's going to need help and I've got to get it!"

Patrick was shoving Mauve's head down behind the bakery counter. "Forget the muffins. Let them burn."

Adam pulled Beth behind the counter with them. "Stay here," he ordered tersely, looking toward the door. "I've got time to make a run for it. Stay right here and you'll be safe."

"Adam!"

"Stay here. I'll be back as soon as I can." He looked at Patrick. "I'll go out your back door. Keep an eye on Beth for me."

"Sure thing, Doc." Patrick's usual ruddy complexion was pale. Mauve was on her knees, reaching up into the cash register and stuffing money into her apron pocket.

Adam ran out the back door.

"He'll be alright. All the fuss is going to be out front,"

Patrick assured her. "Tanner's got it all worked out. Just stay down like a good girl. I can hear the bastards coming!"

Peering carefully over the counter, Beth saw masked men gallop by, firing randomly into buildings. Glass shattered in the bakery window. Mauve shrieked.

"You're not hit!" Patrick cried.

"They broke our window!" she wailed.

Beth gingerly pushed herself up to look across the counter again. She could hear wagons rolling and rifle fire, men shouting; a horse screamed. The masked men galloped by the jagged window again. She ducked as another shot thudded into the wall behind the counter. Mauve screamed and clasped her hands over her face.

All the conversations between Beth's father and the men who had come to the cottage these last few weeks jelled. They had blocked off the gang's escape from both ends of town. That's why she'd heard wagons.

Where was Logan? Was he alone out there?

The gunfire seemed louder. She heard a man cry out in pain. One of the masked men flipped backward off his racing horse. "I've got to see. . . ." Beth said half to herself, and looked toward the door that led to the stairs of O'Herlihy's upper-story rooms.

"You're going to get yourself shot, Miss Beth!" Patrick said, making a grab for her. She scooted around the end of the counter and ran for the door. Raising her skirts, she raced up the stairs and peered out their parlor window to the street below. She had a good vantage point from up there and could see the main street and several alleyways.

Mac Slate was still sprawled in the dust, the masked riders riding right over him as they tried to find a way out. They kept firing their guns. She saw Matt rise up from the hotel roof and fire a rifle. One of the outlaws grabbed his shoulder and bent forward.

Giving up on riding out, they dove from their horses for cover. Rifles blasted from several rooftops and upstairs windows, flicking up dust near the outlaws' hiding places. One was behind the watering trough a building down from the bakery. Beth could see him plainly. Another used his body as a battering ram to break open Maddie Jeffrey's front door and lunge in for cover.

The man behind the trough had a deadly aim. He ducked out and fired, hitting Antonio Sanchez, one of Avery's men. He sagged out a second-story hotel window and didn't move. A second shot from the outlaw's gun sent another man off a roof. He fell, hit the landing over the boardwalk, and dropped to the street, where he lay still.

What could she do? Friends were being killed. She ran across the room to the stairway. "Mr. O'Herlihy! Do you have a gun?" Perhaps she could fire near the outlaw and scare him off.

"I don't own one, Miss Beth."

She went to the back of the building to go down the stairs, and as she opened the door, she saw three gunmen coming down one of the sidestreets. They had come in the back way through the hills. One was signaling to the others as he dismounted. He ran between the shops and pressed his back against the wall as he edged his way toward the main street of town. His gun was drawn and he was grinning ferally.

Beth ran back to the front windows.

She saw Logan. He was working his way down the opposite side of the street, ducking from doorway to doorway to shield himself from the man firing from behind the trough. Rifles were firing from somewhere along Beth's side of the street. Glass shattered and paint and wood chipped off the millinery shop where one of the outlaws had gone in. The man fired back. She saw him raise himself up, jerk back, and fall. He didn't get up again.

The gunman who'd gone into Maddie Jeffrey's house came out with one of her children held in front of him as he fired. The child was screaming and crying in fear. He reached his horse and flung the child aside as he mounted. He yanked the mount around to make another try at escaping. Logan stepped out from the doorway, raised his gun shoulder high, and fired once. The man's arms went wide as he pitched off his horse and bounced off the boardwalk, rolling face down in the street.

Logan had to dodge back as the gunman behind the trough fired on him again. Wood chips flew from the doorframe as the man came close to killing Logan. Logan made a signal with his hand. Beth saw her father rise up from the hotel roof and begin firing one shot after another from a rifle, cocking it between each blast with amazingly swift jerks of his wrist. He was pinning the man down behind the trough so Logan could move closer. Each shot her father fired hit the trough, sending streams of water out into the dusty street. When he emptied his gun, he ducked down. The man rose to fire back. It was his fatal mistake.

Moving one more doorway down had brought Logan into better range. He fired. The outlaw fell backward, mouth ajar, eyes wide open, blood staining his chest.

Spine-tingling silence fell. It lasted only a few seconds before she saw men she knew standing up and shouting. Matt Galloway was up on the hotel, raising his rifle and cheering. Her father raised his as well, grinning broadly. McAllister was whooping from somewhere down the street. They had hemmed them in and picked them off once and for all.

They all thought it was over!

Beth tried to raise the window and warn them. It was stuck tight. She banged on it but no one noticed her. Frantically she turned and ran for the stairs that led down into the bakery.

"They got them, Mauve! They got 'em all!" Patrick was laughing, hugging her.

"No!" Beth cried. "Stay down!" She ran across the glass-covered floor and yanked open the front door of the shop. She ran out.

The alleyway where the other gunmen were hiding lay just two doors down from the bakery. Logan was up the street, stepping down off the boardwalk and striding toward one of the wounded outlaws. He took the gun and flung it a safe distance away.

"Logan!" Beth shouted. "Three more!" She turned and saw them surging into the street, the townsmen who were hidden before now clear targets. Matt Galloway. McAllister. Her father.

Logan!

"No!" she screamed, and ran into the street. "Get down!"

Logan's face went chalk white. "Beth, get off the street!"

But it was too late. She stood between him and Kane.

"Get down!" Logan roared.

She turned and looked into glowing, opaque eyes. The man heard Logan's shout and grinned as he raised his gun. She saw the flash and felt something strike her, catapulting her backward. She hit the ground and lay there, stunned, unfeeling, hearing Logan's cry of pain-filled fury and the sharp staccato blasts of a gun.

Chapter Twenty-five

"Beth!"

She lay in the dusty street, the sun blinding her, and heard Logan running toward her. A jumble of confused, excited voices came closer.

What had happened? She couldn't seem to move. A heavy weight inside her was pulling her down into a dark haze. She felt warm wetness oozing from her side.

"Buchanan!" Logan roared, coming down on his knees beside her.

"Went for his bag," she managed thickly. She blinked slowly, her vision cloudy.

Logan looked so frantic, his face white, his eyes wild, as he shouted again. He looked down at her body. "Damn you, Beth! Why did you come out into the street?" he railed at her, his face wet as he bent low over her. She felt his hand, hard and pressing against her ribs just below her breast. "Buchanan!" He swore hoarsely.

She stared at Logan helplessly, feeling it hard to breathe

at all with the fiery pain growing. She drew a rasping breath and coughed, tasting blood. His face convulsed.

"Get back, everybody," Adam shouted from the outer ring of people. He shoved his way through and hunkered down beside her.

"Where in hell were you, you son-of-a-bitch?" Logan raged across Beth. "Where were you? I told you to keep her safe!"

Adam's face was white and pinched. "Take your hands away so I can see the wound." Beth's face was colorless. She was staring up at him, uncomprehending. Her dilated eyes were changing slowly, and Adam knew she was going into shock. "Take your hands away, damn it!" he shouted at Logan.

Logan did. He leaned back, staring down at his hands covered with Beth's blood.

Adam bent close, his stomach turning. He pressed something hard against her side. She moaned softly before letting out a soft sigh and losing consciousness.

"Beth," Logan groaned. "Jesus, God . . ."

"We've got to get her inside fast," Adam said. "She's losing too much blood. I can't do anything out here."

Frank was running toward them, his face gray. "Beth!"

Logan shoved Adam back roughly and lifted her himself. She sagged limply in his arms.

"Into the hotel. Put her on a table," Adam said, and gave short, curt orders to two men, who ran for the house on Elm Street. Adam strode after Logan grimly.

She roused briefly as he laid her down carefully on a table. She saw Logan's face before Adam was there, bending over her. He tilted her head up and gave her something foul tasting to drink. She could hear voices. Her father was somewhere close. She listened, frightened. "Logan?" she managed thickly.

Someone took her hand tightly. "I'm here," he said softly. "Hang on."

She turned her head toward the voice, but pain spread through her so she could hardly breathe. Her head swam dizzily.

"Lay still," Logan groaned, bending over her, putting his hand against her cheek. "Beth . . ."

"Move back, Logan," Adam ordered sharply. "I've got to have room!"

Logan moved. His hand loosened from hers. He felt the tremor in her fingers as she tried to hold on to him.

Adam put something over her mouth and nose. "Just breathe naturally, Beth," he whispered, his hand stroking her shoulder. The cloying odor filled her senses, making her nauseated and light-headed. She wanted to push the soft cloth away, but when she raised her hand, Adam pushed it down, gripping her wrist.

Logan moved back against the wall and watched Buchanan work. People stood outside in the street, talking and waiting. Frank was sitting down, shoulders hunched forward, fingers gripping his gray head.

The bloody bandage Adam had pressed against the wound to stop the bleeding was removed and dropped. Logan saw her side for an instant before Adam shifted his position and blocked his vision. It was the first time the sight of blood had ever made him sick. He closed his eyes tightly and fought his gorge down, his heart tripping hammer beats. His eyes burned and he felt his throat closing.

Logan kept seeing Kane's face as he'd grinned and pulled the trigger. Even knowing in another second he was going to be dead himself, Kane had enjoyed what he had done, hearing in Logan's own outcry what it meant. And Logan kept seeing Beth flung back by the force of the bullet. He kept seeing the blood welling from her side. Over and over the vision rolled in his head.

He remembered again his own fury and hatred and violence mounting uncontrollably. He'd killed Kane and then another and then another, walking forward as he blasted his gun until no bullet remained to fire. Behind his own fierce pain, he had felt a primeval, triumphant surge of demonic satisfaction in taking life.

"Just stop," Beth had said only last night, seeing more in all this than he ever had. Until now, when it was too late.

Frank raised his head, hearing the sound that came out of Logan. He glanced up at the younger man standing with his back pressed hard against the saloon wall, his head lolling back and forth, his eyes squeezed shut in a mask of self-condemnation and agony.

"It wasn't your fault, Logan."

"Wasn't it?"

"She didn't stop to think."

"She wanted to warn us. She wanted to warn *me*." Better him dead than her fighting for her life because she had been caught in the middle of the very violence she so abhorred.

Kane's violence.

His own violence!

"Just stop," she had said. *Just stop!*

He looked across at Buchanan working to save her life and prayed for the first time in his.

Adam finished removing the bullet and bandaging the cauterized wound. He bent and kissed her tenderly and brought the blankets up to keep her warm.

She was moved back to the white cottage because Adam and Frank knew it would be better if she awakened in her own home than to strange, alarming surroundings. She awakened once, half-drugged, and whimpered Logan's name.

"With proper care and plenty of rest, she may make it," Adam said. Frank rested his forearms on the mantel and stared at the bouquet of roses and daisies and greens she had arranged in the tin pot that morning. "I'll stay with her," Adam told them. "The next few days will be critical."

Logan turned.

Adam put a hand to his face. "You were right. I should've stayed with her," he admitted brokenly.

"We were all at fault," Frank said simply, slumping into his chair. "Every damned one of us."

Chapter Twenty-six

"YOU'VE GOT TO eat more, Beth," Adam said firmly as she sat up against the headboard of her bed. She shook her head, eyes downcast. He put the tray back on her lap. "The fever's finally gone, but so's most of your strength. You can't get it back without good food and plenty of fluids. Now come on."

"I'm just not hungry, Adam," she whispered. "Maybe later."

"It'll get cold." He sat down on the edge of the bed and dipped the spoon into the nutritious chicken-and-vegetable soup and lifted it to her lips. She swallowed obediently. Her eyes filled with tears, and she tried to avoid his intent scrutiny.

"All of it," he ordered. She was waif thin from the ordeal. Her skin was so pale it was translucent, and the glow was gone from her eyes. After weeks of illness and fighting infection, the wound had finally healed, but inside a worse one sapped her. He knew what it was and that it had be faced.

"One more bite. There. Good." He kissed her cheek.

He sat for a long time, her hand in his. Finally, he sighed heavily. "I'd do almost anything to keep you, Beth. I think you probably know that, but it's just not going to work. You're never going to love me the way you love Logan Tanner. So, we might as well settle this whole thing right now and put it behind you before you starve yourself to death."

He looked so drawn and resigned that Beth began to cry softly. "I'm sorry."

Adam drew her close and sighed as he stroked her hair. "I know I'm a prize, after all," he said ruefully, striving for some lightness. "First things first. The wedding is off."

She nodded, and he felt her muscles relax. It was one thing off her mind, he knew, and he felt grim and hurt. He had his own confessions to make, and they were hard coming. "I should've stayed with you just as Logan told me."

"You couldn't know what would happen."

"What you did was typical of you. I knew how you felt about him. I've know since the day of the picnic that I've been fighting a losing battle with him. You already belonged to him, Beth, and you're not the sort to stand by or hide safely away in a bakery if someone you love is in danger. That day your father and Logan went into the street against each other, I had all I could do to keep you in that alley and out of harm's way. I should have known. . . ."

He cupped her face, kissing her gently. "Logan did, Beth. It's why he said what he did just before the firing started. He was telling me to keep you safe. And without thought, I went tearing off for my medical bag."

"You can't blame yourself."

He let it pass. "Listen to me, Beth. The truth is, medicine is my life, my first love if you will. You should've been foremost in my thoughts that day, the way you were with Logan, the way he was with you."

"But he's gone now, Adam. He said he would leave town when it was finished. And it is."

Adam knew then, without doubt, that she had been living under a complete misconception and grieving over it. He kissed her again, taking the last opportunity he'd ever have, and then stood.

For as long as he lived, he'd never forget Logan Tanner's face as he'd hunched over Beth lying shot down in the street. Never had he suspected the man of the depth of emotion he had seen. Yet there it had been, stark and raw and wide open for everyone in town to see and never forget.

If anyone had wondered about Logan Tanner's reasons for pursuing Beth Tyrell in the first place, it was clear to all now that the gunfighter loved her.

After they carried her home, Logan had stood by during the worst, his back against the wall, self-hatred etched into his hard, bleak face, his blue eyes dead of everything but fear and regret. Frank had been the only one to talk to him, and Logan hadn't said much.

Adam had stayed by Beth, relieved by Frank when he needed rest. Logan had sat silently in the parlor, just staring at his hands.

When Beth had roused several times and moaned Logan's name, not his, jealousy and anger had eaten into Adam's insides. Logan hadn't been here to hear her, and Adam hadn't told him later.

But he knew Logan knew of Beth's love. She had made it plain enough when she'd turned away from Logan and put herself directly in Kane's way. Acknowledging that love, finally, Adam had felt his first stirring of pity when

Logan withdrew entirely once he knew she would live. It was the first unselfish thing Logan Tanner had probably ever done in his grim life.

Yet Adam had never expected Logan to do what he had then, nor had anyone else in town who heard about it later. It was Frank who had found him in the hills outside of town.

He closed his eyes tightly, facing away from Beth. "He's not gone, Beth."

Her head came up, her eyes wide and questioning. For the first time in weeks he saw color in her cheeks, and it hurt him deeply knowing the brightness was for another man. "He isn't?" she asked faintly.

"No," he said flatly, but couldn't tell her the rest.

"Where is he?"

"Living in his cabin." A sizable reward had been placed on Kane's head, as well as on his brother's. Enough to start a herd.

She frowned, studying his face. "Is he alright, Adam?" She knew he hadn't been shot during the fighting that day. It was the first conscious thing she had known when it was all over, because she had asked.

Adam turned away. "He's getting by. He'll probably be down to see you in a few days."

"What aren't you telling me, Adam?" she asked very quietly.

"Nothing," he said. She'd know when Logan came to see her, if he did.

Though Logan didn't come, Beth regained her strength over the next few weeks. Faraday Slate brought whatever she needed to the house, and she began to work a few minutes each day in her flower garden. Pastor Tadish stopped by several times to visit, as did Avery and Edwina. Even Faith Halverson came by one day, with little Terence in tow, and said she wanted the Sunday jacket and knickers after all, as well as some school clothing for fall. Beth almost cried.

In the evening, she sat on the porch swing while her father took his daily walk to the saloon for a whiskey. He always teased her from the front gate while he rolled his cigarette.

But still Logan stayed away. She never saw him in town.

"I guess he's waiting for me to come to him."

"No," Frank said firmly over the evening meal. "He'll come. He just needs to think things through for himself." He smiled wryly. "Sooner or later, he'll know he can't do anything else."

Beth wanted to believe him, but she couldn't be sure. No one would talk about Logan around her, and she wondered at all the secrecy.

"I'm going to the saloon for a drink," Frank said one evening, bending to kiss her on the cheek as she sat on the porch swing watching the sunset glow on the horizon. He knew how often she looked toward old Kilkare's hill and how that patient, hope-filled look would come into her wide hazel eyes.

She smiled up at him. "Just two, Papa. You know what Adam said," she teased.

He pinched her cheek lightly, then stood at the gate to roll his cigarette. "I'm going to have to marry Vinnie O'Keefe just to get out from under your thumb."

Beth leaned forward and laughed delightedly. "Are you really thinking about it?"

He drew deeply on his cigarette. "Some." His cigarette bobbed between his lips as he added with a half smile, "She's been wearing me down."

"I like her, Papa."

"She'll have me riding herd instead of wearing a badge again."

Beth stood and came to the rail, understanding what he was saying. "Will Logan take the job?"

"No. John Bruster."

"Oh." Beth lowered her head.

Frank exhaled slowly, watching her. He had played out his only hand. Bruster wanted to marry one of the saloon girls and would have need of this cottage. With the wedding off, Beth's plight was obvious.

Something was going to have to bring Logan Tanner down off his hill. Frank hoped this would do it. If it didn't, he had a mind to go up there and shoot the stupid bastard and put him out of his misery.

Beth looked up again. "John will make a fine sheriff, Papa."

"I've trained him well." Frank smiled lopsidedly. He'd never be the gun that Logan had been, but time was coming when that wouldn't be what was needed most anyway. Pray God. "I'll be back a little later, honey. Want anything?"

Nothing he could give her. She smiled faintly. "No."

She sat on the porch swing, pressing her toe against the porch floor to rock gently as she listened to the crickets. A soft rose-scented breeze stirred the soft lace at her throat. She leaned her head back and looked up toward the star-studded evening sky. She closed her eyes, trying not to think of anything, just to feel the warm, companionable stillness of the night around her.

The gate latch clicked.

Beth opened her eyes and looked down toward the pathway. A tall, broad-shouldered man was silhouetted there. She stood and came to the rail, her heart thumping wildly. "Logan?"

He wasn't wearing his gun. He didn't move and seemed undecided. He turned slightly, and she moved quickly to the column beside the stairs. "Please. Don't go, Logan."

He heard the catch in her voice and glanced up at her. "Buchanan said the wedding's off."

It sounded an accusation. "Yes," she answered simply.

Logan came a step closer, then stopped again. "And your father's decided to marry that widow lady with the ranch?"

"Yes."

Logan came closer. She could see the faint sheen of his blue eyes as he stopped at the front of the steps and looked up at her grimly. "Beth, marry Buchanan."

She shook her head.

A muscle moved in his cheek and he looked away from her. He said nothing for a long moment. "He'll give you a proper home. He's got background and he's educated. He's going to have plenty of money a few years down the road. He's a fine man, Beth. He saved your life."

Her eyes burned. "He's everything you say and more, Logan, and someday Adam will find a girl who will love him as deeply as he deserves, but the girl won't be me."

He didn't move, but just stood looking up at her. Nothing showed in his face, but she felt the power of the emotions he held under strong, tight rein.

"You're making a big mistake. You've got to listen," he said hoarsely.

"Logan, it's no mistake to love you," she told him quietly. He flinched.

"What have I got to give you?" he demanded in that hard, implacable voice. "A reputation as a gunfighter, a piece of land with a ghost, a cabin not fit for—"

"None of that matters to me," she told him, coming slowly down the steps. She drank in the sight of him, painfully noting the new lines about his blue eyes, the flatness of his hard mouth, the rigid way he held himself. He backed from her as she reached the bottom step.

"It should matter," he bit out. "You shouldn't waste

yourself on anyone less than a man like Buchanan."

"All I want is *your* love."

A grimace of pain tightened his face briefly. "You'll always have that," he said deeply. Reaching out with his left hand, he lightly stroked her cheek. "But you're far better off with Doc."

She raised her hand to his, pressing it against her cheek as she closed her eyes. "What arrogance, when you've always made it so clear that the only man I've ever wanted or ever will want is you."

"Oh, Beth," he groaned, and pulled her forward, seeking her mouth hungrily. He raised his head, his fingers deep in her hair. "What a damn fool thing you did . . . " he said, and kissed her again, over and over, unable to get enough of her.

"I couldn't see you killed." She reached up, sliding her arms tightly around his shoulders, pressing herself against him and hearing his ragged indrawn breath before he kissed her again.

He dragged his mouth away. "You can't . . . you'd be out of your mind . . . listen to me. . . ." His face was agonized. "Look what knowing me has done to you already."

"Oh, Logan," she sighed, cupping his face. "Only a small scar and so little pain compared to what I'd have felt if I'd lost you."

"Listen—"

"Are you compromising my daughter again, Logan?" Frank Tyrell demanded from where he stood watching them at the open gate.

Logan caught hold of her arms and pulled them down. She heard him draw a sharp breath and hunch over slightly. She stared up at him, but before she could say anything, he turned away from her.

"John said he saw you coming down off your mountaintop," Frank said wryly, rolling another cigarette and licking the paper to seal it. "I had a feeling something like this would be going on." He put the cigarette in his mouth and lit it. "Whole damn town will be out watching you two in a few minutes unless you go on inside and work things out properly."

"You talk to her," Logan said roughly. "Make her see some sense. She doesn't belong with me, Frank."

Beth looked up at him and saw he had made up his mind.

Well, so had she. She stepped forward. "Everything's been settled, Papa. It has been ever since the day Logan took me up on that hill and consummated a marriage."

"Beth!" Logan groaned.

"Damn right," Frank said, nodding, satisfied. "How about I stop by the Tadishs' and talk about some wedding plans?"

"Do that, Papa, and then take a nice long walk about town and have your two whiskeys at the saloon. You might even want to stay for a long game of cards."

Frank grinned broadly, seeing how Logan stared at her. "Now, I don't know about you, Logan, but when a woman uses just that tone, I think it's best to go along with her wishes." He laughed, turned, and walked away.

Beth looked up at Logan. *"Please,"* she insisted.

His eyes glistened.

She came close and put her arms around his waist, hugging herself against him and hearing the quick surge of his heart. His hand was gentle on her hair.

She let go of him slowly and walked toward the steps, then paused as she glanced back at him. She knew a war still waged within him. She held out her hand. He didn't take it, but nodded toward the cottage door.

When they were inside, he nudged the door closed behind them. Beth moved to the fire glow and held out her palms. "I want to see you hands, Logan," she told him softly.

His blue eyes narrowed briefly.

Her heart pounded heavily as he approached her and raised his hands for her to see. His left one was hard, brown, square, its fingers long, straight, their nails clipped and clean. His right was badly crippled. Scars still showed pink from recent healing.

"Oh, Logan," she said softly, and put hers gently around it. "Why did you do this to yourself?"

"It was the only way I could be sure I'd never use a gun again," he said simply.

She kissed it and gazed up at him, seeing the still-faint rebellion working against what he wanted: her. "Just let all of it go, Logan," she whispered, "and love me."

"I do, but it's never going to be that simple," he said grimly. "I'm the same man now that I was when I wore a gun. Doing this," he said, holding out his crippled gun-hand, "hasn't changed what's inside me and what I am."

Beth smiled tenderly. "The same man, Logan, but with a new direction. You're right. It won't be simple. It won't be easy. What of any value and importance ever is?"

He sighed heavily. "The battle is harder for some of us."

"Easier if it isn't fought alone."

They stood looking at one another, the very depth of their emotions making them feel restrained. The old sparkle was back in Beth's hazel eyes, radiating from the inside out. Logan looked half-frightened and less in control than when he had stood in the street wearing a gun. Killing and putting an end to things had always come easier than living fully, opening himself wide.

"Would you like me to make some coffee?" Beth asked softly.

His mouth curved slightly. His gaze was direct, dark, and very warm. "No."

Color rose faintly into her cheeks.

Logan came close and lifted his left hand to the front of her high-necked dress. The lengthy, half-coordinated effort he made to unbutton it heightened their longing.

When he reached her waist, Beth moved away, her eyes dark and luminous. She went to the kitchen door and pushed it open, one hand holding the front of her dress closed.

Logan followed. "No coffee," he said deeply.

She smiled, her dimples peeping shyly in her flushed cheeks. "No coffee, Logan."

She led him into her small bedroom. He closed the door behind them, glancing around briefly to see that it was simply furnished, with touches of her everywhere: a shawl over the chair near the corner, everything neatly put away, the narrow bed covered by an intricately patterned quilt, flowers on the little dresser, two small porcelain figurines on the windowsill, two fine embroidered pictures of wood scenes on the walls.

Logan looked at her again and saw the shyness in her eyes. He came forward and finished what he had started. Unlike the time up on the hill, he wouldn't be satisfied this time until he could see her as God had made her. When she stood naked before him, he undressed himself. He was grateful she didn't try to cover herself or look away from his body.

His embrace was almost careful. He kissed every precious feature, her eyes, her cheeks, her nose, her chin; her mouth parted for him as she quested in her turn, making his senses reel and his heart race. It had been so long since he had held her and it had never felt like this.

He gently brushed the edge of his teeth along her sensitive collarbone. Lowering his mouth to her breasts, he kissed each tenderly. He knelt, his hand warmly and slowly moving down her back as he kissed the scar beneath her right breast, then her smooth, pale velvet-skinned belly.

His hands moved lower, slowly coursing over each curve and valley, passing from her waist over her small firm buttocks, to the backs of her slender thighs, her knees, her shapely calves. He lowered himself still further until he was sitting back on his heels. One hand clasped her fragile ankle while the other moved up along the back of her calf in an easeful caress to her knee. He leaned forward slowly.

"Oh, Logan, I think I'm going to faint."

His hands coursed up again to her buttocks and kneaded her warm flesh as his passion mounted. She was shaking violently and making soft sounds that drove his heartbeat faster. He knew in another moment her legs weren't going to hold her. With the same pulsating slowness, he raised himself until she was clasping him close.

"There's only room for one on your bed," he murmured, kissing her again and again. He sat slowly and stretched out on his back, bringing her down on top of him, hugging her against him. He edged over and rolled onto his side. Putting one hand between her legs, he raised her knee. He sought and found her and watched her eyes darken and close and felt her hips roll forward as he went into her body. He kissed her, opening her mouth and giving in to everything he felt. When her soft hand touched his hip and explored the hard muscles of his thigh and went back up against his back, he rolled her again, holding himself up on his forearms as he moved with slow, cautious, deep strokes inside her.

He loved the way her eyes looked, the way her lips parted with her soft exhalations, the way her hands felt on his body. He loved the sound of her voice, cloud soft in passion as she whispered his name. He loved her body folding around him, moving with natural rhythm beneath his, drawing his life into hers.

She uttered a cry.

He drew back. "Am I hurting you?" he rasped.

"Oh, Logan, *no* . . ."

He took her mouth, stifling his own outward cry of release as it came.

After a long moment, he eased over onto his side, taking her with him so their coupling would not be broken. They lay facing one another, both stroking, admiring, breathing in the essence of one another. He kissed her long and tenderly, his hand exploring the full softness of her pale breasts, the smooth curve of her hip and leg.

"I love you," he said thickly.

She heard the faint fear behind the words and stroked his cheek, kissing him reassuringly. Sighing, she snuggled against him, but he made a slow circling motion with his hips. She gazed up at him, dimples showing, and answered with her own body.

He chuckled softly, drew her leg over his hip, and made love to her again, slowly. His hand lay spread against her breasts so he could feel the rapid heart-song soaring. He felt an overwhelming tenderness and peace even as his body was hotly consumed with the giving of himself to her. They lay together for a long time afterward, saying nothing.

He thought of the years of hard work ahead of them, the possible trouble that would come. "I wish I could protect you from what could happen," he whispered against her hair, breathing in the scent of her, her flesh a part of his.

She wished the same for him, but didn't voice it. He wouldn't understand her feeling that way. A man thought he had to stand alone, but in truth he never really did. No one did, if they could but see.

Holding Beth, Logan remembered grimly how easy it

had been to live the other way, to give in to rage and violence and let it mount and conquer, to gain a primitive bloodlust satisfaction from laying waste to an enemy. It was part of his nature, deep-seated, but the aftermath had emptied him. Not much had been left of him when he had come to Kilkare Woods, but this young woman had filled him up fuller than he'd ever been before.

His old life had touched her in the worst possible way, almost costing her her life. Yet, none of it had changed her or her convictions. She remained gentle yet unyielding in her inner strength. He knew his old life would touch her again many times before they had grown old together and were buried side by side on that hill where Kilkare had roamed, for it was all still there inside him, an ancient wound inflicted even before his birth.

He had wanted to prevent anything from happening, but even the act of destroying his gun hand had been committed in violence and rage, a vengeance turned on himself for what had happened to Beth.

Men were violent from the womb. It was there, a part of him, an essence that was human nature itself. Yet, Beth believed in another essence of human nature, the capacity to change, to trust, to love, to seek a better way to live. Logan had seen and lived the worst of himself, and Beth had found the best and refused to accept anything less.

Becoming a peaceful man would be a lifetime battle harder than any Logan had ever taken on in his past. "It's going to be so damn hard, Beth," he said raggedly, coming closer than he ever had before to admitting his own human frailty and vulnerability.

"Yes," Beth whispered, knowing, "but it's a beginning."